BIRD WITH A BROKEN WING & THAT SUMMER

*Two Sweet and Scary
Tales for All Ages*

Theresa Dale

Paper Doll Publishing

ISBN-13: 978-1-989897-05-8 (Book)
ISBN-13: 978-1-989897-06-5 (eBook)

Cover design by: Theresa Dale

ALSO BY THERESA DALE

Rose's Ghost
Heather's Grave
Dmitry's Shadow
Rose's Ghost – the Trilogy
Chrysalis

CONTENTS

BIRD WITH A BROKEN WING

First published in May, 2019 by
Paper Doll Publishing.

This is a work of fiction. Any similarities
between real life and the characters and/
or events within is purely coincidental.

ISBN-13: 978-1999277314 ISBN:
978-1999277345 (eBook)

For Shannon, Allyson, Sarah, Lyndsay,
and the rest of the neighborhood
gang of my youth.

CHAPTER 1 - A BOY ON THE TRACKS

The first time he appeared to her, Margot was walking along the tracks, humming. She balanced first on the right rail, switching to the left with a quick step in the middle when she lost her balance. Sometimes she'd jump from tie to tie, one foot to the next, before hopping back up.

She didn't mind being alone. Her friends were all at school - there were no voices in the cow pastures aside from a lowly 'moo' now and then. The apple orchard beyond the trees to her right was silent; if you didn't know it was there, you'd never guess that after school, sounds of kids playing in the trees would carry out to the tracks. And when enough of the fruit had dropped to the ground to provide ammunition for an apple fight, those sounds erupted into shouts and laughter.

The girls mostly avoided the orchard when the apples were overripe; they hated getting the sour-smelling flesh of the bruised and rotting fruit on their clothes. Besides, being pelted with an apple hurt. But the boys showed off their bruises with pride, each battle a legend to be celebrated and boasted over for days or months afterward as they debated who had won. It seemed a futile exercise to Margot; they never reached a consensus.

She and the other girls would sit on the bridge over the river, their ears habitually pricked up for the sounds of an approaching train, the boys' shouts travelling to them from the orchard. Ella would confidently sit on the wooden rail at the edge of the bridge, or sometimes lay across the ties in the sun. Sometimes Margot's breath would catch as she watched her friend coolly dangling her sneaker-clad feet over the edge, suspended thirty feet above the rushing water below.

Ella and Margot were the same age, but in the maturity category, Ella had eclipsed Margot (and perhaps all the other kids in their grade, too!) long ago. Ella had an undeniable air of sophistication about her. She waited at the bus stop one driveway over from Margot's house every morning, the rest of the neighborhood kids forming a circle as they arrived. Even when the older boys would join them, Ella was the focus at the head of the group, whether she had anything to say or not. Their close friendship had suffered a bit in those preteen years as Ella grew up and Margot got left behind. She knew Ella had a group of friends at school that she probably didn't fit in with, and mostly that didn't bother her. She'd never felt compelled to blend in with the crowd - but she couldn't deny the feeling of being left out as everyone else shopped for the latest trendy clothes and learned the words of new songs together.

Being homeschooled meant that Margot was always behind when it came to the latest trends. It also meant her family depended solely on her father's income as a scientist - it sounded prestigious, but it was hard to get a well-paying job as a scientist in a small town. Both of her parents had made sacrifices so they could raise their children how they felt was best. So, Margot knew they didn't have a lot of money; her clothes were either home-made or found in the bins at the local *Frenchy's*, and they never ate at restaurants like the neighborhood kids talked about doing.

But they had advantages, too. Her parents were of the opinion that the public-school system underestimated a child's ability to learn, and was stuck in traditional teaching methods. According to them, the curriculum was sadly bereft of life skills, too. So, having finished school early herself, their mother was only too happy to take on the challenge of teaching her children in creative and exciting ways. They tackled the mandatory curriculum and then explored further, their mother letting them lead as she filled in the gaps.

Consequently, the three were eager to learn and ended up being far advanced in their studies, often able to wile away at least part of the day as they wished. For the twins, that usually meant building Lego or playing with their dinky cars in the sandy ditch by the house. For Margot, it meant long walks on the train tracks or to the dead end at the top of the street.

Which was what had brought her to the tracks that day, despite her mother's warning of impending rain as she ran out the front door, the metal frame of the screen smashing hard against the door frame as she went.

It *was* a grey-sky day, and cool, especially in the shorts she'd outgrown the summer before. She was aware of gooseflesh prickling on her skin as a cool breeze tickled her bare legs and arms. Taking a moment to look up from the wooden ties of the track, she searched for the bridge far behind her. She'd come further than she'd realized, the green earth rising to the fenced land on the right of her, and the left dropping suddenly into the thick forest of pine, oak and maple.

The air smelled like rain. Though she'd been looking forward to seeing Ella and the rest of her neighborhood friends after the bus dropped them off, it seemed likely their jaunts through the woods and along the tracks would have to wait until tomorrow. She shrugged as she turned back around. An afternoon listening to music in Ella's bedroom would be OK, too.

She decided to take the tracks all the way

to the edge of the cow pasture at the dead end of the street. She stepped onto the right rail, her arms reflexively reaching outward on either side of her as she balanced, and immediately stepped down again, hard, when movement ahead of her caught her eye.

There was a boy on the tracks.

He was sitting to the outer right, his right leg bent over the rail and his foot resting on the ground inside. His left appeared to be folded beneath him. It seemed an awkward position, making Margot wonder if he was hurt. Something in her gut said she should find out, but she paused. She didn't recognize him. Inherently shy, she typically counted on her more outgoing friends to ease her into comfort when new kids came to the neighborhood. But they were all at school today.

How come this guy isn't? Margot wondered.

He was quite a distance from her, probably close to the dump - a notorious place between the tracks and the road for locals to throw their unwanted furniture, equipment and the like. She considered turning back toward the bridge, but the sky was ever darkening, the formerly innocuous shades of grey deepening into massive rainclouds. It would take twice as long to go back that way, and it would also mean negotiating the narrow trail through the woods to Greenwood Square afterward. That was unpleasant enough when it wasn't raining, thick as

17

it was with mosquitos and cursed with mud and damp from the little brook that trickled through.

The boy turned his head toward her now, his neatly-cut, sandy blonde hair shining in what was left of the sunlight as he did. She took a step back. He waved. She paused, then raised a hand, waving back.

It was something. She continued toward him.

His head resumed its downward position, a shadow across his profile. He seemed to be digging at the ground with something. Margot approached him, now able to see a large railroad spike in his hand coming down on a wooden tie. He'd already gouged it considerably.

"What are you doing?" she asked, stopping on the tracks beside him.

He looked up at her. "I found this on the tracks," he said, holding it out for her examination.

She took it from him gingerly. "We've found these before," she said, handing it back and adding, "The tracks are old."

The boy nodded, his gaze finding the trail to the dump just beside the tracks.

Margot followed his gaze, a thought occurring to her. "Oh! Are you one of the new kids who moved in at the bottom of the hill?" she asked, already feeling pleased she'd be able to place him when she told Ella about this later.

He squinted up at her again. What sunlight remained uncovered by dark clouds seemed determined to shine into this boy's eyes. "Sure," he said finally, and Margot nodded.

Thunder rolled in the distance. Margot looked toward the sound. She was walking straight into it. Making a quick decision, she gestured toward the trail that would take her past the dump. "Rain's coming. I'm going to go home through there; do you want to come?" She offered her company, excited to be the first in the neighborhood to show the new kid around a bit as they walked home.

He shook his head. "Nah, not yet," he answered.

She looked at him doubtfully. "OK, but you don't want to be back here when lightning's coming down," she said, thinking of her lessons about the power of the electricity that could come down from the sky.

The kid went back to gouging at the rail tie with his spike. His distraction allowed Margot a longer look at him. She was sure he was older than her. His lightly freckled cheekbones jutted out under his unusual crystal-blue eyes. The one leg he'd stretched out before him was long and lanky, his kneecap a bony protrusion where his leg bent. The leg folded beneath him showed the top of a dirty sock, but no shoe as far as Margot could see, his toes protruding from beneath his backside as he sat on his foot. She looked back at his other foot. That one sported a sock, too, but ended in a scuffed-up sneaker, the brand of which she was unable to identify.

"Where's your other shoe?" she asked.

He shrugged.

Margot was ready to give up. She jumped over the rail and began walking toward the dump.

"You coming back tomorrow?" the boy called out from behind her.

She stopped, turning to look at him again. He'd pulled his left leg over the rail now, too, and had wrapped his arms around both of them, pulling his knees up to his chin. His skin looked dirty; his left leg in particular was smeared with rail grease.

"Maybe," she said, then pointed at his leg. "Did you hurt yourself?"

"A while ago," he said, squinting at her.

The breeze made her shiver. She turned around and started off again, hurrying now as the thunder boomed closer overhead.

"See you tomorrow," she heard him call, but didn't look back as she started to run.

Weird kid, she thought as the first cool drops hit her. *I'll see what Ella thinks,* she decided, but immediately changed her mind. The thought of Ella's easy popularity and the fact that the boy would probably start waiting at the bus stop with the rest of the neighborhood kids gave her pause. She decided she'd rather keep him to herself, at least until she knew more.

The rain came down harder, the sound of it hitting the grass in the field ahead of her a relief. She was almost home.

But she would come back tomorrow.

CHAPTER 2 - THE WILLOW

"Margot's wake-dreaming again!" Aaron exclaimed gleefully, bouncing in his seat.

Margot tore her eyes away from the window to look at her brothers, who sat across from her at the dining room/lessons table. Aaron smiled hugely, his dark eyes sparkling, while Mason giggled, his little fists balled up in front of his mouth.

She rolled her eyes and gathered her papers. "I'm going to finish this in my room," she said as she stood.

Mom looked up from her book, her glasses perched on the end of her nose. "Oh, no you don't. Math's done at the table, Margie, you know that. She looked over at the twins, asking, "Are you two done?"

The boys straightened up and bent over their work, Mason still stifling his giggles. They were likely motivated by the thought of free time later. Mom raised her eyebrows at them, then looked back at Margot, giving her head a shake.

"The rain had them cooped up yesterday."

Sighing half-heartedly, Margot sat back

down. She picked up her pencil, but leaned forward before she begun, whispering, "It's *day*dreaming, twerp!" to Aaron, who only rolled his eyes back in his head, his eyelids fluttering, and used his hand to mock his sister's mouth as he moved it.

Margot made a sound of annoyance, then looked down at her answer sheet. She'd escape after she was finished – and she was on the last question. Sneaking another peek at her brothers, who were now preoccupied with poking each other beneath the table with the business end of their pencils, Margot couldn't help but smile a little.

She remembered a time when she'd have given anything for a sibling, super-annoying or not. Her parents had tried and failed to get pregnant for six full years after she'd turned one. As a last-ditch effort, they decided to give in-vitro a try, and BAM! – they were thrilled to inform Margot that they'd in fact be having babies two and three.

Margot remembered the feeling of being suddenly overwhelmed at the prospect of having two little brothers. She'd cried, the words, "Why can't you just have one girl?" escaping between sobs.

Her parents had laughed, but Margot failed to see the humour at the time.

Fraternal twins, the boys looked about as different as they could. Aaron got Mom's colouring like Margot; his hair dark brown and straight, hanging down to his large, hazel eyes. He was built solidly, standing a full inch and a half taller than his brother.

Mason was smaller in every way but heart - his skinny arms and legs giving off an air of fragility. He'd inherited their father's fairer colouring; blonde, curly hair and bright blue eyes. Aaron was the trouble-maker, but Mason happily followed his brother's example. When Aaron wasn't looking, though, he'd cuddle up to Margot on the couch while they watched TV.

She looked at them again, softening. She guessed two brothers were better than no siblings at all.

Margot flew through her last algebra question, handing the answer sheet to her mother as soon as she was done. Mom looked over the paper quickly, lifting her chin as she peered downward, beneath her glasses. "Good," she remarked, then looked up as Margot stood.

"I'm going to read in my room," she said, then turned toward the stairs, bounding through the living room in giant leaps.

"Read at least two chapters!" Mom called after her as she climbed the stairs, and Margot only laughed in response. They both knew reading enough wasn't Margot's issue - tearing her away from her books was the real challenge.

Margot jumped into the air, landing belly-first on her bed and reaching for her book on the opposite end table. Opening it to her bookmark, she got an idea. She glanced toward her window, then bounced backward, pushing herself up with her hands. She stuffed her book into her multicolored backpack, pausing to pull a cardigan on before swinging it over an arm to her back.

Bounding down the stairs and then holding onto the rail as she reached the landing, she called, "I'm going to read outside!"

Mom's head appeared in the archway. "Where?" she demanded.

"By the tracks, probably," Margot answered.

Mom rolled her eyes. "You know I hate that you kids hang out over there!"

"I'm always careful, Mom," Margot sighed.

"Fine, just stay away from that bridge!" she called, Margot already turning to leave.

"Always do!" she lied, bursting outside.

The screen door smashed back against the wooden door frame, as usual, as she jumped over the three stairs from the porch to the ground. The grass was still wet from the rain, which had continued late into the night. Today it seemed reluctant to leave completely, the sky once again filled with varying shades of white and grey clouds.

Skipping up the gradual incline as the road rose ahead of her, she relished the wet slapping sound her runners made on the pavement. She decided to avoid the tall, wet grass of the field by the dump, instead heading toward the dead end at the top of the street. Ten minutes later, she approached the vine-covered fence, the gate itself having been unused for years now. She glanced around, catching her breath. It was deathly quiet, no houses to be seen since she'd reached the top of the hill and the road had levelled off.

The older boys had told them stories about an abandoned, broken-down house beyond the trees to the left, but Ella had rolled her eyes. "They're just trying to scare us," she'd said, and Margot had been satisfied to believe her. From the stories they'd been told, proving the boys right or wrong didn't seem worth a visit into the woods.

Margot cut across the land on the right, the ground too covered by small stones for much to grow. Cheerful daisies popped up here and there, as did little bunches of purple clover. At the height of summer, Mom would ask all three kids to bring home wildflowers from their daily excursions, and it was always an easy request to fulfill. Dad said it was a blessing in disguise that Mom preferred the messy, but charming bouquets they'd bring home for her over the expensive, store-bought cultivated roses you could get from the flower shop in town.

Reaching the corner of the fence, Margot launched herself up the steep grade of rocky ground to the tracks, then paused to catch her breath as she searched for movement in both directions. The damp air was heavy in the silence. It was days like today that shook her confidence in walking the tracks by herself. The sun hid entirely behind the clouds, giving the landscape a washed-out appearance, and the cool air ruffled her hair and made her glad she'd remembered to put on a sweater today.

Her eyes focused on the track ahead of her, Margot shuddered. It wasn't that she'd expected to see the new boy right away. Her hesitation was rooted in the fact that she'd been surprised by the older boys too many times to trust she was alone. Jumping out from the trees or over the fence at the top of the hill by the orchard, they'd scared the daylight out of the girls and younger boys alike, laughing hysterically at their reactions.

Taking comfort that she'd likely be the only kid around on this school day, Margot carried on toward the spot beside the tracks where the trees thickened into forest. She thought about the giant willow by the river beyond the orchard ahead, and smiled. She loved reading there, her back resting against the familiar bark of the tree, the sounds of the rushing river a soothing soundtrack to whatever story she was reading.

Decision made, she ran along the wooden

ties, now and then jumping to land on one of the rails, trying to keep her speed as she stepped lightly along. Breathless, she bent over double as she reached the spot the kids used to get into the orchard. Winding her way through the blueberry bushes on the hill, she arrived at the fence and hoisted herself over it.

Next, she ran through the quarter-acre of dense forest between the fence and the orchard, bursting joyfully out of the trees in quick time. She inhaled. Besides the damp earth, she smelled a pungent mixture of rotting apples from the season before, and fresh cow manure. The trees were rarely picked these days except by the neighborhood kids who climbed them, so the farmer let his cows pasture here when the grass got too high.

Margot headed in a beeline to the slope descending to the water's edge. Spotting her willow, she sidestepped down the wet grass, her legs tense as she anticipated slipping. Making it safely to the bottom, she reached into her pack for her book as she rounded the large willow trunk, then squealed in surprise. The strange sandy-haired boy was there, his back precisely in the spot on the bark where hers should be.

He laughed at her reaction, slapping his thigh.

"What are you doing here?" she blurted, her face burning.

"It's a free country," he said, squinting up at her.

Margot wondered briefly if it wasn't the sun in his eyes that made him squint like that; maybe it was just the way his face was.

"What are *you* doing here?" he asked.

Margot pulled her book out of her bag. "I was going to read! This is sort of...my spot!" she replied, trying to add strength to the end of her sentence. To her ears, she sounded defensive. And a bit whiney. She bit her lip.

The boy sat up straight now, his legs bowing out in front of him slightly as his knees bent. "Are you telling me," he started, casting his arm in an arc to demonstrate the space all around them, "that of all the places you could have chosen, this was the only spot where you could -" he paused, eyeing her book "- read?"

"No; I'm just saying this is my favorite spot to read!" she replied, clutching her book in front of her.

He leaned back against the tree again, pulling at the tall grasses beside him and popping the end of one in his mouth casually.

Margot muttered, "Ugh," putting a hand on her hip. "Well, it's your turn; what are *you* doing here?" she demanded.

He gestured toward the water's edge, and Margot saw a fishing pole rigged up between two rocks, the line listing to the right with the current.

She looked back at him. "Surely this isn't the only place you can fish!" she exclaimed.

He looked at her. "No, but it's my favorite."

"Argh!" Margot raised her voice in exasperation, stomping her foot like a toddler, and the boy sat forward, laughing again.

"It just so happens I need to recast, so lucky you! You get your spot back," he said, rising to stand.

Margot felt her jaw drop as he did; he was a full head taller than her at least, his sandy hair messed up, no doubt, from the bark of the willow. He smiled down at her, and Margot was forced to admit that not only was she wrong about his face being permanently contorted into a squint, regardless of the cloud cover, but he was quite beautiful.

"Well?" he asked, his chapped lips still pulled into a smile.

Margot shook her head, once again aware of warmth spreading to her cheeks as she blushed. She put her weight on her left leg, the other pulling straight, trying her best to look defiant. Ella had this pose down pat. "Well, what?" she asked, tossing her head.

He gestured to the abandoned spot in front of the tree as he walked toward his fishing rod, looking smugly back at her.

Margot jumped, then hurried to sit, opening her book on her bent knees. Her eyes, however, were still on him.

He was skinny, the length of his legs exposed below his short shorts.

What kind of boy wears shorts like that? Margot thought absently.

She watched him bend to retrieve the pole, his back flat and muscular beneath the fabric of his t-shirt. He drew back, then cast, his right arm stretching long in front of him as the left held the reel, then turned a couple times to catch the line and prevent it from spinning out until it was empty. He was squinting again, this time clearly affected by the rays of the sun as it peeked out from behind the clouds. He looked out over the water, lazily pulling the line now and again.

His profile to her, she noticed the straight line of his nose, the slight jut of his chin, the strength in his jaw. Margot tried again to guess his age. *Sixteen, maybe?* That would make him two years older than her, in grade ten. Right or wrong, he was surely too young not to be in school.

Margot cleared her throat. "Why aren't you in school?"

He looked back at her. "I could ask you the

same," he replied, tugging the line.

"I'm homeschooled," she answered, seeing no reason to hide the fact. Unless, of course, this guy planned to steal her spot every day just to spite her. She lowered her head. She should have thought of that before she spoke.

The boy nodded, squinting back at the water, now. He deftly replaced the rod between the rocks, turning back to her. As he approached, Margot studied his shirt: a glittery photo of two men, a scantily-clad woman and an orange car beneath equally shiny "Dukes of Hazzard" lettering occupied the majority of the front. She recalled the black and white "01" numbering she'd spotted on the back and shook her head. Where was this guy from?

"Me too," he said as he sat on the large rock beside her, his long arms resting on his legs, fingers intertwined in front of him.

"Huh?"

"I'm homeschooled too, like you," he said, picking up a flat stone and turning it over and over.

"Oh, my God. Really?" she asked, smiling. When he only looked at her, Margot continued, "Mom is going to freak out. It's her dearest wish to be able to meet other homeschooling families nearby."

"Why?" his face scrunched up.

Margot laughed. "I don't know. So we can do field trips together?"

The kid shook his head, looking at the ground between his legs. "My family sort of keeps to themselves," he said finally.

Margot was blushing again. "Oh. That's OK. No problem. I mean, it isn't me that wants to – it's my Mom. Anyway. Ugh," she trailed off, and the boy shook his head then stood again, this time walking to the water as he pulled his arm back, the stone flat in his grip as he prepared to skip it. His arm moved in a broad arc as he released it. It seemed to hover above the water for a moment before it skipped, first in a grand arch above the rushing water below and then jumping rapidly several times as it skidded to a quick stop.

"Cool," Margot said, impressed.

He picked up the rod again and fiddled with the line. "It's much better with a flat surface," he muttered.

Margot nodded.

He picked up the rod again, falling quiet as he became engrossed in his task.

She opened her book, but her eyes kept going to him, and she ended up reading the first sentence on the page three times before realizing she had read that page before. Irritated with herself, she found her place, then settled back against the tree.

She could see him casting his line out again over the top of her book. Several minutes went by, the sounds of the river filling the air. She noticed the grease marks on his outer left thigh - the ones she'd seen the day before. She felt her brows knit as she scowled. Had those been there the whole time?

He turned, seeming to sense her eyes on him.

"I was just wondering about your leg," she explained in a rush, pointing to the grease marks.

He looked down. "Shit," he said.

"It's OK. I just – I saw that yesterday. Are you hurt?"

He swiped at the marks with his left palm, the line jiggling in his right hand. "Oh!" he exclaimed, now using both hands to give the rod a jerk.

"Did you get one?" Margot asked, her voice high and excited. She stood and ran to stand beside him as he nodded.

He reeled in the line in spurts, giving it quick tugs in between. At her questioning look, he explained, "Just making sure to keep him on the line."

Margot startled as the fish jumped, landing back in the water as it violently turned its body this way and that.

"A pike!" the boy enthused, his face appearing

younger in his excitement. Reeling in the last of the excess, he pulled the rod backward, the grip resting on the muddy ground behind him. His face alight with his accomplishment, he grabbed the line just above the struggling fish's mouth.

Margot squealed in shared excitement. "What are you doing to do?" she asked, hoping she wouldn't have to witness a messy fish beheading. She'd seen Jack and Adam, the older boys, do that more than enough times to last her the rest of her life.

He didn't answer; he merely held the rod out to her, saying "Hold this, would you?"

"No way!" she exclaimed. It was one thing to witness the next bit, but quite another to involve herself!

He smirked, grabbing her right hand and placing it on the rod, curling his fingers around hers. Margot felt a new heat burst into flames in her belly, despite the chill of his hand. Overwhelmed by his unexpected touch, she complied, taking the rod from him as he used both hands to grab the fish.

Holding it up, his hands on the belly of the wriggling thing, he bounced it up and down slightly. "It's gotta be seven or eight pounds!" he yelled in his excitement, and Margot cheered, though she had no idea whether that was considered a big catch.

He met her eyes for just a moment, his clear

blue and lit up by his smile. Her stomach did a somersault.

She watched as he got to work. He carefully removed the hook from the pike's gaping mouth. It seemed frozen as is awaited its fate, the only sign it was alive its gills, which opened and retracted slowly. Margot held her breath as he dropped the hook. He'd smash its head against a rock now, or pull out a pocket knife to do the job. She squinted in anticipation, but was unexpectedly flooded with relief as he waded into the shallow water, using both hands to lower the fish into the current.

Mesmerized, Margot watched the fish pause as though it couldn't believe its luck, then twitch, then propel itself away like a shot. It wiggled deep into the river, its scales flashing in triumph.

Margot looked at the boy in admiration. He caught her eyeing him as he walked back toward her, reaching for the rod. "What?" he asked.

She handed him the rod. "Why did you do that?" she asked, still breathless from the excitement.

He shrugged, examining the hook.

"My name is Margot, by the way," she said.

He wiped his right hand on his dirty shorts, then held it out to her. She laughed, then took it, seeing the seriousness in his eyes. She'd never shaken any kid's hand in introduction.

This guy is different in more ways than one, she realized.

"I'm Wren," he said.

She giggled, her hand still within his. "Like Ren and Stimpy?"

He looked confused.

She covered her mouth, appalled she'd made fun of his name. "Oh," she said quickly. "Like the bird."

He nodded. "I have to go," he muttered, feeding the hook through one of the eyes of his rod, then pulling it taught with a half-turn of the reel.

Margot backed up. "Oh," she said, astonished at her disappointment. She'd had crushes before, but none had ever given her this half-sick/half-elated feeling. She was dizzy with it.

He glanced at her as he walked past. "Thanks for helping with the fish, Margot," he smiled.

She watched him walk away from her for a moment, noticing his filthy leg again and – she squinted, leaning forward to see better. She had been sure he was wearing both shoes today. She'd even made a mental note to ask him where he found the left one while she was watching him from behind her book.

She felt like a creep. What was wrong with her? Raising a hand to wave at his back, she called, "You're welcome, Wren!"

He glanced over his shoulder, raising a hand in farewell as he twisted.

Margot looked around. The clouds had cleared a little, revealing a blue sky just hinting at the lateness of the afternoon. Her belly growled. She needed to get home for supper. Not wanting to follow Wren, she put her book back in her bag and started off in the opposite direction, toward the bridge and the narrow trail through the woods beyond.

CHAPTER 3 - THE KISS

Ella sucked in on her bubble, popping it loudly. Margot giggled on cue. They sat on Ella's back porch, overlooking the sloping lawn where the neighborhood kids played frisbee.

This was typical for a Friday night - Ella's lawn was the biggest and everyone wanted to start the weekend off doing something fun.

"What do you think of the new kid, Ella?" Kim asked as she swung her legs back and forth on the bench beside Margot. Margot squirmed. Kim was two years their junior, and yet she had a leg up on Margot; she knew everything about everyone and loved talking about it. All the time.

And now it was she who was bringing up Wren with Ella, when Margot had been waiting to do just that - after she found out a little more about him. But she hadn't seen Wren today; Mom had taken she and her brothers to the science museum, much to the twins' delight.

Margot usually loved those trips too, but today her heart hadn't been in it. Mom had noticed, asking, "What are you thinking about, Margot?"

She had blushed, mumbling something about the new exhibit on comparative fuel consumption based on vehicle velocity.

Mom had looked at her critically, one eyebrow raised, but Margot turned, saying "Where's Aaron?" It was always a guaranteed distraction when needed. Which was good, because she'd really been thinking about how it had felt to have Wren's fingers pressing gently on hers, curling them around the fishing rod – and she wanted to get back to it.

By the time they'd gotten home, it was late afternoon and Mom had given Margot two options: to either keep the boys occupied while Mom made dinner, or peel and chop vegetables for the soup. Margot was crestfallen. Regardless of the option she chose, she'd be stuck home instead of heading back to the tracks.

After dinner, she'd walked to Ella's with Jack, whom she'd met on the road between their houses. Regardless of his questionable decision-making when he and Adam were together, Jack could be a decent guy when he was on his own. He'd asked her if she'd met the new guy yet and she'd nodded before she'd even thought about what she wanted to say about Wren. Instead, she'd turned the question on him; what did he think of him?

Jack had shrugged. "He's in my grade," he said, but before Margot could ask how he'd met him, given that Wren was homeschooled, they were joined by Jack's little brother Martin, who was running to catch up with them, yelling his brother's name as though the world was ending.

Jack looked around. "You ate your broccoli after all, eh, sport?" he said, messing up Martin's hair as he fell in between them.

By the time they reached Ella's, they'd been joined by Sharon and Stevie, who'd run from the farm to catch up with them, Stevie sporting his baseball glove, as always. Sharon had the frisbee that was currently being thrown back and forth, the kids standing in a disorganized circle, most of them joking and goofing around more than focusing on the spinning disc. It always started like this: non-competitive and relaxed, until somebody started crying or one of the older kids got bored and devised a new game. Margot looked at Ella anxiously, awaiting her answer.

"Hmm, I don't know yet," she started, regarding Kim curiously. "Why do you ask?"

Kim shrugged. "All the girls in grade seven are talking about him."

"Oh yeah?" Ella raised her eyebrows.

Kim nodded. "They think he's gorgeous," she finished, exaggerating the last word.

Margot couldn't help but roll her eyes.

Ella spotted her reaction and asked, "Have

you met him, Margot?"

Margot tried to be casual even though her heart had sped to a gallop in her chest. "Uh-huh."

Kim whipped her head to look at Margot. "Do you think he's gorgeous?" she asked, smiling.

"I don't know about that, but he could use some tips on fashion," she said, deflecting.

Ella laughed, "I know!" she said, leaning forward, now. Fashion always got her interested. "Those shirts!"

Margot was caught between laughing with her friend and acting non-committal. Something felt wrong about making fun of Wren behind his back.

Before she could decide, Ella continued, "He said he'd come over tonight. I guess Stevie invited him."

Margot gasped involuntarily. "Really?"

Ella nodded, seemingly bored with the topic now.

Margot lowered her head, her emotions clashing. She wasn't sure she could articulate her interest in Wren, but there was one thing she did know: if Ella showed any interest in him, Margot could count on losing his attention. Maybe that would be good; she had no idea what she'd do if Wren was interested in her, anyway.

She was brought out of her reverie rudely; one of the kids had found the garden hose and was spraying the girls on the deck.

"Adam!" Ella cried, dripping wet and pissed. "Just you wait!"

Margot watched, surprised, as Ella sprinted across the deck, down the stairs and toward Adam, a playful smile on her face. The younger kids squealed in excitement as Adam turned the hose on again, the water shooting wildly around the yard as Ella reached him, grabbing his arm and squealing herself.

"Stop!" she screamed, protesting as he used his free hand to tickle her.

Margot laughed, shaking her head.

Ella was nothing if not unpredictable. She looked over at Kim, who'd turned around to view the excitement.

"Oh, my God!" Kim exclaimed, looking at Margot and pointing.

Margot looked over her shoulder again and gasped.

Adam had been disarmed. Ella had gained control over the hose, but it lay useless in her hand, the dripping water puddling in the dirt below. Instead of trying to regain his weapon, Adam had wrapped his arms around Ella and lowered her toward the ground, his lips pressing on hers. Ella seemed momentarily disarmed herself, but then shoved him, hard, and he stood them both upright.

Margot was fascinated by the look on Adam's face as he looked at her friend. She didn't think she'd ever seen him so serious. Or quiet, for that matter.

Ella backed up two steps, dramatically wiping her mouth on her arm. The whole yard was in chaos; the younger kids screaming and the older kids hooting and hollering, Jack patting Adam on the back, his face swallowed up in a smile.

Ella snapped back to reality. "You giant SHIT!" she screamed, and wasted no time aiming the hose and firing.

Finding its target immediately, Adam was soon soaked from head to toe, but he didn't seem to mind. He had a dorky smile on his face as he looked at Ella. He looked almost handsome.

Kim was giggling beside her. "Oh, my God," she said again. "I knew he liked her."

Margot scoffed as she turned back around. "Everyone likes Ella," she said, but she was happy. Not only was she excited to get Ella's thoughts on the events, but she now had hope that Ella would be too preoccupied with Adam to worry about Wren.

Ella climbed back up the stairs, resuming her seat on the picnic table in front of them. She squeezed her dripping hair, looking at her friends in exasperation. "What an asshole," she said quietly, but a smile played at her lips.

CHAPTER 4 - THE FALL

Saturday arrived spectacularly bright. After the rainy, grey days of the week, Margot was thrilled when she awoke to the sun shining on her face through a gap in her curtains.

Her first thought was of the tracks – and of finding Wren.

He hadn't shown up at Ella's the night before, nor had he joined them during their game of hide and creep - a neighborhood classic, supposedly invented years ago by their predecessors - once the sun had gone down. It was more an exercise of scaring and getting scared than of trying not to be found, and the hiders/scarers always won. The older kids paired up with the younger ones, and screams of terror and delight echoed through the neighborhood until they were called back home by their parents.

She knew she wouldn't be alone today, no matter where she wandered. The weekend meant getting outside and playing, every kid heading out to find their friends as soon as they were up and fed. The regular haunts were known by all. If you didn't find who you were looking for, you'd likely find someone who could point you in the right direction.

After scarfing her breakfast of peanut butter toast and a banana, she was halfway out the door before her mother came down the stairs, saying, "Whoa, whoa, whoa, Margie-Mae. Where are you off to so early?"

Margot threw the door open, catching it as it sprung back toward her. She gestured outside. "Look! It's beautiful!" she cried, and her mother's hands flew up in front of her face, her eyes squinting as the sun hit her.

"Bah!" she muttered, reaching the bottom of the stairs. "Just go. I need coffee."

Margot sprung forward, hugging her mother before bounding out the door. "Free!" she yelled, and she heard Mom chuckling from inside.

She hit the street, the pavement already heating up in the sun. She paused, looking down at her flip-flops. Not the best choice for the tracks, but she was reluctant to go back. In truth, she was eager to find Wren before the other kids did.

She cut across the field to the dump, the tall grass getting caught between her feet and her shoes and making her pull her knees up high as she ran.

Her thoughts raced. Her efforts were likely futile, especially the way Kim has spoken about Wren the night before. Margot scowled. *How are all the grade sevens so impressed with his looks? He doesn't go to school.* She slowed. Had he lied to her?

She felt something cool wrap around her ankle and knew what it was without looking; grass snakes were the main reason one didn't take leisurely walks through this field. She let a high-pitched scream loose, taking off at a run again and feeling the thing slide off her leg. "Blaaaaaaah!" she yelled, mortified.

She looked around self-consciously as she reached the dump to her left. There was nobody around. "Thank God for small blessings," she muttered under her breath, trying out one of Dad's favorite sayings.

She looked down at her shoes and cursed herself. She really should have worn her sneakers. Besides the snake issue, it appeared she'd dragged half the grass from the field as she'd run; it stuck out in clumps on both sides of her flip flops. She kicked her feet, flexing her toes and shaking the grass to the ground first left, then right.

Catching herself again, she looked around. Still nobody there to giggle at her, despite her apparent ongoing efforts to look like a total dork.

Shaking her head, she carried on toward the tracks. She shuddered inwardly as she remembered the feeling of the snake coiling around her lower leg.

The tracks were unusually bare. It was true she'd come out early today, but she was still surprised, especially considering the weather. Maybe a group of kids had found someone to drive them to the community center - there were outdoor pools there. Still, Margot started in the direction of the bridge.

She heard voices as she rounded the lazy left curve of the tracks. The bridge would come into view in seconds. *There must be some kids there, already.* Margot paused, listening.

A girl's voice – surely Kim, Margot thought as she heard, "Oh, my GOD!" Laughter followed, and Margot thought it was from a girl and a boy. Had she already missed her chance to find Wren first?

She started along the tracks again, this time leaping over every second tie. The bridge came into view in no time.

She'd been right; Kim sat with a petite blond girl at the start of the bridge. Easy to scramble off of should they hear a train coming, but still benefitting from the cool, damp air emanating up from the rushing water below. An older boy sat on the other side of the new girl, his curved back and the back of his blonde head just visible to the left of her. It had to be Wren.

Margot didn't let the shot of adrenaline that sped up her heart stop her; she called, "Hey, Kim," as she approached, determined to join them.

Kim squinted up at her. "Margot! I was just telling these guys about Adam and Ella last night!"

Of course, she was. Margot feigned a laugh as she reached the little group, plopping herself down on the rail to sit beside Kim. In her efforts to be casual, she avoided looking at the boy, raising her eyes, instead, to the girl. Light brown eyes gazed back at her curiously.

"Are you the girl who's homeschooled?" she asked.

Margot nodded, then began, "Just like -" she gestured as she finally allowed herself to look at the boy, but faltered, her hand falling to her side limply. It wasn't Wren.

He was grinning at her, but his eyes were questioning.

"Uh, -" Margot said, embarrassed. Again.

The girl tittered. "I'm Nancy. This is Chris. We just moved here."

The boy added, "Well, sort of. My dad used to live here like, twenty years ago. He came back to teach at the high school." He looked at her kindly, his dark eyes still curious.

Margot nodded. "Ah, I see," she said lamely.

Kim giggled. "Nancy's in my grade, but Chris

is two years older than you, so he's in grade -" she looked at Chris, fluttering her eyelashes. "Ten, right, Chris?"

"Eleven," Chris said, still looking at Margot. "My birthday is in December, so I end up being the youngest in my grade, most of the time.

Margot studied him, feeling entitled to it, given his unbroken gaze on her. Who did he think he was? He wore a blue t-shirt with a glittery "Magnum, P.I." print on the front. She met his eyes again. "You don't – have a twin brother, do you?" She thought of her own brothers, so different in appearance. And Wren didn't look entirely different from Chris; they had similar coloring – *except the eyes,* Margot thought, remembering Wren's almost eerily clear blue eyes - and their fashion sense was identical. She looked at Chris's feet. Two shoes. Not identical, then.

Chris knotted his eyebrows together, then laughed. "No, why?"

Margot shook her head, looking down the tracks toward the orchard.

"Well?" Kim pressed, eager as always for gossip.

Margot brought her gaze back to the group with some effort. "I, uh, met this guy a few days ago." She looked at Chris's hair. "He's blonde, too, but he has blue eyes. He's homeschooled, too -" she trailed off, thinking. At least Wren hadn't lied to her about that.

Kim leaned over, waving a hand in front of Margot's face. "Hello?"

Margot focused on her friend. "I think he was hurt. His leg – anyway, I think there was something wrong with him."

Kim giggled, Nancy joining in enthusiastically. "What are you talking about? If there was another new kid, I'd know," Kim laughed, bringing her hand to her chest.

"Yes, you certainly have a gift for knowing everything there is to know," Margot remarked without thinking, and now Chris was laughing.

Kim blushed, looking hurt.

"Hey, it's a compliment!" Margot hastily added, backpedalling.

Kim smiled good-naturedly. "It's a full-time job!"

Now they all laughed.

Margot stood. "I'm going to look for Ella," she announced, though in truth, she was thinking of the orchard.

"She's at the pool. She was looking for you earlier," Kim informed.

Margot shook her head, smiling. "See? You

know everything!"

Kim smiled. "Hang out with us!"

Margot shook her head. "It's getting hot. Besides, I have homework."

"On a SATURDAY?" Nancy asked, disbelieving.

"My teacher's nuts," Margot said as she started walking. She called, "Nice to meet you!" over her shoulder.

"Wait up!" Chris called, his footfalls loud as he caught up to her, running with some difficulty on the gravel beside the tracks.

Why is this guy following me? Margot looked sideways at him, half-smirking. "It's easier to walk on the tracks," she said, hearing the condescension in her own voice and regretting it. She had fallen into the habit of acting like a jerk when she was feeling shy. It was easier than letting her awkwardness show, but she'd learned the hard way that it gave off the impression that she was a snob. She stopped, then scooted over a bit. "Here," she gestured to the tie she was standing on. "It's a lot faster, too."

Chris smiled, hopping over the rail and joining her. Margot blushed, realizing the track was too narrow for the two of them to comfortably walk side-by-side on, and yet she'd been the one to suggest it. She reflexively took a step back, hitting the rail with her heels, her arms whirling as she tried to keep her balance.

Chris caught both of them, saying, Whoa!"

Giving in, Margot let him pull her up, his hands warm on her skin. She thought of Wren's cold hands, then pulled her arms back, looking up at Chris. "Thanks."

"You new at this, too?" he joked, gesturing at the tracks.

Embarrassed, Margot rolled her eyes before turning again and starting off, hopping expertly from tie to tie. She heard Chris start after her, working to keep her pace. *I'll show you who's new at this,* she thought.

"How often does the train come?" he asked, and Margot was relieved to hear he was a bit breathless.

"Hardly ever, now," Margot answered. She actually hadn't thought about it in a while, but couldn't remember the last time she'd needed to vacate the tracks.

"Too bad. Have you ever put a penny on the rail?"

Margot scoffed. "Of course."

Chris seemed to be at a loss, saying nothing more.

Margot slowed as they reached the hill to the wooden fence. "Have you been to the orchard?" she asked, pointing toward the trees that towered above them.

He looked up, shielding his eyes from the sun. "What kind of orchard?" he asked.

"Apple," she answered. There was something refreshing about this kid. Unlike the neighborhood kids, Chris didn't seem to need to have the answer to everything.

He looked back at her. "Want to go?" Margot was momentarily taken aback, quickly deciding she didn't want to be alone with Chris so far back in the woods. She didn't know him at all, really.

She shook her head. "I have to get home. But if you want to go, just climb the hill, here, and over the fence. There's a few paths through the trees, and they all lead to the same spot."

He raised his eyebrows.

"The orchard?" she said, a sarcastic question in her words.

Now he looked embarrassed, and Margot couldn't help but empathize, laughing.

"Sorry," he said. "I think I'm overheating. We stayed inside a lot of the time in the city." He wiped his forehead with his shirt, bringing the bottom edge of it up to his face with both hands, inadvertently revealing his taut belly.

Margot let out a small gasp, then covered her mouth as a giggle escaped.

He moved his hands to his mouth, looking at her over the edge of the shirt.

"Uh – nice abs?" she said, glancing at his bare skin again.

He lowered his shirt. "Whoops."

She laughed, then started walking again.

"Hey," he called, seemingly deciding to stay behind.

She turned to look at him.

"Too bad you're homeschooled," he said, smiling shyly.

Butterflies took off in her stomach, and she was disarmed. No sarcastic remark to be found, she only smiled. "I'm here every day!" she said, then turned back around quickly, cursing herself. Did she just give this guy another invitation? She did not want to give him the wrong idea.

And what would that be? her thoughts challenged her. She was fourteen years old. Practically everyone else her age was thinking about the opposite sex in ways she'd never been compelled to do. Sure, she liked boys, but the thought of a boy having any sort of – expectations – made her nervous.

Contrary again to the other girls her age, Margot hadn't yet started filling in – there was still a skinny kid looking back at her in the mirror when she brushed her teeth at night. She was pretty sure she was the only girl her age waiting for her period, and she wore a bra more to fit in (at Mom's insistence) than to fulfill a need. *Not much to support there, she thought,* looking down at her boyish chest.

She turned toward the dump, momentarily forgetting her inappropriate shoe issue. Remembering as the tall grass came into view, she turned back around, then automatically stepped back, gasping. Wren was there on the tracks, where she'd been just moments ago.

She bent forward to catch her breath. "Wren!" she yelled. "You scared me!" She straightened, smiling, but her smile slid off her face at the blank look on Wren's. "Wren?" she asked, starting toward him in concern. He was filthy, his hair smooshed flat on the left side of his head, and he was gripping his left thigh, where Margot had noticed track grease before. He stared at her, seemingly confused.

Margot stopped. Blood was seeping from his leg and head, flowing between his fingers and dripping down his forehead. "Oh, my God!" she screamed in a panic, and his face changed as she ran toward him. It was like it cleared – he actually started to smile at her before she tripped.

Her flip-flop bending beneath her, she fell forward, squeezing her eyes shut as she braced for impact. Her forearms scraped on the gravel path and bolts of pain shot through her legs as her knees met the ground, hard. Her face was largely spared by some miracle, but her chin did bounce off the ground in a final insult.

"Oooh," she groaned, laying flat on her stomach and assessing the damage inwardly, first. She opened her eyes a crack and a few blades of grass came into focus. Her knees hurt the most, but almost as bad was the discomfort of having bits of gravel stuck into her palms and forearms.

That was good. If that was the worst of it, she'd be good to go in a few days, tops. It wasn't her first clumsy move.

"Margot?" a voice cut across her thoughts. She looked up, remembering Wren. He still stood on the tracks, his face contorted with worry.

What the -? He was clean. No flat hair, no blood. Had she been imagining things? Had her own fall placed the memory of him, hurt, in her brain? She shook her head. The bump on the chin must've knocked a screw loose.

"I'm OK!" she called, pushing herself back to her knees, which protested forcefully. She fought the grimace that threatened to take over her face, and was appalled to feel her eyes brimming with tears. Expecting Wren to run toward her, she urged them back.

But he wasn't coming. "Are you hurt?" he called, still standing in the same spot on the tracks.

She shook her head, using her palms to brush the gravel off her scraped-up forearms and palms, a few particularly sharp rocks refusing to budge, half embedded in her skin. A tear escaped to her cheek, but she swiped it away. She stood, a bit wobbly, and brushed at her knees now, taking note of a deeper cut amongst the scrapes and gravel on the right kneecap. "Shit," she muttered.

"What is it?" Wren asked.

"Come here and see!" she yelled, surprising herself at how angry she sounded. But what kind of person didn't rush to help someone when they fell? She threw her hands up in exasperation as he shook his head no. "Fine!" she yelled, turning toward the field, her tears refusing to back off, now.

"Margot, wait!" he called, and Margot turned, uncaring if he saw her crying. "Margot – do you know Harris?" he asked, and she was momentarily shocked into silence.

"What?" she finally replied.

"Harris – do you know him?"

"Harris who?" she shouted, her hands gesturing dramatically at her sides.

"Harris Chalk. He's my best friend -" he trailed

off, looking at the ground, then raising his head again, adding, "I need to find him."

Margot shook her head. Was this guy for real? "Whatever!" she shouted, but it felt weak. She turned, her back to him as she limped away, adding "Jesus Christ!" at the top of her lungs.

That felt better.

He called after her again but she was tired of him, and she hurt all over. She wanted her mother and a bath.

She didn't pause as she reached the tall grass, even as she remembered the snake from earlier. At the end of her rope, she yanked both flip-flops off her feet, holding them in her hands, and took off across the field as fast as her limp would allow, yelping now and then as her bare feet met something squishy or rough.

When she arrived home and her mother gasped at the sight of her, she fell into her arms, crying.

Her father looked up from his paper in the living room. "What happened to you? He asked, pushing his glasses up his nose.

Margot could only continue crying.

The twins stared at her, mouths agape, from their puzzle on the table.

"Come on, sweetie," Mom said. "Let's get you

into a bath."

Margot sobbed in relief. She spent the rest of the weekend recovering in bed with her Walkman and her books, stubbornly turning away visitors, even Ella. She only wanted to see one person, and as soon as all the other kids were back in school, finding him was her first priority.

Wren had some explaining to do.

CHAPTER 5 - I'M SORRY

Margot sat on the edge of her bed on Monday morning, peeking under the bandage on her right knee, having already examined her left. While the scrapes and the larger cut on her forearms and knees had scabbed over and felt much better, they looked much worse.

The angry red of the skin all around her injuries had deepened and expanded into a rainbow of bruises, the ugliest of which being an impressive snot-green colour. The purple one on her right knee was almost pretty, though. She hadn't even looked at her chin since Saturday. She'd let herself live in denial about that one all weekend. It was such a little-kid thing to have: a big ugly scrape on your chin.

Her mother had fretted over her as she washed and bandaged her hurts, asking what happened and chastising Margot for her shoe choice. She just as quickly apologized when Margot's face crumpled into tears over her own stupidity.

Margot hadn't mentioned Wren – especially the part about seeing him badly hurt when he actually wasn't. That would guarantee a trip to the emergency room, and Margot couldn't imagine a more boring way to spend the rest of her day.

Still, she felt weird about the whole thing. She had seen Wren like that, whether it was her own imagination or not, and despite her efforts to stay out of the hospital, she wondered whether she had given herself a concussion.

But there were other things, too. She'd recalled how Chris had walked with her along part of the tracks on Saturday morning. The warmth of his hands on her arms. The energy of him beside her. She couldn't quite put her finger on it, but it had felt so – different – than her encounters with Wren had. And – the way Wren had refused to come to her when she'd fallen, not like he didn't want to but like he couldn't. She'd been angry about it at the time, but now it just seemed...odd.

Last but not least, his desperate calls after her about this friend he needed to find. So random, especially considering the circumstances.

In the end, after having gone over it a million times while she lay in bed recovering (and stubbornly hiding from the world), Margot wasn't angry with Wren anymore. She just wanted to see him. And ask questions.

Walking down the hall, she noticed her limp had disappeared, and was glad. Maybe her chin was back to normal, too! Leaning over the sink as she examined it in the mirror, she groaned. She guessed she shouldn't be surprised that it was bruised like the rest of her scrapes and cuts, but did it have to be the green colour? And yellow?

"Ugh," she muttered, considering the foundation she'd bought because Ella was getting some, but hadn't ever used. She decided against it, reasoning internally that an ugly, bruised chin with foundation on it would look worse than an ugly, bruised chin without.

She brushed her teeth, then went downstairs, her brothers' raucous voices greeting her from the kitchen before she could see anyone.

Her mother peered around the frame of the archway, a flipper in her hand. "She lives!" she announced, and Margot did a little spin, curtsying neatly at the end. Her Mom disappeared, presumably going back to the stove to flip something. "Don't do anything too fancy there; you don't want to complicate your injuries!" Mom giggled, and Margot entered the kitchen rolling her eyes.

"Margot! Can I pick your scabs?" Aaron yelled, smiling hugely.

"Ew!" Margot squealed. "You're gross, Aaron." She grabbed an apple from the fruit bowl and sat on one of the stools at the island.

Mason tugged on her shirt, a mischievous smile on his face as he looked up at her.

"Yes?" she asked, looking down at him.

"Can *I*?" he asked. Margot glanced over at Aaron, who was flying a paper plane, making broken engine noises, then screaming as it plummeted to the floor.

Looking back down at Mason, she said, "Maybe later."

He scurried away, whispering, "Yesssss!"

"You shouldn't do that, you know," Mom said from the stove.

"Oooh, pancakes!" Margot said as Mom flipped a fluffy, blueberry-dotted disc. "Do what?"

"The boys and I went blueberry picking yesterday," she smiled, then added, "You know what! Treat them differently!" she gestured toward the boys, who were fighting over the plane, now.

"But they *act* differently!" Margot protested.

Mom looked at her, then shook her head.

"Right?" Margot challenged.

"Well, you still shouldn't do it," Mom huffed, and Margot laughed.

"Oh!" Mom looked at her again as she carried two plates to the table. "One of the new kids from the bottom of the hill came by last night! Boys, come eat!"

Margot thought for a second. "Nancy?" she asked.

"No, the older boy – Chris?" Mom answered, going back to the stove. "Wow, Margot, he's *handsome!*"

"Mom! Why didn't you come get me?"

Her mother eyed her, incredulous. "Are you kidding? After you yelled at me to turn Ella – YOUR BEST FRIEND, INCIDENTALLY – away, I stopped trying! Kim came by, too!"

Margot threw her hands in the air. "You still could've told me!"

Mom sighed.

"Why are we fighting?" Aaron called from the dining room, his mouth full of pancake.

Mom said, "Don't talk with your mouth full!" at the same time Margot said, "Stop being so nosy!" and they looked at each other, pausing before bursting into laughter.

Mom placed a plate in front of her now, gesturing at the syrup. "OK, look," she started. "The truth is, I forgot to tell you last night. The boys made a huge mess during their bath, and Aaron insisted on wearing his Superman pyjamas, which were in the wash -"

Margot softened. "It's alright, Mom," she interrupted.

Mom patted her hand, then returned to the stove. Margot took a giant bite of pancake, moaning as she chewed. "So good," she mumbled.

What could Chris have wanted? She wasn't surprised he'd found her. With the social network the neighborhood kids formed, it would have been as simple as yelling the question into the air. You'd get an answer back from someone. She giggled out loud. That was a bit of an exaggeration, but when there were people like Kim...*aha! Kim!* How could she even have questioned?

"Math first this morning," Mom reminded them as she sat at the table with the twins.

"Yep, and then I'm done!" Margot reminded her back.

"You probably read enough to last you the week, I'm sure," Mom replied, "but we have history, too, and there's an activity sheet."

Margot groaned. She'd forgotten about history.

Mom sighed. "You can do history right after math, if you like," she offered.

"Yeah!" Margot enthused. It would get hot later in the day, and she was eager to find Wren.

She finished her math in no time, her brothers protesting as they struggled through theirs. History took longer, only because the activity was tedious.

Regardless, she was out the door by ten, her feet safely clad in runners this time.

She was surprised to meet Mr. Albert, the farmer, on the tracks. Warily, she raised her hand as she approached him. Most of the time he was friendly enough, but when his cows had been bothered or his fences had been damaged, he spread his wrath in a wide net, reprimanding every kid in his path.

Today he seemed friendly, his return wave a good sign.

Exhaling, Margot yelled, "Hi, Mr. Albert!" in greeting as she approached him.

He stopped as she drew near, and Margot held her breath again. Maybe she'd read him wrong.

"Hey there, uh, Margot. How are you?" he asked, then jumped back theatrically when he spotted her bruises. "What the hell did you get yourself into, girl?" he asked.

Margot sighed. This would be the first of many such reactions, she supposed. "It's no big deal, I just fell, on the weekend," she explained.

"I ain't never seen that many scrapes and bruises from a simple fall!" the farmer replied, eyeing her knees.

Margot shrugged. "I excel in clumsiness," she offered, lamely.

He laughed. "Not the best subject to be good at, I imagine," he remarked, scratching his chin through his beard.

Margot started walking again, getting ready to say her goodbyes as she left the farmer behind.

"Now, just wait a second," he said, his fingers finding her arm as she moved to pass him.

She stopped, looking up at him. "Huh?"

"I wanted to ask you about a kid, tall guy, real skinny?" he held his hand up to demonstrate the height.

Margot scowled. "Do you mean Chris? He and his family just moved in at the bottom of -"

He shook his head, stopping her. "Nope. I seen that kid, too, and his little sister, to boot. This other kid, he's blonde, too, but more of a sandy color, you know what I mean?"

Margot nodded. "You mean Wren."

He raised his eyebrows. "That his name? Huh. Feels like I heard it before." His eyes looked distant for a moment. "Anyway, I never can seem to get close enough to him to ask. I see him in the orchard, mostly," he gestured with his thumb behind him, "but have seen him on the tracks, too, at a distance. Always seems to be avoiding me."

Margot felt her brows knit together as goose-bumps raised on her arms and legs. There was that feeling again, of something being off.

The farmer continued when Margot didn't respond. "I only want to introduce myself, and maybe find out a little about him. I find it cuts down on the vandalism, you know, when the kids know me."

Margot nodded. "If I see him, I'll tell him. Promise."

"Good girl," the old man said, hooking his thumbs into the straps of his dirty overalls.

"Is that all, Mr. Albert?" Margot asked politely, unable to keep herself from glancing past him and down the tracks. He raised a hand and moved to the side to make room for her, to Margot's relief. "Bye, then, Margot. You have yerself a good day," he said, before loping down the track in the opposite direction.

Margot skipped from tie to tie, focusing on her footing. Approaching the hill to the orchard, she moved to the right of the track, craning her neck in an effort to see the bridge.

She was still too far back.

She looked again toward the trees beyond the wood fence. Which to try first? Remembering the feeling of triumph when Wren had pulled in the big pike, she started for the hill. It was closer, anyway.

The forest beyond the fence was still cool, thick as it was with shadows as the sun slowly climbed in the sky. Just past noon, there'd be some heat as the sun shone straight down to the forest floor. Otherwise, the trees stood too close together to let much light in. The other kids avoided this part of the woods as much as possible if they were alone; there were other ways to get to the orchard, but they took too long for Margot. If they were with friends, though, these woods were the best for finding salamanders, toads, worms and other slithery creatures.

Margot was relieved to feel the sun on her skin when she entered the orchard. And it didn't take long to spot Wren; the sound of his reel letting line out as he cast met her ears right away. A few steps toward the sloping hill to the river, and Margot caught sight of his blonde head, his short hair neatly combed back today.

I was starting to wonder if he owned a comb, Margot thought, and chuckled to herself as she started down the slope.

Wren looked her way, then shoved the grip of his rod between the same two stones as last time so he could come greet her. As she reached the bottom of the hill, he held his hand out to her. She smirked, but grabbed it as she hopped down the last few feet. It would be just like her to deny his help and fall in front of him, again.

Rather than letting her hand go when she landed beside him, he grabbed her other one. "I'm glad to see you," he said, studying her face.

She blushed, remembering her chin as he released one of her hands to reach for it, grimacing. She turned her head and he pulled his hand back.

"Sorry," he said. "It must still hurt a lot."

She looked back at him. "Not really," she answered truthfully. "It's just – gross."

He shook his head, taking her hand again. "I want to tell you I'm sorry," he said, his cool blue eyes holding hers steadily, just like their hands.

She grew confused, her feelings of warmth and excitement mashing together with the more familiar discomfort. "For what?" she asked, willing herself not to pull away too fast. She wasn't sure she was ready to be touched like he was touching her, but she didn't want to offend him or seem like a prude – a name she'd been called more than once. After all, he was only holding her hands. But no eyes had ever looked at hers like his were in this moment. With regret, sincerity, and interest as well.

He smiled, and it changed his face entirely. Margot had to focus on not getting overwhelmed by the butterflies that swarmed in her belly.

He really is beautiful, she thought.

"About the other day, of course!" he replied, finally letting her hands go.

For a second, she thought she'd fall without

him to hold her up. Amazingly, her legs held her with nary a wobble. "Yeah..." she paused, not knowing how to continue. She didn't want to get angry with him - that urge was gone. But she wanted to ask why. Gathering her courage - which she was sure would have been more difficult if he'd still been holding her hands – she continued, "That was sort of...weird."

He looked down at his feet, shoving his hands deep into his pockets. "Exactly," he said quietly. "I should have come to help you," he raised his eyes to her in sincerity.

She held his gaze, brimming with questions but having no words to form them. "It's OK," was all she could manage.

A sound from behind them had Wren snapping his gaze toward the river. She whirled around as he took off at a run, yelling "Oh, no!"

She ran to catch up, the sound of fishing line being reeled out reaching her ears.

He must have a fish on again! she thought, and she was right, though Wren hadn't gone for the rod where he'd left it; he was running awkwardly beside the river in the direction of the bridge, half bent over, his arms outstretched in his effort to catch it as it was dragged at high-speed down the bank of the river.

Margot stopped, her hands going to her

mouth as she wailed in sympathy for her friend. She hopped up and down a little, her cheeks hurting as she smiled despite the trouble Wren was having recovering his property. She lost sight of him as he carried on and the river bent to the right, the trees obstructing her view. But she did hear some splashing and swearing, making her laugh behind her hands again.

He returned to her some minutes later, looking dejected.

Margot made a herculean effort to banish her smile. Noticing he was empty-handed, she cried, "Oh, no!"

Wren looked up at her, then spun around, making an offensive gesture back in the direction of the lost fishing gear.

She couldn't help it; she giggled again.

He stopped at the willow, sitting hard on the ground, his back scraping audibly against the bark. "Shit," he said half-heartedly, his hand going protectively to his back.

Margot ran to him, squatting beside him before sitting down gingerly, babying her knees. "I'm sorry you lost your rod," she said, trying to catch his eye.

He turned his head, looking over the water. "I'll get it back," he replied. Then with a decisive nod, "I always do."

Margot narrowed her eyes. "This happens often?" she asked, a note of humour in her voice, but he didn't reply. She sat back, hugging her legs. He was wearing the Dukes of Hazzard shirt again, but today he had tied a sweatshirt around his waist.

"I have to get going," he said, still looking at the river.

"OK," Margot replied, suddenly feeling an urgency to ask him more before he left. She spotted his left foot, again bereft of a shoe. She was sure it had been there before, this time. "Wren," she laughed, pointing to his foot, "you lost your shoe again!"

He looked at his feet, then stood, a new feeling of urgency radiating off of him. His hair was messed up, too. Margot felt gooseflesh crawling across her skin again. "Wren, last time you asked me if I knew somebody -" she blurted as she got up.

He was hurrying now. "Don't worry about that," he said quietly, already starting up the slope to the orchard.

Margot followed him. "Wren! Wait up!" she called, feeling like a little kid as she worked to catch up with him. It didn't happen until they were halfway across the orchard. "I want to help you find your friend!" she said breathlessly, laughing a little as she caught up. H e didn't answer. Margot looked at him, a question freezing on her lips. He looked different.

"I have to go!" he said, louder now. "Wren? Wren!" she called as he sped up, ahead of her again.

"Wait a second!" She yelled now, a desperate quality to her voice.

Amazingly, he stopped.

She ran up to him, planting herself in front of him, her face contorted in confusion. She looked him up and down. There was no way she could blame Wren's dash through the brush for the change in him, now.

His left thigh was a mess - bleeding, just as it had before she'd fallen the other day. She hadn't imagined it. A concussion, whether she was suffering one or not, did not plant the image in her brain. Remembering, she raised her eyes slowly to his head, then took a step back, her hand flying to her mouth in shock. His hair was flattened on his left side again, and now she could see a mess of gravel and blood in his exposed scalp.

"What's happening?" she screamed, but he only stared, his eyes strangely blank.

"Harris Chalk," he said, and to her horror, a gooey line of blood-tinged drool flew out of his mouth, stretching as it hung from his lower lip.

Margot screamed again, shrinking back from

him as he passed her. He smelled of sweat, blood and something else. Earth. Frozen, she could do nothing but watch him walk away from her, through the dark woods.

When she realized he was almost to the fence, she snapped back into herself, and sucked her breath in to scream "Where are you going?" after him.

"I don't know," he answered, his voice reaching her as though from a great distance as she started to run again, her legs shaking as she did.

"I'm in shock," she said aloud, remembering her first aid course.

He was at the fence. Too far to catch, but not too far to hear her. "You don't know?" she wailed, tears welling in her eyes as she tried to process everything she'd seen, even as she continued to run toward Wren.

He disappeared over the fence, and she fell to her knees in defeat, letting out a desperate yelp as she landed, her previous injuries reopening.

Then he answered her, and it seemed like his voice was coming from all around her. "I don't remember the times in between," it said, like a whisper, but loud in her ears.

She put her face in her hands, falling back onto her bum, her knees straightening painfully in front of her.

And cried.

CHAPTER 6 - A CONVERSATION WITH CHRIS

Margot didn't go home that afternoon. She couldn't face her mom with fresh blood oozing from her knees – and yet she was exhausted and ached for her bed. Still on the forest floor, but quiet now, her tears dried up for the time being, she looked up through the trees at the sky.

The sun had reached its peak and had started down again. Margot estimated it to be around one o'clock. Comforted by the swaying trees, she lay on her back, the earth cool beneath her. Her fingers moved at her sides, picking at the fallen pine needles and bending them absently. Some were dry enough to snap in her fingers. Some weren't.

Her mind wandered as she watched the clouds float by in the blue-sky-filled gaps between the treetops. And eventually, she fell asleep.

She awoke with a shiver, the sky above her grey, now. But then something moved on her leg, and she knew the shiver had been in response to that rather than the slight change in temperature. Sitting up, she squealed as she spotted a spider on her leg. "Get OFF!" she screamed, her frenzied swats far more violent than needed. The spider had disappeared in seconds, but she kept swatting away at herself as she stood, jumping up and down for good measure as she did.

Somebody laughed, and she froze. This time, she was out of luck. There was a witness to her ridiculous display, and it served her right. *Why am I such a spaz?* she wondered inwardly before she turned to find out who it was. *As long as it's not –*

It was Chris. "Jesus," she whispered as the feeling of defeat overwhelmed her. At this point, she had two options: she could either fall back down and hope to hit her head hard enough on one of the tree roots to knock herself out (and thusly avoid having to explain anything to anyone), or she could just let go of the last tiny bit of hold she had on acting like there was anything normal about this day.

She lowered her head, her hair falling in front of her face, leaves and pine needles poking out here and there. She raised her hand to pick a particularly crunchy leaf out of it. Given her choices, she decided the latter was her best bet.

Chris was walking toward her. Margot smoothed her hair back, sniffed, and brushed herself off.

"What was that?" he asked, then stopped when he saw her face.

She pointed at her chin, acknowledging the target of his stare. "This is the least of my worries," she said, and it felt good to just say what she thought without a care for what he would think.

"Ella told me you'd been hurt," he said, and real concern showed on his face. "I came by last night to see how you were."

"Yeah, my mom told me this morning. Sorry, I felt pretty miserable all weekend."

He nodded, then looked at her knees. "Are you OK?" he asked.

"Let's just say it's been a rough day," she said, looking down. Her bandage had soaked through with blood.

Chris stepped toward her. "Did something happen? Did someone – hurt you?"

Margot was touched by the anger in his voice. She shook her head no, but tears filled her eyes. "Oh, man," she said, wiping them away. Option one was looking more attractive. She scanned the forest floor for tree roots.

"Hey, hey," Chris said, reaching out to her. Overwhelmed, she stepped into his arms, folding her own arms between them and letting her tears come. He held her until her tears slowed. She was warm. No longer feeling overcome by the events of the day – or the last few days, really – she allowed herself to take note of Chris's arms around her. His breath, rhythmic and soothing. His scent – soap, maybe a touch of sweat, and – coffee?

She pulled away slightly, looking up at him. "Do you drink coffee?" she asked, and he laughed. She looked at him more closely. Had he been crying, too? "Are *you* alright?" she asked, her arms still folded against his chest.

He ducked his head, stepping back. The cool air felt cruel against her skin after his warmth. Margot hugged herself, rubbing her arms.

"Yes, and I'm not sure," he finally answered, looking at her again with a smile.

Margot thought back, placing his answers with her questions. "Huh," she replied. "Coffee's gross."

He laughed. "You're – different than other kids, Margot."

"So are you," she said, pointing at his shirt. "For example, you have a weird wet mark on your chest," she smiled.

He looked down. "I don't mind," he said, patting the damp spot made of her tears.

They looked at each other, the seconds drawing out as each considered what to share with the other.

Margot surprised herself by reaching for his hand. "Come on," she said. He didn't hesitate in taking hers. She led him back toward the fence.

"You don't want to go to the orchard?" he asked.

"Not today," she replied. She let his hand go as they climbed over the fence and down to the tracks, then walked in companionable silence until they reached the bridge. He stopped as she started over it. She looked back. "Coming?"

"This thing makes me nervous," he confessed, and rather than push, Margot simply turned and walked back to him.

"We can sit here," she said. When they were seated – she on the rail and he on the tie, his back against the opposite rail, she said, "You first."

He picked at a hangnail. "Huh?" he asked, not looking up.

She stared at him. Still without the desire to push, she started. "Remember that kid I mentioned the other day?"

He looked up, grinning. "My twin?"

She laughed. "Yeah. I saw him today."

Chris sat up straight, locking his eyes on hers. "Did he hurt you?" he demanded.

She held her hands up in front of her. "No!"

He relaxed back, but his face was still tense as he studied her.

"No," she repeated quietly. "But -" she considered her words. "But he scared me. There's something wrong with him."

Chris leaned forward, resting his upper arms on his knees, his hands clasped in front of him. "You said that the other day, too."

She nodded. "I'm sure of it, now."

"What is it? What's wrong with him?"

She sighed. "You'll think I'm crazy."

"Too late," he joked, then looked at her seriously. "Tell me."

"Ah," she said, looking down at her shoes. She undid the laces on the left sneaker, then redid them. "He – he changes," she said.

He looked confused. "And yet – some things stay the same," she finished, her voice sounding dreamy as she said her thoughts out loud for the first time.

"What?" he asked, and she had to laugh. She couldn't blame him; she wasn't sure what she meant, either.

"I don't know," she said, looking back along the tracks. "It's hard to explain…" she trailed off, her ears perking up. She turned her head back to him, meeting his eyes. "Hear that?" she asked.

"What?" The whistle blew again, closer this time, and his eyes widened. "Train?"

"Yep!" she said, and he grabbed her hands again. They pulled each other up and got off the tracks, skidding down the rocky incline and coming to a stop at a patch of grass halfway down. The train blew over the bridge, the wooden structure creaking as it bore the weight of the huge machine. Then it passed them, car after car, their hair blowing back in its wake. Chris grabbed her and she was surprised to feel him trembling. She looked up at him, but his eyes were riveted on the looming monster above them, his face impossible to read. It was past them in seconds, but Chris's head turned as he watched it fade.

"Oh, wow. You're afraid of trains," she said, and he shook his head.

"No?" she asked, watching his face as he let go of her.

"No," he said. "Not trains."

"I'm confused."

"Come on," he said, reaching for her hand, and it was Margot's turn to reach back. They climbed back up the shallow slope and back to their spot on the tracks. Chris put a hand lightly on the rail.

"Wow," he said. "I've always wanted to see that."

"Chris," Margot began, "you looked – scared - when it went by!"

He looked at her, settling back into his spot on the tie in front of her. "I guess it's my turn anyway," he mumbled, turning his head in the direction the train had just disappeared in.

She said nothing. Just waited.

"I told you on the weekend that my Dad is actually from here, right?" he asked, his gaze still fixed in the distance.

Margot nodded.

"Well," he said, looking at her again. "He didn't just move back because there was an opening for him at the school."

"OK...?" "

Something happened here when he was a teenager, to a friend of his. But he was there."

Goosebumps again. Margot steeled herself for what he'd say next.

"He never really got over it."

"What happened?" she whispered, not altogether sure she wanted to know.

He shook his head. "He moved away soon afterward. Said it was just too hard to be here. Then he sort of just – lived his life. Married my mom, had us kids – me and Nancy," he added, redundantly.

Margot rolled her eyes. "I remember," she said, teasing just a tiny bit to lighten the mood.

"Then Mom died," he continued, and Margot groaned.

"I'm so sorry, Chris," she said, but he waved it away.

"It's OK. I mean, it sucks balls, actually, but it was almost a relief -" his eyes filled with tears again and he grimaced as he fought them. He met her eyes. "She was so sick," he said, trying to explain his last words.

"You don't have to explain," Margot said, her heart hurting for him. She found herself fighting an impulse to hug him as he had her, when she'd cried in the woods.

He wiped both of his cheeks, taking a steadying breath. "Anyway. After that, it was like it all came back for Dad, what had happened when he was a kid. That and losing Mom – it just all mixed together and – it was too much for him." He shook his head again. "He tried to kill himself," he said, and despite his efforts, a sob escaped him.

Margot gasped, then moved to sit beside him, taking his hand in both of hers and waiting quietly for him to recover.

"He did all kinds of therapy," he said, finally. "We did, too." Margot looked up at him. "And the therapist said he needed to make peace with both of the terrible things that were weighing him down, or he'd break under the pressure of them."

"Wow," she said now, honestly blown away by the story and at a loss for how to comfort this boy she'd only met a few days ago.

"Yeah," he said.

"So, he moved back here to make peace with what happened?" Margot asked.

Chris nodded. "Only it's not having the effect he hoped for. He's miserable. Says being back here just makes it that much more painful."

"I'm sorry, Chris," she said.

"Ah," he sighed, wiping at his face. "I just wish I knew how to help him."

She understood that.

"I think teaching is good, though," he added.

"You're scared he's going to try it again, aren't you?" she asked.

He only looked up the tracks again.

"I can't even imagine -" she trailed off. She thought of Wren, and how she wasn't sure how to help him, either. Maybe she *could* imagine, a little bit.

Approaching voices from the narrow trail in the woods had Margot dropping Chris's hand – which he laughed at – and Chris standing and wiping his cheeks with his shirt – which Margot laughed at. He looked at her, then down the track in the direction they'd come from. She nodded, and they were off, leaping the ties two at a time, laughing a bit. Once they rounded the curve, they slowed down, breathless.

Margot suddenly wondered how late it must be. "Oh, God. What time is it?"

Chris raised his bare wrist in front of his chest, studying it. "Time to get a watch," he answered, and she rolled her eyes. "Hey," he said, serious now. "Can we keep this – everything -" he gestured in a wide arc, implicating all the events of the day.

If only he knew, thought Margot.

"Between us?" he finished, and Margot nodded.

"Yes, please." He smiled, and they were quiet for a few moments. "I should get going," Margot said, starting to back away, her hands in her pockets.

He looked regretful, but said, "Me, too. Dad will be home from school by now. He stays late tutoring kids."

That triggered a memory for Margot: Ella had talked about the new teacher tutoring Adam. "Oh!"

she said. "I think he tutors Adam!"

Chris nodded. "Yep. Comes home with stories about him already, and it's only been a week!"

Margot laughed. "I bet. What's his name again? Your last name, I mean?"

"Chalk," he said.

Margot inhaled sharply, her heart pounding.

Chris was already walking back toward the bridge. "Guess I have to face these guys now, huh? All alone, too!" he called over his shoulder.

Margot was frozen. She'd just found Wren's friend, or a relative of Wren's friend. And deep inside she knew that the event that had Chris's father suffering for the last twenty years had to do with Wren. And no matter how she felt about it, she'd have to find out how, if she wanted to help him.

She shook her head, going over everything Chris had just told her. She wouldn't just be helping Wren. She'd be helping all of them.

"Shit!" she said, and then said it again, for good measure.

"Shit."

CHAPTER 7 - A RELUCTANT REALIZATION

Ella twirled a lock of hair around her finger, looking at Margot as she did. "Like, you want to know his first name?" she asked.

Margot gritted her teeth. "Yeah. I know his last name is Chalk," she explained again.

Ella shrugged. "OK. I'll see if I can find out at school tomorrow. I'll go to his office if I have to."

Margot relaxed, sinking into the pillow she'd shoved between her back and the wall. They both sat on Ella's bed on Tuesday night, forced inside by rain.

Ella leaned toward her, crossing her legs. "Adam handed me this note today," she said, digging in her shorts pocket and pulling out an intricately folded piece of paper. She held it out to Margot.

Margot took it, giving her friend an excited smile, though she truly didn't want to read a love note from that doofus to her best friend. She unfolded it, looking back up at Ella. "Impressive folding!" she said, and Ella nodded, bouncing on the bed a bit in excitement. "

Read it, Margot!" she said.

"OK, OK," Margot said, sitting up to lean over the paper. It was scrawled all over in clumsy printing. Margot read it aloud: "I think I love you, Ella Trenton!" She couldn't help but smile. "That's kinda cute," she admitted, then laughed at the twinkle in her friend's eyes. "Hm, it's kinda obvious you feel the same."

Ella fell backward, her strawberry blonde curls bouncing in a fan around her head, clutching a pillow over her stomach. "Oh, Margot. He's different than he used to be."

"I should hope so," Margot said, and Ella swatted her with the pillow. Margot took a breath and changed the subject, trying her best to be casual. "Hey, do you know about something happening here, like, twenty years ago?"

Ella rolled onto her side, resting her head on her palm. "That's kind of vague, Margot."

It was true, but she didn't have much more to go on. "I know." She laughed. "Something happened to a teenager."

Ella looked intrigued. "Oh yeah? Who told you that?"

Margot shook her head. "I just heard someone talking about it."

Ella narrowed her eyes, blowing a bubble and then popping it.

Margot wilted under the scrutiny. "Really, Ella. I don't even remember who was talking about it!"

"Probably Kim," Ella said, and they both giggled. "Hmm," she continued. "If it happened twenty years ago, you could ask any of the parents that lived here back then."

Margot sat up. Her friend had surprised her again. "Stevie and Sharon's family have lived here forever!" she said, excited.

Ella nodded. Her phone rang, lighting up on her bedside table. As she reached for it, her eyes widened. "Mr. Chalk lived here then; you could ask Chris or Nancy to find out for you!" she turned her attention to her phone. "Hello?"

Margot sunk back into the pillow again. That option was out. Chris had avoided her gentle probing for details the day before. Her next thought had her cringing with guilt before it was even fully formed. Nancy might be more forthcoming... She shook her head. If the topic had reduced seventeen-year-old Chris to tears, she couldn't imagine what effect it would have on Nancy.

What else could she do? She supposed she could check the library. She sighed, resting the back of her head on the wall and looking up at the '90210' poster on the ceiling, Luke Perry raising one eyebrow at her.

"What should I do, Luke?" she asked aloud, and Ella kicked her in the shin playfully. Margot shot her friend a dirty look, then, noticing the look on Ella's face, sat up a bit to listen in.

"Really?" Ella inquired into the phone, her heavily-lined eyes widening. She looked at Margot, moving the mouthpiece under her chin. "It's Kim," she said.

"Ask her about it!" Margot said, and Ella pointed at the phone, shushing her. Apparently, she already had.

"Oh, my God," Ella said, and Margot bounced impatiently. "How come nobody talks about it?" Ella asked now. Then, after a few seconds, "NO, WAY!"

Margot thought her head might explode.

"OK, talk to you later," she finished, replacing the phone on its base. "Holy shit, Margot, you are not going to believe this!"

"WHAT, already!?!" Margot yelled, exasperated.

"Chill, sheesh!" Ella said, stuffing a pillow between the arm she was resting on and her bed.

Margot took a breath and held it, counting down from ten. Her friend was enjoying having her on tenterhooks, and she didn't want to encourage her. Exhaling, she picked up a Sweet Valley High book from the bedside table, opening it to a random page.

"Margot!" Ella exclaimed. Margot regarded her over the top of the book.

"I haven't read this one," she lied. She'd read everything her friend had in her room.

"Don't you want to know what Kim said?" Ella asked, her voice shrill.

Margot put the book down. "Sure," she said. *Score*, she said to herself.

Ella bounced up, crossing her legs again. "I asked Kim if she knew about anything that had happened about twenty years ago, to a teenager!" she started.

This was not news. "Yeah?" Margot asked, sitting upright, too.

"She said that was the reason she was calling!"

Margot's frowned. "What?"

"I know, it sounds fake, right?" Before Margot could reply, she went on. "But, it's true! She said she'd been hanging out at the train bridge with Nancy after school and -"

"Was Chris with them?" Margot interrupted.

Ella frowned. "I don't know...why does that

matter?"

Margot shrugged. "Just wondering."

"ANYWAY!" her friend continued, "I guess Nancy told Kim that a friend of her father's got hit by a train when they were kids!"

Margot's stomach knotted. "What?" was all she could manage.

"I KNOW!" Ella said, chewing her gum in short, loud snaps. "But there's more – Kim asked her mom about it -"

Margot leaned forward, gasping. "Kim's mom's one of the ones who's been here forever, right?"

Ella nodded, curls bouncing. "Yep. And she re-members it! She told Kim that Chris and Nancy's father moved away soon after it happened. She said the whole town was a mess over it!"

Margot's thoughts raced. She picked at Ella's quilt as she tried to piece everything together. This had happened twenty years earlier – Wren wouldn't even have been born. Maybe he was the son of the kid who got hit? She smacked her forehead with her palm, then looked at Ella, who seemed to be holding her breath as she watched her friend think. "The kid that got hit -" she began, her stomach feeling sick. "Did he die?"

Ella rolled her eyes. "Of course, he did, you

twit! He got *hit by a train*," Ella enunciated each syllable, then looked toward the window, her face going blank. "Oh, my God. On our tracks, Margot," she looked back at Margot now, fear in her eyes. "He was killed on our tracks!"

"Crap," said Margot as she pushed herself to the edge of the bed and stood, pacing.

"Margot?" Ella asked.

Margot was quiet. *Wren's not the son of the dead kid, but he could be another relative – a nephew, maybe –* she reasoned in circles, avoiding the glaring answer on purpose.

"MARGOT!" Ella's voice but through her thoughts.

She stopped mid-pace. "What, Ella?"

"Didn't you say you'd met a kid that looked sort of like Chris? Blonde, but with blue eyes?"

Margot scowled, asking, "How did you know –"

"Kim," they both said in unison, and Margot shook her head, angry she couldn't have anything of her own around here.

"Well?" Ella pressed. Margot was reluctant to share Wren with Ella. She had no idea how to describe him, especially now, and she'd already told Chris more than she'd intended to. Ella raised her eyebrows, annoyed.

"I have to go," Margot said, hastily heading to the door.

"Oh, no you don't!" Ella shrieked, bouncing off the bed and grabbing Margot's arm.

"Ella, let go!" Margot said, her voice laced with panic. She made an effort to relax, her shoulders lowering away from her ears. "Please?" she added, desperate to get out, though she wasn't sure why.

"Margot, we're best friends!" Ella exclaimed, her voice pleading. "Just tell me – who was that guy you talked to Kim about?"

Margot felt her eyes well with tears. Her thoughts swam in confusion as she looked down at the carpet, then back at her friend. "I don't know who he is, but I'm going to find out," she replied, realizing she needed to talk to Chris right now.

"I'm coming," Ella announced, releasing Margot's arm and crossing the room to grab her hoodie.

"No, Ella!" Margot cried. "I don't want to spook him!"

"Who? The mystery kid?"

Margot frowned. "What does that mean?"

Ella cocked one hip, her opposite leg straightening to the side slightly as she crossed her arms.

Damn, thought Margot, *that really is effective. I*

need to practice more.

"Kim says nobody else has seen him!" she said accusingly.

"That's not true!" Margot shot back defensively.

Ella merely raised her eyebrows in an unspoken challenge.

Margot brightened, remembering her chance meeting with old farmer Albert. "Mr. Albert has seen him. He asked me about him the other day!" she said triumphantly. "Besides, that's not who I'm going to see," she finished.

"Of course not," Ella said sarcastically, tossing her hoodie on the bed.

Margot was torn. "I'm going to see Chris."

Ella picked her hoodie up again.

"No!" Margot yelled, and Ella jumped, clutching her hoodie to her chest and staring at Margot with wide eyes. "Margot, you're scaring me!" she said, and her face crumpled as she started to cry.

"Oh, Ella. I'm sorry," Margot said quietly, going to her friend. She hugged her for a few moments, feeling Ella relax a bit as she did. She pulled away, holding Ella at arms length. "I'm going to figure this out. And then I'm going to tell you everything, I promise."

Ella, still crying, wiped a tear away, and Margot dropped her arms. "You're really going to talk to Chris?" Ella asked, her voice high and shaky.

Margot nodded.

Ella looked moderately comforted, then looked at Margot again, asking, "But why won't you let me meet the other kid?"

Margot sighed.

"Because I'm worried he – Wren – might be the kid who died twenty years ago."

Ella's eyes widened in shock, and Margot reached out to gently wipe a trail of mascara off her cheek, succeeding only in smearing it into a jagged, black mess.

"Whoops. You have some makeup on your face," she said lamely.

"Margot," Ella whispered, and now it was she who held her friend's arms as she continued, "you think your friend – this 'Wren?' – is a ghost?"

Margot shrugged, trying for nonchalance, but failing as she shuddered visibly, images of Wren's on-and-off injuries flashing through her mind. His cold hands. The smell of earth about him. The way he only seemed to exist back in the woods and on the tracks. How his – condition – seemed to deteriorate while she was with him, until suddenly he was eager to leave. The words she'd heard echoing around her in the woods after he'd disappeared the day before, after she had asked him where he was going.

I don't know. And when she'd challenged him, *I don't remember the times in between.*

She felt sick.

"Holy shit," Ella whispered, and Margot nodded, meeting her friend's eyes. Ella dropped her hands. "Suddenly I don't feel like joining you," she said.

Margot grinned, almost tempted to change Ella's mind. "I'm just going to Chris's," she said.

Ella sat on the edge of the bed, her hands in her lap and looking, for once, like the fourteen-year-old she was rather than the adult she was working on becoming.

Margot went to the door and opened it.

"You'll tell me everything?" Ella asked from behind her, and Margot turned.

"I promise."

Ella nodded. "Be careful."

Margot nodded back. "I will." A thought struck her and she raised her pointer finger with her free hand, targeting Ella with it, adding, "And until then, *don't tell Kim anything!*"

Ella laughed wholeheartedly, then made an

'x' across her heart. "She wouldn't believe me anyway."

"That wouldn't stop her from telling the whole world," Margot noted, and Ella nodded in agreement. "Hey, Margot?" Ella called again as Margot made to leave.

She turned around, her eyebrows raised at her friend.

"I'm sorry about before," Ella said, her tears welling up again.

"Me too. Still best friends?"

Ella smiled, nodding through her tears, and Margot left, taking the stairs down to the front door as quick as she could and grabbing her shoes as she flew out the door.

Next stop, Chris's house. And if she was lucky, his father would be there, too. And she'd ask him his first name.

If it's Harris, she thought as she jumped from foot to foot, pulling her shoes on as she continued toward the road, *that'll mean I've been making friends with a dead kid.* Her heart hurt. She shoved the thought aside, determined to focus on her next task. She wasn't ready to put that final piece into the puzzle of Wren just yet.

CHAPTER 8 - MEETING HARRIS CHALK

Margot had slowed down.

A lot.

By the time she'd reached the bottom of the hill, she was positively dragging. She'd had way too much time to analyze things as she made her way to Chris's house. What exactly was she planning on saying once she got there, anyway? She guessed it depended on who answered the door. Chris and Nancy were easy – but what if it was Mr. Chalk? Would she just go ahead and talk to him? What if the man was so unstable that any questions from her that even hinted at his past would push him over the edge?

She was standing across from the house now, having come to the end of Ella's street, which turned off of her own. So, technically, all the kids on Ella's street lived at the bottom on the hill, but for some reason, the one house at the bottom was called – *why am I thinking about this now?* she asked inwardly, stopping her rampant thoughts in their tracks.

Focus.

She looked to the right. If she turned up the hill now, she could just walk home.

"For God's sake, you're just asking him his NAME, Margot!" she said aloud, chastising herself.

She took a breath.

It wasn't just the Chalks who'd feel the impact of Margot's next move. If she was right, it would affect Wren, too – whether in a strictly corporeal sense or not.

Which brought her to her next question, existential as it may be: *if Wren is really – if he isn't – OK if this kid is the spirit of the kid who got hit by a train and killed twenty years ago and through some as-yet unexplained cosmic event, he's been triggered to appear by the return of his best friend whose entire life has been devastated by his death and who has moved back home to hopefully get some closure –*

"Holy shit," Margot said aloud, and sat on the rocky dirt shoulder of the road with a thud.

If all that is true, why am I the one seeing Wren? she finished her thought, staring absently at the pavement in front of her.

"God help me" she said, the summed-up version of the Wren situation, as fractured as it had been as an internal monologue, momentarily overwhelming her.

"Are you OK?"

Margot's head snapped up in search of the voice, although she was unsure it was meant for her.

"Miss?"

Nobody to the left or to the right. Footsteps. Directly in front of her. Margot shielded her eyes with her hand as the sun appeared from behind a cloud. A shadow fell over her, and the person became a silhouette looming over her, the sun glowing around him. The next thing she knew, he was pulling her up, exclaiming, "Are you OK? What happened?"

The urgency in his voice finally brought her back down to earth. "Oh! Oh, no, it looks worse than it is," she started, stuttering over her words as she rushed to explain.

"You look like you've been in an accident!" the man said, panicking. He looked up the road, then back to the spot on the shoulder where he'd found her. "Oh, my God! Were you hit by a car?" He gently took her arm, walking her across the street.

"No! No, there haven't even been any cars – I mean, I sat down of my own free will!"

The man stopped as they reached the opposite side of the street and looked down at her, his eyebrows knotted. His hand still gently around her arm. "What?" he asked.

"I'm not hurt!" she managed. Where was this guy when she'd fallen? Remembering her injuries, she laughed. "Oh! You're seeing all this", she said, gesturing up and down her body. "But, look!" she pointed to her bandaged knee. "It's already been bandaged up, see? I fell on the weekend -"

He let go of her arm, his hand dropping to his side. "Why were you on the ground, then?" he asked, still studying her.

Margot laughed again. "I – I was thinking," she offered lamely.

A look of understanding softened his features.

Of all the things I could have said, I choose the truth and this guy gets it – what it's like to be so overwhelmed by your thoughts you're literally knocked over, she thought with some humour.

"So, you've had those moments, too?" she asked, smiling up at her would-be rescuer, taking note of his fair coloring, save the brown eyes. Something clicked in her brain and the shock of her realization made her gasp, an "OH!" escaping her involuntarily.

He looked confused, but smiled beneath a rather untidy moustache, and she saw it even more clearly, remembering Chris looking at her the exact same way.

"You're Mr. Chalk, aren't you?" she asked, already positive she was right.

"I am," he nodded, gesturing toward the house whose driveway they were currently occupying.

Margot slapped her forehead with her palm for the second time that day.

"You alright?" Mr. Chalk asked again.

"Yep, I'm just – sometimes I can't see the forest for the trees – or the opposite of that," she trailed off, cocking her head. She was *mastering* this first meeting with Chris's father. "Shit," she said, her hand flying to her mouth as soon as she heard it.

The man's eyes first widened in surprise, then crinkled up as he laughed.

"I'm so sorry, Mr. Chalk. I just – I'm friends with Chris and I was just realizing what an awful impression I'm making!" the words tumbled from her mouth. "I don't even swear very much – at all – usually!" She groaned. "I should just go," she finished, more than ready to give up and revisit this particular meeting another day.

Or maybe never. Chris could confirm his father's name. *He can't lead him to Wren, though,* her thoughts reminded her. She hated her thoughts sometimes.

In any case, Mr. Chalk was looking thoroughly amused. His eyes lit up and he pointed at her, shaking his hand as he connected the dots. "Ah-ha! You must be Margot?" he asked, his huge smile seemingly stuck on his face.

Margot nodded. "Can we just forget this whole thing happened?"

"No way!" he answered. "I've heard a lot about you, and my son can't seem to think of anything else." His eyes flickered, his smile finally faltering. "I probably shouldn't have said that," he said.

Now Margot smiled. "Seems we both have the same affliction," she said, and when he looked confused, she explained, "The no-filter-between-brain-and-mouth one."

He was laughing again, and Margot relaxed a little.

Thunder rumbled distantly, and she glanced up at the sky. The sun was hiding again.

He shook his head. "I had forgotten how quickly the weather changes in Nova Scotia. When I was a kid, my friends and I just gave up and fished in the rain," he said, his eyes suddenly distant.

Margot was quiet as she thought of Wren.

After a few moments, Mr. Chalk seemed to snap back to the present. "Do you – uh – fish?" he asked, half-heartedly.

Margot remembered holding Wren's fishing pole as he took care of the pike he'd caught. She shrugged. "Sort of," she said.

"Well, I should get inside," he said, sidestepping further into the driveway and gesturing to his car. "I was only supposed to be grabbing something I forgot in the car. Tomatoes," he finished, his voice trailing again.

Margot nodded. "Nice to meet you, Mr. Chalk."

He smiled.

Margot turned away, thinking, *this did not go in any sort of way I could EVER have predicted.*

"Hey, you're not a student of mine; in fact, you're homeschooled, right?" Mr. Chalk called after her.

Margot turned. "Yep!"

He smiled again. "Then you can call me Harris."

"Shit," she said again.

"What was that?" he asked, cupping his hand around his ear.

"Nothing," she called back to him, relieved she'd said it under her breath, this time. "Nice to meet you, Harris," she managed, before turning again and starting up the hill at a sprint, her thoughts racing.

I guess it turned out, after all, she thought, and

then focused on running as the thunder rumbled again, this time ominously close in the darkening sky.

CHAPTER 9 - TRAIN!

"Margot?" … "Margie-Mae!"

Margot snapped her head up, her mother's voice rousing her. Disoriented, she looked around, and then down. Her math sheet was smeared with what Margot could only assume was drool. "Ick," she said.

"Jeez," Mom said quietly, sitting at the head of the table.

Beside Margot, Mason giggled and Aaron, curious, got up on his knees to look at Margot's sheet. "What's that?" he asked his brother.

Mason covered his mouth, his eyes sparkling over his hands.

"Your sister was sleeping on her work and DROOLED all over it," Mom said.

Aaron pointed at Margot, laughing uproariously.

"Thanks, Mom," Margot said, rolling her eyes.

"I left the room for two minutes to get a tea, Margot. What's gotten into you?"

Margot put her head in her hands. "I didn't sleep well last night," she mumbled. That was an understatement – she'd spent the night tossing and turning, her previous day's conversation with Mr. Chalk on a continuous playback loop in her mind.

And thoughts of Wren, too. Wren, who seemed likely to be dead. But who was somehow here, anyway.

She took a napkin from the middle of the table and laid it over the offending puddle, then returned her hand to her head. She closed her eyes.

"Margot!"

"I'm not sleeping!" Margot said defensively, startling a bit in her chair. She looked at her mother.

Mom studied her, a look of concern on her face. "Are you OK?" she asked.

Mason, whose head had been turning back and forth as he followed the conversation, gasped, looking at Margot with worry.

"I'm OK, Mason," Margot answered. She looked at her mom. "I really am."

"Something's going on with you," Mom said.

"I told you, I didn't sleep well," Margot replied, growing tired of the third degree. Growing tired, period. Oh God, she was tired.

"Margot!"

"Shit," she mumbled, shaking her head in an effort to wake herself up.

Aaron was laughing and pointing again.

Mason still looked worried. "What's wrong with Margot, Mom?" he asked, and Margot felt a little bad for worrying the kid.

"MARGOT DID A SWEAR!" Aaron shouted, standing on his chair.

"Get DOWN from there!" Mom admonished, and Aaron complied, though he was still laughing and bouncing as he sat.

"Mom?"

"Yes, Mason?" Mom, answered, exasperated.

"What's 'shit'?"

Aaron's entire face lit up with mirth as he burst into laughter again.

Mom made a face. "Don't you worry about that, Mason, she said, sternly, then stood. "I'll be right back, boys." She motioned for Margot to follow her, and to her surprise, Mom led her all the way up the stairs, and into Margot's room.

"What are we doing?" Margot asked.

"You're going to bed," Mom replied, pointing sternly at Margot's bed. Margot only stared. "Margie, you need sleep. Anyone can see that. I'll let you have two hours and then you're going to do today's work on your own. Deal?"

Margot hugged her mom.

"I'm worried about you," Mom said into her hair.

"No need to be worried, Mom," she reassured her again.

Mom stepped back, meeting Margot's eyes. "Is this about a boy?"

"What?" An image of Wren popped into her head.

"That new boy – Chris – he seems to really like you."

Margot rolled her eyes. "Yes, Mom. A boy likes me so now I'm tired."

Now Mom rolled her eyes. "I only wondered if maybe you were worried, or if you had anything you wanted to talk about -" she trailed off, raising her eyebrows as she continued to study her daughter.

Margot looked down at the carpet. "Not really. I mean, I'm a little concerned that Chris might like me…"

"Concerned? Kim says all the girls want to date him!" Mom laughed at Margot's surprised look, adding, "That girl can talk."

"When did she…oh, the weekend."

Mom nodded. "When she came to visit you, she ended up talking to me." She smiled.

The twins started screaming downstairs.

Mom looked toward the bedroom door, yelling, "YOU TWO BETTER BE FINISHED YOUR WORK!"

The screams diminished.

"I should get down there," Mom said, looking back at Margot. "But first, why are you concerned that a handsome, nice young man might have feelings for you?" She brushed a lock of hair off of Margot's face.

Margot laughed. "Because I'm not – I mean, I feel like a little kid still, Mom. I see kids my age holding hands or going to the movies or even kissing, and it makes me feel...WEIRD!"

Mom looked at her sympathetically. "You know, I was a late bloomer, too. I didn't get boobs until after I had you, really."

"Oh, my God!" Margot cried. "You were, like, *thirty*!

"I was not! I was twenty-seven, thank you very much! And I – I meant that before I got pregnant, I was still quite, uh, modest in the chest area. But I had something. Hmmm...this isn't going as well as I'd hoped it might."

Margot giggled. "So – wait – when did you get

something?" she asked, hoping for fourteen, fifteen, tops.

"Your age. Just wait. It'll happen. And there's no need to rush it, honey. You don't need to be like anyone but your own perfect self."

"Thanks, Ma," Margot said, blushing.

"Speaking of which, you'd tell me if you'd started your period, right?"

Margot made a face. "Of course. Who else is going to keep me stocked in feminine hygiene products and reassure me that my mood swings are completely normal?"

Mom smiled. "So, it hasn't happened yet, then?"

Margot shrugged. "Nope. Nothing. Nada. Zilch. And again, I feel weird. I feel like I'm not normal. And trust me, I know I should be excited about Chris, but the truth is, I'm scared."

Mom hugged her again. "Margot, if Chris is as nice as he seems, you can be up front with him! If he asks for more than you feel ready to give, just tell him no! You don't even have to explain! You have nothing to be embarrassed - or especially scared - about! And believe me when I say there's no rush, my love. Just because you might be a little different does NOT mean you're not 'normal' – whatever that means, anyway." She looked Margot in the eye, bending slightly to make sure she had her attention. "Alright?"

Margot nodded, sniffing the beginnings of a cry session away with a giggle.

"I love you, my Margie-Mae. Now go to bed." Margot did as she was instructed as Mom blew her a kiss from the doorway, closing the door as she went to deal with the twins.

"I'm a lucky girl," Margot mumbled, then fell hard into a deep sleep.

When she awoke, her work was beside her bed stand, along with a glass of water and a sandwich. She checked her alarm clock – "Three?" she asked aloud. Mom had let her sleep for well over two hours. And now, time to go back to the tracks had for the most part passed, given the work she had to catch up on.

She reached out for the sandwich, hunger growling in her stomach. As she ate, she pondered her next move. Talking to Chris was the obvious thing to do, but part of her – perhaps the larger part – wanted to find Wren and confront him once and for all.

She shook her head. *That would be selfish, though,* she thought. Wren wasn't here for her, after all. Nonetheless, his presence had affected her.

Besides, what would she tell Chris? Everything? Wouldn't that make her crazy? She thought about her conversation with Mr. Albert, the farmer, and wondered if anyone else had seen Wren and just hadn't thought anything of it. Would Chris be able to see him? What if she confessed to him and he couldn't see him? What would stop him from thinking she was making up a story based on his confessions to her on Monday? He wouldn't like her so much any more, she bet.

Margot finished her sandwich, washed it down with some water, and then grabbed her work from the table. With no easy solutions for the Wren/Chris/Harris situation apparent, she decided to put it all aside for now and do something much simpler: her school work.

She finished her math (her puddle of drool having dried into an odd, warped circle on the sheet), then pulled out geography, reading the text pages that Mom had marked and answering some follow-up questions. She was still far ahead in English, but did an outline for a reading response anyway.

She didn't just want to finish the requirements, she wanted to impress the teacher tonight. Regardless of her indecision about her next steps, she knew she wanted to get outside and roam around a bit.

The phone rang, but Margot continued her work.

"Margot! It's for you!" Mom called up. "Are you up?"

"Yes! Thank you for the food! Oh, and I'm almost done my work!" she yelled back. She grabbed the phone, yelling, "Got it!" so Mom would hang up.

"Hello?" "Hey Margot. It's me," Ella said, and Margot could hear her cracking her gum.

She rolled her eyes. Surely her friend was calling for an update and Margot wasn't ready to give her one. "Ella! Hi, how's it going?"

"OK; Adam asked me to the end-of-year dance today."

"Oh? What'd you say?"

"Yes, of course!" her friend replied, making a sound of annoyance. "I mean, even if I didn't like Adam, I'd still want to go to the eleventh-grade dance. Hey! I bet I can get Jack to bring you...?"

Margot shut that down pretty fast. "Oh, good Lord, no. Jack's a nice guy. He deserves to go with someone who likes dancing."

"Ugh, come on, Margot," Ella replied, unimpressed.

"Or *wants* to go to the dance!" Margot added with a laugh.

Ella didn't join her. "OK. I get it. You don't want to go."

Margot was quiet. It seemed like she should feel bad about that, but she was at a loss for why.

"Margot, do you know how excited even the grade seven girls would be to go to this dance?" Ella asked.

"Um, not really," Margot answered, but didn't want to alienate her friend. "I'm sorry, Ella. I really hope you have a great time and I'll tell you what, if somebody invites me who isn't just bringing me because they've been pressured to, I'll consider it. If I want to go with them." She shook her head. It was a lame apology, even to her own ears.

She tried to start over, but Ella stopped her. "Someone like Chris?"

Margot frowned. "Actually, I didn't have anyone in mind. I just meant -"

"Oh, don't worry, Margot, I know what you meant. Hey, maybe your ghost will ask you!" she replied, and Margot could hear giggling in the background.

"Is that Kim?" Margot asked, frowning.

Ella avoided the question. "Anyway, I have to go. Give me a call when you figure that whole thing out. You did promise, remember?"

Margot had the feeling it didn't matter how she replied, and frankly she was more than a little pissed that it seemed like Ella had blabbed to Kim, so she just said, "Whatever."

click

Margot hung up, still frowning. She knew most of Ella's side of that conversation had been for effect, especially if Kim was with her, but it still sucked. Her feeling of being overwhelmed with situations she had no idea what to do with refreshed, Margot lay back on her bed, staring at the ceiling.

"Everything OK?" Mom asked from the doorway, and Margot jumped.

"Jesus!" Margot said, rising and walking past her mom to the bathroom.

"Margot!" Mom yelled after her. She was waiting for her in the hallway when Margot finished in the bathroom.

"I'm sorry, Mom. I had an - unexpected - conversation with Ella. I shouldn't have taken it out on you."

Mom pressed her lips together in a tight line, folding her arms, but didn't say anything.

Margot needed to turn this around. "Thanks for the sandwich. Was that your homemade blueberry jam?"

"Yep," Mom replied.

"*So* yummy!" Margot gushed, then skipped

to the bedroom, recovering her school work. "And look! All caught up, and then some!"

Mom took the work from her, looking over it slowly while Margot danced impatiently beside her.

"I was thinking – since I feel so much better, and I've done all my work, AND I've already had something to eat, maybe I could go outside for a while?" She smiled as Mom looked at her.

"That sandwich was lunch, Margie." She was using her nickname. That was good.

"I love it when you call me that. You're the only one who does, you know?"

"You hate that name!" Mom protested, but she was smiling. "You know, you're named after my Mom, who -"

"– insisted on being called Margie, with the hard 'g', because it's unusual!" Margot finished.

Mom put her arm around her and led her to the stairs, and Margot internally celebrated. She was totally winning, here.

"And easier to deal with than the -" this time she waited for Margot to finish.

"– silent 't'!" Margot finished, on cue.

They reached the bottom of the stairs and Margot raised her eyebrows at her mother, smiling again.

"Oh, you," Mom said, but there was defeat in her tone. "Go ahead. You haven't been outside at all today and you've been through some challenging stuff lately. Just be home before dark!"

Margot jumped up and down, hugged her mom, then stuffed her feet halfway into her shoes and burst out the door.

"Put those shoes on right, Margot!" Mom called after her. Then, "I'll save a plate for you!"

Margot waved without turning around. She headed up the street, deciding against the tracks for now. She'd sit in the quiet at the dead end.

It was a gorgeous evening - the Spring air was deliciously sweet with the scents of flowers and mowed grass. All she wanted was to be alone, smelling this smell and watching the sky change as the sun dropped slowly down to the horizon.

She saw the gate at the dead-end long before she reached it; the road levelled off at the top of the hill. And the distance between she and the gate consisted not of houses, fences and trees, like the rest of the street, but widened into empty fields as the trees shrunk back away from the road and to the thicker woods beyond the fields.

Margot sat on the pavement in front of the fence facing the side with the supposed abandoned house first, wondering about it. Imagining what it must be like behind those trees, who would have lived there – and why.

Thinking maybe she'd like to go back there, just to see it for herself.

She heard the cows in the fields beyond the tracks behind her, and used her feet to turn herself on her butt, hugging her legs to her chest. The air felt cool and moist on her arms, the breeze hinting that the rain wasn't quite done with them yet.

It was so peaceful. *She* was so peaceful.

She looked toward the woods, the tracks carving a gap through them, and wanted to go. Nobody would be out right now; it was nearly dinner time on a school night. But Wren might be there. She inhaled. She focused on how the cool air felt in her lungs, then exhaled.

But maybe he isn't.

Margot thought about the last time she'd seed him – gravel and congealed blood matted in his hair, his leg – ugh. It turned out she didn't want to think about it, after all. But she didn't want to have to steer clear of her favorite spots just to avoid him, either. It was probably true he wasn't there for her, but that didn't mean she had to go out of her way to hide from him.

She stood. That was logic that made sense.

Letting a feeling of lightness overtake her, she sprung forward in a run across the gravelly field toward the tracks. When she reached them, she was happy to find them bare as far as her eyes could see. She skipped along the ties, letting herself get lost in her thoughts, but not letting her thoughts wander to Wren. Or Chris. Or Ella. *Or Kim,* she thought with a smirk.

The cows were at the fence, so Margot said hi, visiting with them briefly and noticing bits of apple on her side of the fence. Someone must have been giving them treats. *That was kind,* she thought.

She turned to go back to the tracks and saw him peripherally, snapping her head back to the left as soon as his image registered in her brain. It was Wren, at the tracks by the trail to the dump again, but his back was to her.

She stood for a moment, conflicted. He hadn't seen her. She could turn back. She could probably even walk in his direction and cut across the field by the dump. She reflexively looked down at her feet. She'd never forget her sneakers again.

She looked back up. He was still there, but getting smaller as he walked away, hands in his pockets. The giant '01' on the back of his "Dukes of Hazzard" shirt was still recognizable, even at this distance.

The heifer closest to her mooed, startling

Margot. She slid down the grassy slope a little, then looked back at the cow. "OK, OK!" she said. The cow looked at her expectantly. "Sorry, pretty girl," she said quietly. "No apples here."

Margot made her way down to the tracks, looking after Wren again. It was strange that he hadn't seen her. Was he just here all the time? Or had he seen her and walked away purposefully, to avoid her?

Her heart sank.

The last time she'd seen him, he'd been working hard to get away from her, and fast. She'd had to run and scream to catch up to him, then to get him to answer her.

Huh. This could be bad, she thought.

What if she no longer had the choice to help Wren? Or Harris and his family, for that matter?

She moved up the tracks, now, two ties at a time. Toward Wren. For a long time, she focused on the accuracy of her footfalls, but as the ground on her left rose into the hill that led to the wooden fence, she had a familiar choice to make. Orchard, or bridge?

She cursed herself for not paying attention to where Wren had gone.

"Wren?" she called, but her voice was weak. She took a deep breath, and remembered how she'd learned to sing – from the diaphragm – and called out again, "WRREEEENN!"

Nothing, despite her impressive bellowing. Just the sound of the river and the light breeze in the trees.

The orchard would take longer; she'd have to go through the trees and then down to the willow to look everywhere. If she went to the bridge first, though, she could easily turn back as soon as she saw it. Assuming he wasn't there, of course.

Good.

Decision made, she continued her run on the ties. Soon she was turning the lazy bend to the left, relieved the bridge would come into her line of vision soon. She almost expected to have to turn around. She'd never found Wren at the bridge.

She slowed down, then, frowning as her mind worked. *If Wren is a – if he's visiting from – somewhere else – doesn't that mean his travel here isn't necessarily linear?* She stopped completely. *In fact, whenever I've seen him before, he had just been wherever I happened to be…*

If Wren didn't want to be found, there was nowhere Margot could go to find him.

"Balls!" she said.

Reluctant to turn around without at least trying, she continued around the turn. When the empty bridge came into view, she wasn't surprised. Still, she stood for a moment, giving him time, maybe, to appear.

"Wren?" she tried again, but with none of the strength she'd had before. She turned and started back in the direction from which she'd come. Starting around the curve, she glanced back at the bridge before continuing. So sure was she that it would still be bare, she automatically turned back to the curve after she took another look, even though there had been a figure on the far side of the bridge.

She stopped. None of the neighborhood kids went over there. It just – wasn't done.

She turned again, and he was there, his back to her now, walking away.

"WREN!" she called running a few steps toward the bridge. He did not look around, but there was a different answer to her call.

She stopped. A train.

"WREN!" she screamed. This really was feeling like the last time. She couldn't chase him now; she'd have to cross the bridge. "WREN! TRAAAAAIIIIIIN!" she shouted, her heart pounding – and her concern for her friend – whatever he may be – so all-encompassing that she forgot to get off the tracks herself until she saw it, like a nightmare, barrelling toward the bridge – and Wren.

She screamed again, leaping over the rail to the gravelly slope, her eyes on the train, and the figure of her friend in front of it.

"Wren," she cried, knowing he wouldn't move.

Is he trying to show me? Oh, God. Trying to show me he isn't – like me?

She could do nothing but stand trembling and watch. It didn't take long. When the train reached him, there was no impact, no body thrown. Still, she howled at the sight of it, a dark monster of a thing running over – or through – this boy she'd come to care for.

It was passing her now, and she was too close. She was repelled backward by the sheer heat from it, stumbling and landing on her ass again, then dissolving into tears.

She whipped her head to the left, her eyes unmoving until the train cleared her line of sight, and she could see Wren again, hands still in his pockets, facing her now. She sobbed in relief.

"Wren," she cried.

Don't try to find me, Margot.

The voice had come from all around her again, and she looked into the woods around her as though he'd appear there. Just the voice, though, and the sound of defeat in it was like a punch in the stomach.

"No! Wren! I found him!" she screamed back, turning to look across the bridge again, but he was gone. "I found Harris Chalk!" she said, more quietly, because she felt it was useless.

But just in case it wasn't, she said, in a normal tone of voice, "I understand now. I'm going to bring him back here. Please don't stay away, Wren. Please." One of her tears fell on a stone below her, turning it dark and shiny. She smeared her thumb over it, transforming the whole thing into something new.

She scrambled up, a new determination filling her.

"I'm not giving up, Wren!" she called across the bridge, her voice mingling with the sounds of the river. Then she turned and followed the tracks back, twilight falling.

I can only hope he heard me, she thought.

Because if she brought Harris back here and failed to find his friend – and hers - she had no doubt she'd only be making a painful situation worse for everyone.

CHAPTER 10 - CHRIS, MEET WREN

Thursday dawned hesitantly, the sun peeking though the clouds in fits and spurts as though it were unsure of its decision to rise that day.

Margot felt much the same.

At least she'd slept. She rubbed her eyes, flashes of her strange dreams fading as she stretched, groaning. Her thoughts instantly turned to Wren, and she felt that sinking feeling in her stomach again.

"Nope!" she said as she pushed herself up and out of bed. *I may not be able to control that whole situation, but I can control how I approach the day.* It was a comforting thought.

She sped through her bathroom routine, then went down the stairs, where she met her father on the landing in front of the door.

"Hey, Margot! My one and only daughter," he greeted her, his arms open for a hug, his briefcase dangling from his right hand.

"Hi, Daddy," she said, allowing herself to be enveloped in his arms.

He looked down at her, still holding her close. "I barely see you anymore. You too busy for your old man?" he teased.

Margot smiled. "I'm a girl in demand!" she said, hiding the truth under her smile.

"Well, I have to get to work, but next time we're here at the same time," he said, releasing her and grabbing the umbrella from the closet with his free hand, "I want a rematch!"

Margot shook her head, remembering the crushing defeat she'd dealt her father the last time they'd played chess. "You sure you want to risk another thrashing? That must have felt pretty..." she tried to think of a term that would hit him where it hurt, as daughters are expected to do to their fathers. "...emasculating." She finished, smiling smugly.

"Jane!" he yelled toward the kitchen. "Stop letting this girl read the thesaurus! She keeps finding new and painful ways to insult me!"

Margot giggled. He'd had a smile on his face as he called out to her mother for her benefit.

He started to mess up her hair, then pulled his hand back, his smile faltering. "You're growing up so fast," he said, his thumb brushing her cheek.

Her eyes welled up at the rare, sweet moment with her father.

He turned with a wave, saying, "You be good for your mother!" and the spell was broken. That was more like it.

Margot went into the kitchen, wondering at the quiet, and immediately saw Mom and her brothers through the patio door. The boys had buckets and Mom was helping them dig.

Worms.

Margot smiled. When the day started outside, it meant Mom was tired of regular lessons (or had noticed the kids were), and was going to teach them differently – which usually meant more fun outside and less question sheets at the table. Buoyed by this thought, she knocked on the door and waved when Mom and the boys looked up, Aaron brandishing a juicy-looking earthworm.

Mom motioned for her to open the door.

"Nice worm, Aaron!" she called, and Aaron puffed up with pride.

"I got two worms, Margot!" Mason announced, trying to outdo his brother.

Aaron laughed. "You mean you cut one tiny worm in half with your shovel!" he taunted, and Mason shrugged.

Mom shook her head, then finally got a word

in, "We're headed for the insectarium this morning. I know you've seen it all, so you can skip this trip if you want."

"Yesss!" Margot exclaimed.

Mom raised a hand and continued: "That doesn't mean a free day, Margie. It means you do what I've left for you on the table."

Margot glanced at the work; it seemed like less than she'd have on a typical day. She looked back at her mother. "Thanks, Mom!"

Mom nodded, adding, "And *then* you can have the rest of the day free."

"I love you, Mommy!" Margot yelled, jumping up and down.

The twins sprung up at the same time, yelling, "I love you Mommy, I love you Mommy" in shrill falsettos.

Margot and Mom shared a look. Despite their differences, these moments of uncanny synchronicity between the boys were always fascinating, even when they were also annoying.

Margot waved, closing the sliding door, and set about making herself some toast.

She was quickly interrupted by a quiet knock at the door. Margot looked around the side of the arched doorway toward the front door, frowning.

Who could that be?

She saw no one from this angle, so walked to the door, butter knife still held upright, blueberry jam slowly making its way toward her hand.

She stood at the screen, peering outside. She could see the kids at the bus stop goofing around, but there was nobody here.

Just a kid playing tricks, she thought, then spun around. It wasn't the first time.

"Margot!" came a whisper from behind her, and she turned back.

"What?" she asked, feeling a bit strange about talking to a disembodied voice.

"Come out!" came the whisper again.

Her toast popped in the kitchen and she sighed. It'd be cold by the time she was back to butter it. Licking the jam off the knife, she opened the door, leaning out.

Chris leaned against the house, smiling at her.

"Chris! What are you doing?" she asked, surprised to see him.

"My dad mentioned your meeting."

"Ugh. That was – bad," Margot said, remembering.

"Come out for a sec," he said, moving backward to make room for her beside the door. "Do you always arm yourself with a butter knife when you answer the door?" he asked with a grin, eyeing the utensil in her hand.

"Uh-" she looked down at the knife. "I'm making toast," she offered, feebly.

Chris laughed, then glanced toward the bus stop. "My dad likes you. He said you were funny," Chris said, squinting as the sun peeked out.

"Really?" she asked, then added, "If he thought I was funny after that disaster of a conversation, you guys must've had some real weirdos around you in the city!"

Chris laughed again, shaking his head. "You have no idea!" Quickly looking toward the bus stop again, he said, "Look, can you be free at lunch time to take a little walk?"

Margot frowned. "You don't have a full day of school?" she asked.

He smiled. "Yeah, but I need to talk to you, and I don't want to wait until everyone else is around tonight," he said, then added, "Crap!" as the sound of the bus climbing the hill became evident. He backed away, nearly falling down the stairs. "Smooth, Chris," he said under his breath.

Margot covered her mouth, a giggle threatening to escape.

"Lunch?" he asked. The bus came into view and he started running backward.

How does he make that look so easy? Margot thought, then nodded quickly, realizing he was waiting for her answer.

He gave her a huge smile and turned, running at top speed for the bus.

Maggie frowned. What could he want to talk to her about that was so important he was going to skip school? Regardless, it was convenient – she needed to talk to him too, after all.

She turned back to the kitchen, remembering her toast. "Ice cold," she mumbled, retrieving it from the toaster. She thought of making two new slices, glancing guiltily out the window at Mom, then shook her head. She went about spreading the butter on the rough surface, tearing it here and there. "Toast is all about timing!" she muttered, annoyed. Then she carried her plate to the table, grabbing a banana on the way.

She started her lessons as she ate - usually a no-no, but Mom and the boys were still out back, closer to the trees, now. And she wanted to be done by lunch.

She needn't have worried; she had finished her math and was well into modern world problems – the local paper laid out in sections all over the table as she wrote the report Mom had assigned

– by the time Mom and the twins left for the insectarium. By twelve, she'd finished all of her work, washed the breakfast dishes, and was sitting on the front porch with her Walkman.

The urge to run back to the tracks made her feet twitch as they hung over the edge of the porch, her arms resting on the middle railing. She touched her chin. The bruises had almost completely gone, and her scrapes had downgraded into pinkish marks, to her relief.

Chris was in front of her before she realized he's been approaching. She jumped, pulling her headphones off and jerking her head to look at the old beater that was speeding away.

"That your ride?" she asked.

Chris nodded as he reached to take her headphones.

"Oh, you probably won't like what I'm listening to," she warned as her cheeks reddened.

Why does revealing my music choices always make me feel so vulnerable? she thought, but was quickly relieved as Chris made an impressed face.

"Prince is amazing," he said.

She nodded, "I KNOW!"

"Wanna walk?" he asked, and her stomach did a somersault, to her surprise.

She rose, opening the screen door to put her Walkman on the table just inside the door.

"It's quiet," he said from behind her.

She turned, then jumped over the steps, landing on the grass rather than the cement sidewalk. She'd learned that the hard way, too.

Chris watched her, grinning. "You're fourteen, right?" he asked, and Margot felt a twinge of embarrassment.

"What?" she asked. "Oh, I get it - you've never seen a teenage girl execute a leap so well, have you? I know," she joked, breathing on her fingernails and shining them on her shirt.

He laughed, his eyes never leaving her.

"Let's go," she said, starting across the lawn toward the road.

"Where are we going?" he asked as he jogged to catch up, his backpack sliding down his shoulder.

"Back gate. Do you have lots of homework?" she asked, motioning to his bag.

He groaned. "I always feel like there's too much homework!" he exclaimed.

She raised her eyebrows at him.

"What?" he asked. "Don't you get the same amount of work as we do?"

Margot shrugged. "I can't really say I have a fair basis of comparison; I've never gone to public school. But I know we follow a mandatory lesson plan, including tests and assignments, in order to progress."

Chris shook his head. "You talk like you're the teacher."

Margot sighed. "People always say stuff like that. It's just because Mom and Dad don't treat us like kids get treated in public schools. They believe our brains are like sponges when we're young, and our capacity for learning is limitless – tempered with proper amounts of play, good sleep, and so on," she explained, then looked at him.

He was staring at her blankly. "What?" he said.

"Uh – Mom uses techniques that have been proven to be really effective when teaching young minds."

He looked ahead, smiling again.

"What?" she asked.

"Nothing," he said. "I heard you were smart."

"Maybe I'm no smarter than any other kid," she proposed. "Maybe I'm just exposed to different things – or exposed to things differently," she reasoned.

"Do you think your mother would teach me?"

he asked, turning around so he was walking backward, facing her.

She laughed, feeling nervous and a bit giddy. What was wrong with her? "I'll ask," she said, grinning at him.

He smiled back, his eyes looking into her own, still.

"You're going to trip, you know," she warned.

"What?" He glanced behind himself then turned back to her, smirking. "I'm far too skilled to fall while walking backward!"

"Huh. What's that like?" she asked, and he smiled again.

When they reached the gate, Margot sat on the pavement and motioned for Chris to do the same. She pointed to the trees on the left. "Anyone ever tell you about the abandoned house back there?"

He raised his eyebrows. "Kim said something about it, but I didn't realize it was here. What, behind the trees?"

Kim. "Apparently."

"What? You've never been back there?" he asked.

She shook her head.

"Why not?" He looked shocked. "You don't

strike me as the type that spooks easily."

"It's not that I'm afraid, really, unless you consider that the house is falling apart. It's probably pretty dangerous, so I don't want to go back there alone. And none of the girls want to go back, either." She shrugged.

He gazed toward the trees. "I'm not even going to ask you why you wouldn't go back with Adam and Jack," he laughed.

She rolled her eyes. "No thanks."

He looked back at her. "I'll go with you! Want to go now?"

"Really? That's awesome, thanks! But – not today, OK?"

He frowned.

"I have something I need to talk to you about," she said, her nerves making her heart skip a beat.

"Wait a sec – you can't hijack this meeting!" Chris protested with a smile, but she detected some jangling nerves beneath it.

She laughed outwardly, but her stomach did a slow flip, too. "Oh yeah. Sorry, what did you want to talk about?" she asked. She'd honestly forgotten he'd asked her on this walk.

He shook his head, saying, "Ladies first."

"Are you sure?"

"Of course. I have all afternoon!" he spread his arms out beside him, looking happily free, indeed.

"OK." Margot looked at the pavement and scratched at it with a sharp rock, thinking. "Remember that boy I was telling you about?"

His face fell. "I had the feeling this was about him," he said.

"Huh?"

"He's your boyfriend, right?"

Margot's jaw dropped. "What? No!"

"Oh. OK now I'm confused."

Margot frowned.

"Go on," he said, gesturing for her to continue.

"OK...well, I think I figured out what's wrong with him."

"And...?" Chris seemed uninterested.

"I think he's dead," Margot finished, deciding it was best to just get it out, like ripping off a band-aid.

Chris's face was completely blank for a moment, making Margot's breath catch in her throat. Then he smiled slowly. "What?"

"I mean, I think I'm seeing a ghost."

Chris looked blank again.

"Look, I know it sounds insane," she started, and Chris rolled his eyes, then looked off into the trees again.

"Margot, if this is some sort of game -"

"I swear it's not."

"I get it if you don't like me. Ella told me I shouldn't ask you to the dance – she said you wouldn't go – but she didn't tell me why."

"You were going to ask me to the dance?" Margot was stunned. "And Ella told you not to?"

Chris only nodded.

Margot shook her head. They were getting off track. "Chris – Chris, can you look at me, please?"

He dragged his eyes away from the trees, then to the pavement on which they sat, and finally back to her.

"Chris, I promise I had no idea you were going to ask me. Ella is mad at me because I told her I had no interest in going – she's going with Adam."

"You have no interest in going?" Chris looked crestfallen.

Margot took a breath and placed her hand on his. "It has nothing to do with you. It's true I don't really get the excitement over these dances – most people just stand around looking awkward anyway

– but Ella was offering to get Jack to take me, and I said he should go with – ugh, the details don't matter. Just please trust me when I say that conversation wasn't about you."

Chris smiled a little, then flipped his hand upward to hold hers. Margot brought hers back to herself without thinking, and Chris's smiled faltered again.

"I don't get you, Margot," he said.

"Me neither," she said quietly, wrapping her arms around her legs tightly and looking into the trees.

"Go on, then. Tell me about your ghost." His voice had the sound of defeat in it, and Margot's stomach twisted, but she had no idea how to make it better.

She took a breath. *Just keep going,* she decided. "His name is Wren," she said, and watched a spark of recognition spread across Chris's face.

He looked at her, and Margot was surprised of the accusation in his eyes. "Who told you that?"

Margot faltered. "Uh – he did," she said, finally.

"I know Nancy went blabbing to Kim about what happened with Dad all those years ago, but -"

Margot held her hands out defensively. "It was *Wren* who told me, Chris! I promise. Either that's the truth or I'm crazy."

He looked unconvinced.

"Kim couldn't have told me – we're not really on speaking terms right now."

"She didn't say anything about that," Chris said.

"She doesn't really know, I guess," Margot said, unable to hold a small smile back.

Chris said what she was thinking: "That's a first."

She laughed, relieved that the tension was broken. "The new guy catches on fast!" she exclaimed, moving her head so she could catch his eye. "Chris – don't be mad. I'm telling you this because I think I'm supposed to."

Chris rocked back on his tailbone, his feet hovering over the pavement.

A breeze rose and while she shivered, Margot watched as it ruffled Chris's hair.

She carried on. "Before I even met you and Nancy – and then your father – Wren asked me if I new Harris Chalk."

Chris looked at her sideways, squinting as the sun said hello again.

"He told me he needed to find him," she added, crossing her legs and sitting forward. "I knew something was off – his clothes never changed, except to get more dirty. Oh, and one day he had a hoodie tied around his waist. His left shoe kept disappearing and reappearing and -" she paused as she tried to form the next bit into words. "– and the strangest thing was that his condition would change. One minute he looked clean and healthy and the next, he was hurt. Like, scary hurt, Chris. It didn't make sense until I met you and you told me something happened here twenty years ago."

Chris mirrored her, crossing his legs and sitting upright. "Why are *you* seeing him?" he asked.

"I've been asking myself the same thing. Last night, I went to find him so I could ask him, but he ran away from me." Margot surprised herself by sniffling, a tear falling from her eye.

"You do care for him," Chris said, but his tone was quiet and without blame.

"I do!" she replied, her voice high as her emotions took control. "He's my friend! I thought he was just a kid like you and me, Chris. And now, I know he died twenty years ago, and I think part of me is mourning the loss of him even though I still see him as though he's alive!"

Chris looked regretful.

Margot stood, feeling like she needed to move or she'd explode.

"Don't go," Chris said, reaching for her as he stood, too.

Margot took a step back. "Chris, I don't know what's going on or why I'm any part of it, but I am. For some reason, Wren came to me."

"OK. OK, I'm sorry. I shouldn't have doubted you. I can't even imagine what you're going through." He looked so sincere that Margot sighed.

"Nobody knows," she said, and she realized how hard it had been to go through all of this alone. "Chris, I started seeing Wren when you guys moved here. Wren told me he needed to find your dad. Then I met your Dad. It seems so simple, right? The path is logical; I know I'm supposed to take your dad to Wren. To help both of them."

"But it's not simple," Chris cut in, and Margot nodded.

"Exactly. I don't want to hurt your father any more than he's already been hurt. I mean with your mom and all -"

Chris nodded, scuffing his sneakers on the pavement. He looked at the trees again.

"Chris -"

He looked at her. "Take me to him."

Margot felt her eyes widen.

"What?"

"You're right, taking Dad to him now, before we even know what Wren wants, really, could push him off the deep end. He's been there before."

"But how will taking you solve that?" Margot asked.

"I don't know. Maybe I just need to see him for myself." He looked up at her, an apology in his eyes. "No offence, Margot. I just think it would be smart."

Margot nodded, though she felt like screaming. She'd confessed the deepest secret she'd ever had, and now he needed proof. *No,* she thought, *he just needs to protect his father.*

"Let's go," he said, and Margot looked across the rocky field toward the tracks.

"Right now?"

"Why not?" he asked, and the feeling he was challenging her hit her again. It didn't feel good. Then again, handling a ghost like Wren all by herself had been difficult, too. "OK," she said. "But first – two things."

He crossed his arms, cocking a hip. *Even he's mastered Ella's pose!* she thought, absently.

"I told you he didn't let me get near last night. I didn't tell you that I watched a train blow through him like he wasn't there."

"Shit," Chris said, grimacing.

"But my brain saw him, so my brain thought he was there at least in some way."

"So, it sucked."

"You bet your ass it did," Margot said, her voice sure and strong.

"And two?" he asked.

"Two, right. Two is that after the train was gone, he told me not to try and find him."

Chris lowered his head.

"So, I'm scared I won't be able to," she finished, a waver in her voice now.

"It's not your fault if you can't," Chris said, looking back at her.

She hesitated, then took a shaky breath. "Right," she said.

"So, now that I know all of that, can we go?"

Margot looked back toward the hill. "I wonder what time it is?"

Chris looked up into the sky. "Probably just before two," he said.

Margot's heart filled up a little. She'd never seen anyone else read the sky to tell time.

"What?" he asked when she continued to stare at him.

"I – I do that, too. With the sun," she said, pointing to the sky as if to show him where it was. Her cheeks got hot as he hid a smile with his hand. "Let's go!" she said, starting across the field, Chris catching up in no time.

"Why am I always running after you?" he asked playfully as he fell into step beside her. They walked in silence until they were on the tracks, and then Chris piped up.

"Why do you think he told you not to look for him?" he asked.

Margot shook her head, hopping up onto the rail on her side. "I keep going over it. I think about the time I spent with him - it always seemed hard for him, somehow. And then – you remember finding me in the woods by the orchard?"

Chris laughed. "Yeah, you were doing a crazy dance like you had bugs all over you."

"One bug, actually. A spider. He woke me up," she replied.

Chris shook his head. "Those three tiny statements make me want to ask so many questions -"

"Anyway -" she cut in. "That time was so strange. I'd been down by the river with Wren. When I first got there, his hair was neatly combed. I'd never seen it that nice. And he apologized to me for not helping me when I fell -"

"What? Really?"

"Yeah. I was pissed, but now that I know what I know, it sort of makes sense."

Chris waited for her to finish.

"I think he has boundaries. The tracks and the river, where he goes fishing."

Chris nodded, to her surprise. "Every time Dad talks about him, there's fishing in there somewhere."

"Well that day, he got a fish on. Wait, what the hell? How does a ghost actually catch a fish?" she looked at Chris.

He held his palms up. "No idea, Margot."

"Ugh. Anyway, his rod flew out of the spot he had it anchored in, and he went running after it!"

"Dad told me that story."

"What? You mean it happened before?"

"Yeah." He raised his hand, scratching his head. "Maybe it's not just location that serves as a boundary for him. Maybe even his presence – his activities – are bound by what's happened in the past."

A light went off in Margot's mind. "Right! Like, maybe it's easier to be here for him if he's doing something familiar."

"Yeah, maybe it's not so much that he's bound

to repeat the past, but that it's like slipping into a groove he's already familiar with, so he doesn't have to waste energy on the circumstances, at least."

Margot was impressed. "Holy cow, dude. I think you got it."

Chris looked pleased.

Another lightbulb. "And maybe that's why his appearance changes, too! When he came back from chasing the rod, he looked different. His hair was messed up, his shoe was gone, the rail grease was on his leg again."

Chris grimaced.

"It gets worse. At first, I could believe it was just from running through the woods. But when I laughed about his shoe, he got upset. Suddenly he was in a hurry to go."

"He was...fading?"

"Yeah. It must have been getting hard to just be here?" she looked at him, and he frowned back, thinking. "But this time, I ran after him. I was so confused and upset, I needed to confront him. But when I finally caught up and got a good look at him, I was terrified."

Chris stopped walking, his hands in his pockets. "Why?"

Margot stopped too, hopping down from the rail so she could face him.

"He was bleeding. His leg was torn open, Chris. And his head -" she stopped short, cringing at the memory.

"Shit."

"Did your dad ever say what the cause of death was?"

"I think it was a train, Margot."

Margot swatted him. "You dork. You know what I mean."

Chris was smiling again, and it felt good to see it. "No, he doesn't go into details. But – well, he always says he tried to help him." He looked at the ground.

Margot looked around. They were by the hill to the fence. She pointed to it, saying, "Let's try the orchard. He seems to be there a lot."

"He was probably happiest there," Chris said. Margot was amazed. "You know," she said, climbing over the fence nimbly, "No matter what happens today, I'm so glad we talked about Wren."

"Me too...I think," Chris replied.

There was nothing to see in the orchard. Chris jumped up here and there, hitting the branches, trying to go higher each time.

"Boys are weird," Margot muttered, but it didn't slow him down. She led him to the slope and down to the willow. It was deserted.

"Wow, this tree is amazing!" Chris said, putting his hand on the bark and looking way up into the drooping greenery.

"Don't get any ideas," Margot warned playfully. "This is *my* spot."

Chris smirked. "Seems like it's Wren's too," he said, and Margot could only nod, raising her shoulders in a shrug. "So, where is he?"

Margot looked along the banks of rushing water in both directions, then turned to Chris. "I don't know why I'm looking for him - if he's here, he sees us, and he's choosing not to make himself known."

Chris nodded, sliding down the tree to sit in her spot, his back against the bark.

"I'm going to try something," she said, an idea forming. She looked at Chris. "Don't laugh."

He crossed his heart, but he was already smiling.

Margot turned her back to him and faced the direction in which Wren had disappeared after his rod. "Wren?" she tried, feeling both silly and hopeful. "Wren, I have a friend here. This is Chris Chalk. Harris is his father."

"That's impossible," a voice said from behind her, and she whirled around.

155

"What?" Chris asked, craning his neck in every direction, but Wren stood beside him, looking down disbelievingly.

"Wren!" Margot exclaimed, overjoyed at his appearance.

Wren looked at her, a bit miffed, it seemed. "Who are you trying to kid? This guy is the same age as Harris, Margot."

Chris was freaking out. "What is it? Is he here? I don't see anyone! Wait a second! Why it is hot on this side? I feel all tingly!" his words came like bullets.

Margot raised her hand, a request for him to calm down.

He looked at her with desperate eyes.

"Wren," Margot started, and Chris scuttled a foot to his right when he saw where she was looking.

"Is he right beside me?" he asked, fear evident across his face.

"Chris, for the love of Pete, could you just take a chill pill?" Margot said, exasperated.

Chris's face went blank. "Sorry, but Margot, I do need to know if he's right next to me."

Wren had squatted down and was studying Chris's face, not a foot away.

"He's – close-*ish*," she said, trying to imagine

what it would be like to be unable to see someone your friend was talking to.

"He does look kinda like him," Wren remarked.

"Why can I see you, but he can't?" Margot couldn't help but ask.

Wren shrugged. "I wish I knew. It's hard for me to be seen...it takes a lot of work. What you guys were saying before was really close to how it is."

"You heard us before?" she asked, her voice rising. "Yeah, but I should tell you something. Margot, you may be one of the select few that see me, but that doesn't mean you see me whenever I'm near."

Margot shuddered at the prospect of having been watched when she thought she'd been alone. "*Really?*"

Wren had the audacity to laugh. "I don't know how to explain it. It's like a conversation. For it to be meaningful – successful, even – there has to be effort and desire on both sides. Sometimes I'm around and you're not looking. And I imagine sometimes you're around and I'm not looking."

Margot nodded now. "That kind of makes sense."

"WHAT IS HAPPENING?" Chris yelled, and both Margot and Wren jumped.

"OK maybe this guy *is* related to Harris," Wren said, snickering.

"He's admitting you're like Harris," Margot said to Chris.

"Admitting? He didn't believe I'm his son?"

"He didn't understand how you could be the same age as Harris," Margot explained.

"Yeah, like twenty years ago," Chris said.

Margot looked at Wren. "Twenty years?" Wren asked.

Margot nodded.

Wren shook his head. "Time isn't the same for me now," he said quietly. "And I'm not always here. Well, I wasn't until you started seeing me."

"Where were you?" Margot asked.

"I can't explain it. It's like I was caught between two places. It wasn't unpleasant. Just – it just didn't feel like I belonged anywhere."

"Wow," Margot said, and Chris cleared his throat loudly. "Oh! Sorry, this is the most informative conversation Wren and I have ever had," Margot said.

"Aw, thanks," Wren said.

Chris said, "How nice for you."

Margot laughed. "If your father is anything

like you, and from what I've seen, he is, I can see why he and Wren were such good friends."

Both Wren and Chris smiled.

"How do I know Harris is really his father?" Wren asked.

"Not this again," Margot mumbled.

"What?" Chris asked.

"He's as suspicious as you," she answered. "He wants proof your Harris's son."

Chris paused, thinking. Wren folded his arms.

"Wren," said Margot, and he looked at her. "Your shoe – it's missing, again"

He looked down at his mismatched feet. "It's hard to hang on," he said, his eyes showing the new sense of urgency he felt.

"Chris, we have to hurry," Margot said.

Chris looked up. "Um, my father always says that no matter how hard he tried, Wren was always the one who got the girls' attention. He felt invisible beside him."

Wren smirked. "That's true, but why?"

"He wants to know why," Margot asked Chris quickly. "Oh, right! He said they both looked similar, but that Wren was skinnier and he was more fit –"

"Ha!" Wren interjected and Margot held a hand up to him, now.

"– but that didn't matter," Chris continued. "It was the eyes. Wren had him beat by a mile with his weird crystal eyes." Chris finished, looking at Margot questioningly.

Margot raised her eyebrows to Wren. "You do have pretty eyes," Margot said, trying to support Chris's statement, but sounding like a lovesick kid instead.

Wren nodded, seemingly accepting the proof.

"Now his turn!" Chris said, standing and wiping the dirt off his shorts. It was surreal to see them standing so close, facing each other, when she knew Chris couldn't see Wren. "He needs to tell me – tell you to tell me – something you wouldn't know."

Margot looked at Wren.

He looked thoughtful. Meeting Margot's eyes, he said, "This might not go well."

"Why not?" she asked.

"Tell him his mother sees him every day, and she's proud of him."

Margot gulped. She opened her mouth to speak, but Wren cut her off.

"Wait! Duh, anyone could say that." Wren tapped his foot, then raised a finger. "Tell him his mom used to sing him a song about the purple bunny."

"Purple bunny?" Margot asked, without thinking.

Chris jerked his head to look at her. "What?"

Wren started to sing,

Purple bunny, hopping hopping

Hopping through the grass

Margot cleared her throat. "You don't have anything where I don't have to sing, do you?" she asked Wren, and Chris's face crumpled into tears, his hands rising to cover his mouth. Margot sung, repeating the words and the tune as best as she could.

"Hey, you can sing," Wren said. He was looking worse for wear.

"Your hair, Wren. It's all messed up."

"OK,

You can try to catch him

But he's hopping way too fast!"

he sung, and Margot teared up as she imagined a young Chris being sung to by his mother. She sung the words, looking at Chris.

Chris lowered his hands. "My mother sung that to me. There's no way you could have known that. We made the song up about my favorite stuffed ani-

161

mal."

Margot nodded. She looked at Wren. "How did you know that?"

"I saw her all the time in the in-between place," he explained, as though it should be common knowledge. He frowned.

Margot looked at Chris. "They were – in the same place - before Wren came here."

Wren shrugged. Apparently, that was an acceptable explanation.

Chris stepped backward.

"What are you doing?" Margot asked.

"I don't know. I need to catch my breath, here," Chris said, not meeting her eyes. He turned and started up the slope.

"Wait! Chris!" Margot called.

"Don't worry, I'll talk to you soon," he called back, but he didn't turn around.

Margot looked at Wren.

"The Chalks are sensitive," Wren said.

Margot looked after Chris as he climbed the hill, then back to Wren. "Thank you for showing up," she smiled.

"I wasn't going to. I saw what being around me did to you." He stepped toward her. "I never wanted to scare you. Truth is, I think you're pretty swell."

Margot smiled at the term.

"I never actually used that. That was before my time. I just wanted to make you smile."

"It worked," she said.

"Anyway, as I was saying, I started regretting showing myself to you. But now, it's strange. When you're not here, it's like I'm not – not fully, anyway - either. And I'm not in the other place. It's like I'm just waiting..."

"Oh, my God. That's awful!" Margot couldn't imagine being dependant on someone else's presence in order to exist.

"No, don't feel bad. I think it just means you're the key."

"The key?" Margot asked. "Yeah. Before, in between, I – Clara and I – that's Chris's Mom." He slapped his forehead. "I feel so stupid. Of course Harris wouldn't be the same age if I was talking to his wife about their son."

"Don't be hard on yourself. Like you said, time is totally different where you – are."

Wren nodded. "I can't explain it in words that would make sense to you. But let's just say that chronology doesn't really matter as much after you leave your body. He paused, then looked at the ground. Raising a finger, he turned and spit, the resulting little puddle in the dirt tinged with blood. "You know what that means, my friend," he said.

"Wait! You didn't finish!"

"That's just it. Something here needs to be finished. Fixed. I know Harris isn't doing well. I think I'm here to stop him from repeating a past mistake that would make things much, much worse for him in death than they are in life."

"The attempted suicide?"

Wren nodded.

"Are you saying you go to Hell if you kill yourself?" Margot heard the disbelieving tone of her voice, but was unapologetic. It just didn't seem right to her.

"No!" Wren said. "But the earthly problems you don't solve here -" he looked all around them. "- follow you. And, as you can imagine, they're much harder to solve when you don't have a body anymore."

Margot nodded, though she'd need some time to process.

Wren was looking worse by the minute, though, and she wasn't afraid to admit she didn't want to see him at his worst. "You have to go," she said, and he took her hands, nodding.

"Thank you for being such a good friend, Margot."

She nodded, her breath catching. "I'll be back soon, with Harris."

He dropped her hands, then turned. "Don't let this scare you. I don't think I have a choice, this time," he said as he walked away from her, his body fading like mist.

"Holy SHIT!" Margot yelled. She understood now why he'd run from her before.

His laughter floated to her as the last of him simply disintegrated. "Oh, Margot -" his disembodied voice came from all around her, as it had before. "Bring both of his kids, too."

Margot nodded, taking note of the moment when she felt him leave entirely. It wasn't until several seconds had passed after his last words. "That's so cool!" she exclaimed, and it sounded odd in the empty space around her.

Her skin crawled and she bolted up the slope, the irony of her being spooked by her own voice in an empty space not escaping her. But she'd have to think about it later. Right now, she needed to get home to where everybody could be trusted to remain solidly there, with actual, living bodies and everything.

CHAPTER 11 - A LONELY SATURDAY

The rest of the week was uneventful; Margot didn't see Chris again, despite being outside every evening. And, for the first time since they were in elementary school, neither Margot nor Ella had reached out to mend things.

By the weekend, Margot was itching for some company – any company - that wasn't her brothers. As she walked the tracks on the hot Saturday morning, she puzzled over how she could smooth things over with Ella. Nothing obvious sprung to mind.

The heat radiated off the rails. Margot brightened; summer was coming! That meant everyday lessons would go on hiatus!

Uplifted by the thought, she was turning the curve to the bridge before she knew it. The sound of laughter brought her back down to earth, and when she looked up, Ella, Kim, Adam and Jack were all looking at her from their spot in the middle of the bridge.

Their positioning had Margot's stomach

churning. After what she'd witnessed happening to Wren, she knew she couldn't go that far onto the bridge.

Feeling painfully self conscious, Margot started toward them, raising a hand to Ella. Ella raised hers in return, but her face was impassive.

"Hi guys," Margot called, slowing as she approached the bridge, and then coming to a full stop about five steps onto it. Nobody had answered her greeting. "What are you doing?" she tried again.

"Talking about the dance," Ella said, a superior tone to her voice.

Margot nodded. "Cool."

"Come sit with us," Jack offered, and Margot exhaled, but tensed back up when Ella shot Jack a dirty look.

"Nah, I was just coming to say hi, but thanks, Jack," she replied, then looked at Ella. "Can I talk to you for a sec?"

Ella smiled, loudly chewing her gum as she did. "Sure." She made no move to get up.

"In private?" Margot added.

"What's wrong, Margot?" Adam asked, a stupid smile spreading across his face. "Can't find your pretend boyfriend?"

Margot frowned at Adam, then looked at Ella

questioningly.

Ella studied the wood slat she sat on.

"So much for secrets, hey Ella?" Margot challenged, trembling as she confronted her friend.

Ella looked at her. "So much for promises too, hey Margot?"

Margot filled with rage. "I never broke my promise to you, Ella! I just didn't know what to tell you, yet!"

Ella put her nose in the air and whispered something to Kim.

Kim looked sideways at Ella. She looked – conflicted?

Adam laughed. "Go find your ghost, Margot. He's probably better company than us real people, anyway," he smirked, hitting Jack on the arm as he laughed.

Jack smiled, but looked at his sneakers instead of joining in.

"Fine!" Margot yelled, turning. Thinking better of it, she whirled back to face them. "And you're right, he is better company than any of you!"

Adam continued to laugh, his voice breaking, but nobody else was smiling anymore.

Margot couldn't help but feel a twinge of guilt as she turned again and started back along the tracks. Sure, they were being assholes, but that didn't mean she had to be one, too.

Wren's still a real person, she thought, regretting that she hadn't corrected Adam on that point, at least for the sake of defending her friend.

She was surprised at the sound of footsteps coming closer from behind. *There's no way that's Ella,* she thought, but didn't turn to find out.

Kim caught up to her, saying, "Slow down; my legs are short!"

Margot was surprised to see Kim – but as she thought back, she realized that the usually vocal girl had kept silent throughout the exchange between Margot and her little group. "What do you want, Kim?" Margot asked.

Kim stopped short, raising her hands. "If that's the way you're going to be -" she said, leaving the rest of her sentence hanging.

Margot sighed and stopped, turning toward Kim.

"I know Ella's mad at you, and Adam – well you know Adam's a halfwit," Kim smiled, and Margot felt herself soften a little toward the petite blonde girl.

"Why is Ella mad at me?" Kim rolled her eyes.

"She says you're being secretive and cutting her out of the whole ghost thing – which, by the way, I totally believe -"

"You do?" Margot crossed her arms, afraid to believe it was true.

Kim nodded. "My mom told me about what happened to Wren Blakely all those years ago – it's terrible, Margot."

Margot let her arms drop as she processed Kim's words. She shuffled her feet. "I never knew his last name," she said, emotion rising in her chest. "It makes it all more real, somehow."

Kim frowned, her pretty lips turning down in confusion.

"That this new friend of mine actually died twenty years ago," Margot added as an explanation.

"So, you really do see him?" Kim asked, her eyes curious.

Margot nodded.

"My mom said all the girls had crushes on him, but all he wanted to do was fish," Kim giggled.

"What happened to him – I mean, how did it happen?" Kim frowned again.

"I'm not sure. Mom just said he was with a group of boys and he got hit. There was talk of the boys playing chicken with the train, but Mom said that Harris – Chris and Nancy's dad – always denied it."

"Really?" Margot was starting to understand why Harris had needed to leave.

Kim nodded. "He swore it was an accident, but there were still rumours, you know?"

Margot gasped. "Wow – that's terrible."

Kim nodded.

"So, whether it was an innocent accident or not, some chose to believe it was the result of a stupid competition," Margot stated, just to say it out loud.

"Can you imagine what that made Harris and the other boys feel like?" Kim asked, shaking her head.

Margot went to Kim and hugged her spontaneously. "Thank you, Kim. You've helped me a lot," she said, sincerely looking down at the smaller girl's surprised face.

"No problem. What I was going to say before – about the reason Ella is mad at you?"

Margot shaded her eyes; the sun was getting hotter by the minute. "Yeah? Because I was being secretive about Wren or whatever, right?"

Kim glanced behind her, then turned, lowering her voice. "I don't think that's the real reason. I think she's jealous that Chris likes you."

Margot burst into laughter.

Kim put a finger to her lips. "He told her he wanted to ask you to the dance."

Margot nodded. "You can tell Ella I've never wanted to compete for boys with her. Chris and I are just friends."

Kim raised her eyebrows. "Really?"

"Dude, I'm too young for all the problems and complexity that comes with those types of relationships. Right now, I'm just trying to get good grades and have some fun each day," Margot laughed, then felt a sense of contentment. It was true. And there was nothing wrong with it.

Kim looked confused. "Well, he still likes you. He told me himself."

"I like him, too. I might even go to the dance with him! But I'm not marking him for marriage just yet," Margot said, buoyed again by the truth of her words.

"Hmm. Everyone always says you're still a kid, Margot, but I think you're smarter and more mature than all of us."

"Wow. That's maybe the nicest thing anyone's ever said to me," Margot said, astonished.

Kim smiled, gave Margot a quick hug, and turned to go.

"Thank you!" Margot called after her. Kim turned, waved, and then spun again, her movement across the wood ties never faltering.

"Weird un-clumsy ballerina kid," Margot muttered in envy of Kim's gracefulness, but the statement wasn't unkind. Margot's eyes had been opened by their little conversation, and she had to admit that she admired Kim's courage and openness.

Margot stepped a little lighter now, the hurt over Ella's snubs and Adam's outright bullying softened somewhat by Kim's kindness.

As a result, she decided to knock on Chris's door. It had been days – either he was still thinking about things or he had decided to avoid her forever, and she was going to find out which it was.

Cutting across the field by the dump, she made quick time arriving at her house to hop on her ten-speed. She loved that her clumsiness seemed to be left behind when she was on her bike. She flew down the hill as she always did, her hands outstretched on either side of her. Sometimes she wondered what would happen if she went off the road, landing in the steep ditch beyond, or even in the little, boulder-strewn brook that passed underneath, but the thrill of the wind in her hair always won out. *It would be a fine way to go,* she always decided.

The car was in the driveway at the Chalk house. Margot didn't hesitate, despite the butterflies in her belly. She dropped her bike and walked up the sidewalk and to the door. It was open, only the screen door between Margot and the breezy interior, the curtains in the kitchen wafting softly in the crosswind.

Margo froze for a second, her clenched hand held purposefully between herself and the door. It smelled like hot dogs and French fries. There was music playing somewhere in the house. It was dim inside, the only light from the windows. She didn't hear any voices. But she liked the comfortable feeling the place gave her.

She knocked, simultaneously calling, "Anyone home?" through the screen. The strength in her voice, despite her trepidation, was comforting.

Light footfalls on the stairs answered her call almost immediately. Margot gave Nancy a wave as she reached the landing with a smile.

"Hi, Margot," she said, opening the door.

"Hi Nancy, is Chris around?" Margot asked.

"Ummm," Nancy made a non-committal sound as she looked back up the stairs.

Mr. Chalk came through the living room, now. "Margot! How nice to see you!" he said, smiling. His beard was growing in.

"Hi Mr. Chalk – er, Harris," she said, switching to his first name when she saw the look on his face.

"I heard voices when I came in from the back,"

he said, motioning toward the kitchen.

"Just me!" Margot said. "I'm just looking for Chris – is he home?"

Nancy looked up at her father questioningly.

"It's OK, Nance," he said, his hand finding her shoulder. He looked at Margot again, but his smile was fading. "I won't lie to you, Margot. He's here, but he's not feeling up to having visitors," he said, in that way adults had of making something awkward sound innocuous, but Margot got the message.

It won't help to challenge the man's statement, she decided. "Oh, I hope he's alright," Margot replied, making her face as sunny as she could. "Can you tell him I was here, and that I miss him?"

Harris knotted his brow as he gave her a smile. "You know how to get him to come out of his shell already."

"Uh, actually I have no idea," she said. "I just haven't seen him in a few days and I wanted to make things better if he was mad at me."

He nodded, his eyes softening. "I don't think he's mad, Margot. He seems more -"

"Confused?" Margot offered.

He pointed to her, then to his nose. "Exactly."

"Are you picking your nose, Daddy?" Nancy asked, gazing up at him mischievously.

He only shook his head, looking back at Margot. "Don't worry, Margot. He does this sometimes. Just needs some time alone with his thoughts."

Margot nodded, remembering Wren's remark about the Chalks being sensitive. "I respect that! I just wanted him to know I'm waiting," she said, and smiled. "See you, Mr. Chalk. See you, Nancy!" she said, skipping down the stairs.

"Margot?" Mr. Chalk called.

She turned.

"It's Harris, remember?"

Margot smiled. At least things were good with she and Chris's dad. She wished she could say the same about her best friend, and Chris himself.

CHAPTER 12 - A BOY, A GIRL AND A GHOST

It was rare that Margot let anything get her down for long, but by Wednesday she was as low as she'd ever been. She had avoided the tracks since the weekend; there was still no resolution between herself and Ella, or herself and Chris, and she couldn't go looking for Wren without Harris in tow, as she'd promised - she didn't want to give him the idea something was wrong and scare him off again.

She'd gone through everything in her head a thousand times, her sleep suffering yet again, and the conclusion she had come to was that the only thing she'd accomplished in the last couple of weeks was getting the people she cared most about angry with her. Even Mom was fed up with her listlessness and solemn silence.

She dragged herself out of bed and to the bathroom, feeling helplessly dejected. Besides everything else, she'd had cramps off and on since dinner the night before.

It's typical that Mom's chili, which has never bothered me before, is now, when everything else is crap, too.

Sitting on the toilet, she put her forehead in her palms, then let out a gasp. *It's happening!* she realized as she got an unintentional view of her underpants.

"I'M A WOMAN!" she proclaimed, raising her fists into the air in victory.

"What? Margot are you OK?" she heard Mom's voice as her footsteps advanced up the stairs.

Margot was overjoyed. She'd be fifteen in two months, so it was about time her womanhood gave a sign it was, indeed, approaching. "I'm better than OK! I'm a WOMAN!" she shouted again, smiling broadly as the sound of her mother's laughter reached her.

"Ah! Congratulations, baby!" she said from the other side of the door. "You know where the supplies are!"

Margot opened the bottom drawer of the cabinet in front of the toilet, pulling out the products whose boxes she'd read countless times, silently willing her body to kick itself into gear.

"Come down for breakfast and some Tylenol," Mom said, her voice fading as she walked away from the door.

The morning breezed by, Margot smiling smugly, her little secret bubbling happily inside her. Even the cramps were something to rejoice over, given what they meant. She kept catching her mother looking at her wistfully. She felt as though she had started anew. Anything was possible today.

Still internally celebrating her rite of passage after dinner that night (though mildly disenchanted after dealing with some of the more messy, painful aspects of being a woman all day), she walked to the top of the street, sitting as always on the pavement, hugging her legs.

She faced the road back to the hill, wanting to have a clear view of everything. It was a beautiful night. It seemed perfectly right that before long, Chris was walking toward her, his hands in his pockets.

Margot regarded his approach with anticipation. No matter what he had to say, at least she'd know where she stood with him.

"Hey stranger," he said, when he was finally close enough to talk to her in a normal tone of voice.

She smiled in response.

He motioned to the pavement in front of her, "OK if I sit?"

Margot swept her arm across the space, welcoming him.

He sat, then looked around them at the sky,

then the trees. "Beautiful night," he said.

"I was just thinking that," she replied.

He looked at her, his face grave. "I'm sorry."

She nodded, trying not to let her overwhelming relief show. "It's alright. I don't know how it feels to have lost a parent and to have your remaining parent -"

"Threatening to leave you, too?" he finished, and Margot nodded.

"But I respect that you needed some time to consider introducing a ghost into an already...precarious-feeling situation."

"Uh, can you just say that in a way that lets me know whether you're pissed at me for avoiding you all week or not?" Chris leaned back on his hands, regarding her with a grin.

"I'm not mad at you," Margot said quietly. "But to be honest, it's been a lonely week."

"I'm sorry," he said again.

"It's not just you," she said, relieved to be able to talk to somebody about it. "Ella's mad at me and hasn't been very nice about it, and Adam was a total jerk to me the other day..."

"You can't tell me *that's* a surprise?" he challenged her.

"It's not, but it still doesn't feel nice, considering Ella's dating him," she said, and he nodded, his smile fading. "What about Wren?"

"I told Wren I'd bring his best friend to him. I've scared him away before, remember?"

Chris nodded.

"I don't want to do it again; he might not come back next time." She shook her head. "I couldn't go to him just hoping for some company when it takes so much effort for him to be here at all."

"I get it," Chris said, hugging his knees again. "And I'm really sorry I made the last few days even harder for you.

She smirked. "I got a lot of school work done. Technically, I'm done the year, exams and all," she said.

"Whoa!" he looked impressed.

She shrugged. "I don't do well with boredom," she said.

"Seems like you do to me! What I wouldn't give to be finished the year already!" he said, and Margot brightened at his words.

"Huh, you're right," she said, looking surprised.

Chris nodded. "Silver linings, baby."

"So..." Margot had to broach the subject of

Wren again, anxious to see what Chris was thinking.

"So," Chris said, slapping his thighs. "I think we need to bring Dad to Wren."

Margot gasped. "Really!?"

He nodded. "After the other day – well let's just say there's no actor on earth who could've convinced me that there was a ghost with us. The only way I would have believed it is if it was real."

Margot frowned, a bit unsure where he was going with this. He laughed.

"And I believed it, Margot. It scared me more than anything in my life ever has, yet felt more real than anything ever has, too. I know it was real." He ducked his head, seemingly fighting some emotion as he took a deep breath. Looking back at her, he said, "When I heard you singing that song -"

Margot took his hand, at a loss for what to say.

"Truth is, I think you're very lucky," Chris said. "It must be amazing talking to someone who actually know what happens after we die."

"Huh," she said for the second time that night. "I never thought of it that way."

"How could you *not*?" Chris exclaimed, his eyebrows raised.

"Well," she started, remembering her conversation with Wren after Chris had left. "It's weird.

It's like our language isn't – expansive – enough to explain things. Wren has a hard time putting his answers to my questions into words."

"Maybe it's not just the language. Maybe it's the limits of our own earthly vehicles," Chris suggested.

"Uh – our bodies?"

He nodded.

"Wow, you really have been thinking," she said, impressed.

"Come on." He reached for her hands and they pulled simultaneously, standing. "Let's walk on the tracks," he said.

"Really?" she asked. He nodded, and they started off, Chris holding her hand.

Somehow it was comfortable. It just seemed natural, no strings attached. They were quiet as they reached the tracks, and until they reached the pasture fence, the cows at the fence again.

Remarkably, Chris dropped her hand to rummage through the pouch of his hoodie, pulling two shiny apples out as he approached the cows.

"It was you?" Margot asked, impressed with him yet again.

He looked back at her. "I hope it's alright with the farmer-guy," he asked. "I just think they're so sweet," he said, patting the girl who was accepting his gift, Chris pulling it back as she bit into it, so he could offer some to the others.

"Wow," Margot said aloud. Chris had said *she* was different. "Takes one to know one," she muttered.

They carried on along the tracks. "Do you think the farmer will get mad?" he asked.

"Hard to say with Mr. Albert," Margot said, truthfully. "I mean, he lets the cows pasture in the orchard when the ground is getting too messy with fallen fruit, so he can't say he wouldn't let them have apples!"

Chris looked at her expectantly. "But?"

"But he's also pretty wary of how we – the neighborhood kids – treat his animals and his land."

"Understandable," he nodded.

"Next time you see him, just ask. I think he'd appreciate it," Margot suggested.

"Good idea," Chris said, stopping by the hill to the wooden fence. He pointed toward the trees. "Should we? -"

Margot looked at the sky. It was already starting to turn orange and pink as the sun descended. "It's getting late."

Chris looked disappointed.

"You want to talk to him?" Margot asked.

Chris looked around them again. Everything was still, even the trees. Finally, he looked back at her, nodding.

Margot walked a few steps away, thinking of Wren. Picturing his eyes. Remembering the way he held her hands when he apologized for not helping her when she fell. She felt her consciousness change, open up to him. "Wren?" she said, her voice barely a whisper.

And he was there.

"Hey, Margot," he said from behind her, and she turned, already smiling.

"You're looking good," she responded. "Healthy," she said, her eyes going directly to his clean hair and complete pair of shoes.

"Enjoy it while it lasts," he joked. He raised a bent arm, resting his elbow on Chris's shoulder.

Margot looked at Chris for the first time since Wren had appeared. He was looking sideways in Wren's direction. Then he looked at her. "I FEEL HIM, MARGOT," he whispered, loudly.

Wren smiled. "Something feels different with you, too, Margot. It was so easy to – be here – this time. I felt you before I saw you. When you said my name, I was just here. I didn't even have to will it to happen."

"I've been thinking. Wondering how it works, me seeing you. I wanted to try and help, so I was concentrating on reaching out to you, even before I said your name."

Wren shrugged, letting his arm drop. Chris instantly raised his opposite hand to his shoulder, looking at Margot.

"You really do feel him," she said, in awe. "Can you see – anything?"

Chris shook his head, his hand still rubbing his shoulder.

"Whatever you did, it worked," Wren said, approaching Margot. Then, motioning with his thumb toward Chris, "Are you aware of how much this guy likes you?" he asked, a twinkle in his incredible eyes.

Margot smiled. "People have told me -" she broke off and looked at Chris.

"Just tell him I saw you first," Wren smiled and Margot was charmed.

It was so easy for him. "Poor Harris," Margot said, thinking of the friendly competition they'd had when they were kids.

Wren laughed. "I know!" he said, catching his breath.

"What's he saying?" Chris asked quietly.

"Um -" Margot struggled with how to respond.

Wren made a motion toward Chris. "Tell him," he said, a challenge in his eyes.

Not one to back away from a challenge, Margot took a breath. "He told me you like me," she started.

"DUH," Chris said, and Wren looked surprised, and then impressed.

"AND he told me to make sure you know that he saw me first!" she finished, feeling giddy.

"Oh, is that so?" Chris said, folding his arms. "How does he plan to compete with someone who's actually here – like, physically?" Chris asked, a smile on his face, too.

"Nobody's competing for anybody!" Margot said, a laugh in her voice.

Wren looked at her intensely. "I really do wish my timing was better," he said, so quietly that the sound of his voice raised the hairs on the back of Margot's neck.

She looked sideways at Chris. "He really is smooth," she said, and both boys laughed.

Wren took a step back, switching gears. "So, you promised me Harris..." he said, leaving the rest of the words unsaid.

Margot looked at Chris. "He wants to see your dad," she said.

Chris looked to her side, where Wren stood. "We'll do it this week," he said. "He doesn't know yet."

Wren looked at Margot. "I hadn't thought about how hard it would be to talk to him about me."

Margot nodded. "We'll be careful."

Wren nodded.

"Hey," Margot said, realizing Wren still looked – intact. "You still look like you did when you first showed up."

Wren nodded. "It's easier this time."

"Wanna walk us back down the tracks?" she asked him.

He raised his eyebrows. "Yeah!" he said.

So, they walked together: a boy, a girl, and a ghost, Chris and Wren communicating with each other through Margot.

Margot was elated. Not only did Chris believe Wren was here, but they were getting along famously. *If only* – she thought, but shut it down quickly. She didn't want to voice her wishes, even to herself, because the truth was too sad.

When they reached the trail that led from the trail to the dump, Wren stopped. Margot turned back, Chris stopping behind her.

"This is where it happened," Wren said.

Margot reached for Chris's hand, suddenly overwhelmed. "You don't look so good," Margot said to Wren as Chris came to stand beside her, taking her hand.

"I can't go any further," Wren said, and then, turning to look down the tracks, added, "I can't even see past this point."

Margot gasped. "That's why you couldn't help me that day!"

Wren looked back at her and nodded. "I can see just to the top of the trail, there, where the hill levels off. That day, when you were leaving, and you were so mad at me, I panicked. I knew you'd just fade away once you reached the top of the hill."

Margot remembered how Wren had faded as he climbed the slope to the orchard. She started to cry.

Wren reached for her, and she dropped Chris's hand, going toward him. It was strange to be in his arms on the site of his death, even as the body he had appeared to her in deteriorated. The smell of earth intensifying, Margot suddenly found her arms dropping. Wren just wasn't – solid – anymore.

"Wren!" she cried, her arms moving through his body as he faded.

"Hurry," he said, and was gone.

Margot put her face in her hands.

Chris was suddenly beside her, his arm around her shoulders.

She looked up at him. "This is hard," she whimpered, then laughed through her tears. He wrapped his arms around her, and she was warmed. It felt so different after Wren's embrace. She pulled back, sniffing. "Let's go," she said. She wanted home.

They walked up the little hill hand-in-hand again.

"You know you're going to have to fill me in on that last bit," he said, finally.

"Oh! I'm sorry – ugh, I forgot -"

"I know," Chris said. "It's OK. But your side of the conversation has me curious," he smiled.

She filled him in as they negotiated the tall grass of the snake field together, Margot pausing now and then with a squeal. When he looked at her questioningly the first time, she told him about the snakes. It was entertaining to see him gazing far more intently into the grass as he stepped through it as a result.

When they reached her driveway, he turned

to her, his hand still holding hers. "What happened?" he asked. "When you were hugging him?"

Margot thought back. "That must've looked strange," she said, and he smiled.

"It looked kind of sweet. He seems like a really nice guy," Chris said, and Margot was touched.

"Remember we talked about how he starts to deteriorate?"

Chris nodded, saying, "Oh."

"He was fading already when he hugged me." She looked at him, begging him to understand her next words. "It was so scary, Chris. He smelled like earth and blood. And then he faded away in my arms."

Chris shook his head. "I can't imagine."

"And then you hugged me," she continued, "And it felt so solid."

Chris was quiet as she wiped fresh tears away.

"I just wish he wasn't -" she faltered, the hurt like a solid thing in her throat.

"Me too, Margot," Chris said, and hugged her again. Margot cried into his shirt.

She pulled away. "Man, I've been crying a *lot* lately!" she said, trying to make the situation feel lighter.

"It's no wonder, though!" Chris replied, his face sincere.

Her father appeared on the porch. "Hey, who's your friend?" he asked, folding his paper beneath his arm.

Chris looked at her, his eyebrows raised, but he didn't drop her hand.

Margot led him to the porch. "Dad, this is my friend, Chris," she said, motioning toward him with her free hand.

"Chris," her dad said, reaching for his hand with his left, cleverly causing Chris to drop Margot's.

Margot stifled a giggle.

"Sir -" Chris looked her father in the eye.

"Francis, John Francis," her father replied with his "stern" voice. Nice to meet you, Chris.

Chris motioned to Margot. "I was just walking Margot home, sir, but I should be getting home, too." He looked at Margot, now. "I read to Nancy before she goes to bed. See you later," he said with a smile. He turned and started down the driveway, waving when he reached the road.

Margot looked at her father. She raised her eyebrows. "*He reads to Nancy!*"

"Is that his little sister?" Dad asked, his stern

face still solidly in place.

Margot nodded.

He raised his eyebrows. "That's pretty nice," he admitted. "Mom says their mother died not too long ago."

Margot nodded again.

"I'm glad he's a nice guy, Margot," he said, his features softening as he looked at his daughter. "I have to say, though, it felt a little strange seeing him holding your hand."

"You don't have to worry, Dad. We just like each other," Margot said, feeling happy that she wasn't scared of the prospect of Chris's admiration anymore. *There's really something powerful about wondering if you've lost someone completely,* she thought to herself.

Dad nodded. "Guess it had to happen sometime." He held his arm out and Margot climbed the stairs. He rested his arm across her shoulders, leading her to the door. Margot was thinking of ice cream, so when her dad broke into her thoughts with, "Mom says you're officially grown up, now," she was thrown for a loop.

She giggled. "Nah, I'm still a kid, Daddy. And right now, this kid wants some ice cream and TV."

"Sounds good; I'll join you," Dad said, and they went into the kitchen together.

CHAPTER 13 - THE DINNER INVITATION

On Friday morning, Chris knocked on the front door again. This time, though, it was Mom who answered.

Margot, who was munching a perfect piece of toast in the kitchen, held her breath as she heard his voice when Mom greeted him.

The twins looked at her from across the table, Mason with a dollop of peanut butter on his chin.

"Who's that?" they asked in unison.

Margot grabbed a napkin and leaned over the table to swipe the peanut butter off of Mason's chin, earning her an appreciative smile. "It's my friend Chris," she said absently, dropping the napkin by her plate and running toward the door.

"Tell your friend we say hi!" Aaron shouted.

"You just did," Margot muttered, rolling her eyes.

"Tell him we love him, too!" Mason piped up, both boys dissolving into giggles as soon as he'd said it.

Margot paused, tempted to poke her head back into the room and tell her brothers to zip it. Taking a deep breath, she fought the urge and continued to the door, where Mom seemed to be pelting questions at Chris as fast as he could take them.

Margot put her hands on her mother's shoulders. "I've got this, Mom."

Mom turned and levelled her gaze at her daughter, some of the intensity with which she'd been regarding Chris still lingering. "We were just getting to know each other," Mom said.

"Didn't you meet Chris when he came to see me when I was hurt?" Margot challenged.

"Yes, darling, but that was before you two started walking around holding hands, so now I'm just doing my job and getting to know your new friend, *capiche*?"

Margot blanched. "*Touché*."

Chris shook his head, laughing. "If I'm right, that was three different languages in one very short exchange."

Mom looked at him once more. "Why don't you come for dinner tomorrow night, Chris?"

"Mom!" Margot said through gritted teeth. She wasn't only annoyed at the plans being made for her, but she was cognizant of Chris's time limit, noticing the rest of the kids waiting for the bus at the driveway next door.

"OK, OK, I'll let you two talk," Mom said as she sidestepped.

"Actually," Chris cut in, stopping Mom in her tracks. "That's sort of the reason I'm here. My family would love it if Margot could come for dinner tonight," he finished with a handsome smile, his thumbs looped casually through the straps of his backpack.

Margot raised her eyebrows at him, but he continued to smile at her mother.

"Huh. Well, that's very nice. Margot, do you want to go?" she asked, turning to look at her daughter.

"Sure!" Margot replied, anxious to know if this had to do with Wren.

"She can go," Mom replied to Chris, making Margot's eyes roll in annoyance again. "But only if you'll come for dinner here, too. Maybe on the weekend?"

"Of course, Mrs. Francis," Chris nodded, obviously pleased. "Let's make it Sunday, then? Given Margot is going to yours tonight?"

Margot tapped her foot as Chris nodded.

"Alright, alright," she said, a smile on her face as she made room for Margot. "We've got English first," she said as she walked away.

Margot protested loudly, "Mom, I'm finished everything!"

Her mother looked over her shoulder as she reached the kitchen.

"I know! You can help the boys!" She disappeared around the corner.

Margot rolled her eyes yet again. It actually hurt a little, this time. *I need to find another way to express my teenage angst,* she thought.

Chris was smiling. "Seems like maybe finishing the year's work early isn't paying off like I thought it would," he joked.

Margot shook her head. "Nah, helping the boys won't take nearly as long – I'm sure Mom will let me go once she's satisfied I've done something useful."

They both heard the distant sound of the bus.

"Walk with me?" Chris asked, motioning toward the stop with his head.

Margot hesitated, seeing Ella at the bus stop, her eyes riveted on she and Chris.

"Part way?" she asked, and Chris nodded after he followed her gaze to the group of kids.

They cut across the lawn.

"Things still aren't very good with Ella, eh?" he asked.

Margot only shook her head, not wanting to take up the last few moments they had with talk of her strained relationship with Ella. "Chris – dinner tonight -" she began.

Chris nodded. "Tonight's the night. I'll suggest a walk after we're done eating. I've already told Nancy she's got no choice but to join us if she wants a story tonight," he explained.

Margot felt her stomach do a flip. She stopped walking, having reached the point where their conversation would be heard by the kids at the stop, should they care enough to listen.

Chris continued to back away as she called, "Does he know?"

He shook his head no, but said, "Not exactly. I'll explain later." He winked, raising his voice to say, "Oh, and by the way, thanks for agreeing to go to the dance with me!"

Margot's jaw dropped, but she snapped her mouth shut as she saw Ella's do the same. Chris was smiling impishly. "You -"

"See you, Margot!" he called, turning as the bus came into view. Margot was frozen on the spot, and it appeared Ella was, too, until Kim nudged her along, sending a big smile to Margot.

Margot waved, smiling back, and then turned back toward her house. "He's in trouble," she said aloud.

The day flew by; Margot spent more time deciding what to wear for dinner with the Chalks than she did helping the boys. Her mind was all over the place.

She wasn't sure she felt right about springing anything on Harris. She needed to find out what Chris had meant by "not exactly" when she'd asked if his father knew anything.

When Chris got off the bus, he headed straight to Margot, who was sitting on the porch.

"You know there's a stop right by your house, right?" she asked.

He smiled. "Yeah, but I thought I'd walk you down the hill."

Margot smiled back. "You know, you're a pretty alright guy, Chris Chalk."

"Even after what I did this morning?" he looked half guilty, half triumphant.

Remembering the little stunt he'd pulled at the bus stop, Margot gasped. "Oh! I nearly forgot! Thank you for bringing that up! Now I can properly kick your butt before we head down to dinner!" Margot was only half joking.

Chris stopped at the stairs, resting one foot on

the bottom step. "I'm sorry. I hadn't planned that, but when I saw Ella watching us – I just couldn't pass up the opportunity to say something – anything – that would remind her you're an awesome person in high demand."

Margot relaxed back into her chair. "Well. That's actually kind of sweet," she said, her urge to punish him replaced by an urge to hug him.

"You don't actually have to go. As long as I know it's because you don't like dances, not because you don't want to go with me..." he reassured her.

She did get up to hug him, now. Stopping on the bottom stair, she wrapped her arms around him, resting her chin on his shoulder. "I'm as tall as you," she said.

Chris was quiet.

She released him, saying, "If you want to go to the dance, I'll go with you. But if you'd rather do something else that night, we could skip the dance and hang out."

Chris looked so happy that Margot almost laughed.

"Sound good?" she asked.

"Better than good!" he answered.

"Just a sec," Margot said, going back up the stairs and yelling through the screen door, "Mom! Chris is here, so I'm going to his place now!"

"Let me know if you'll be home after dark! I'll walk you if need be!" Mom answered back from upstairs.

"OK! Love you!" Margot yelled, for good measure, and they were off.

As soon as they reached the end of Margot's driveway and started down the hill, Margot asked Chris about the plan.

"You said your dad doesn't exactly know what's up tonight. What does that mean?"

Chris took her hand, walking on the inside of the street. The gesture wasn't lost on Margot. "Yeah, so all week I've been asking him to tell me more about what happened here all those years ago." Margot brightened, but Chris shook his head. "Don't get too excited; I didn't learn much. But it did get him thinking about things. He talked about Wren a bit, and what it was like after he died. Things were pretty hard for him, Margot," he said, his eyes on the road.

She squeezed his hand. "I don't doubt it."

"Then, this morning, I asked if you could come for dinner, and I said that you had learned some things about Wren that he might want to hear."

Margot stopped in her tracks.

Chris turned to face her, his palms already

raised in defense. "I had to give him some sort of heads-up, Margot. I didn't know what else to do."

"Well, now you've left it up to me to broach the subject of Wren – *ghost* Wren – with your father!" she exclaimed, raising her hands and then letting them fall in frustration.

His expression was pained. "Shit, that's not what I meant to do...I'm sorry!" he said. "It's just – if I'd told him the whole truth, he might have shut down before you even got in the door."

Margot raised her hands again, turning on the spot as she digested his words. She looked back at him. "So, you want me to bring it up?"

Chris looked into the trees, thinking, then looked back at her. "I'm not saying that. I'll be there to support you the whole time."

Margot folded her arms.

"I'll bring it up myself!" he said, taking a step toward her. "But I can't see him, Margot. I need you to talk to Dad about him, too."

She sighed, looking down at her feet.

"I didn't want to wait until he was ready, Margot. That could take forever, and who knows how much time we have. Remember what Wren said last time?"

Margot looked at him.

"He said, 'hurry'. You told me that."

Margot nodded, remembering. "I'm just so scared of being responsible if this all goes wrong," she said quietly.

"Don't you see? Things are already wrong, and none of that is your fault. The only thing you're trying to do is help."

"Crap," Margot said, wiping a tear off her cheek. "Say something happy; I can't be crying as I walk into your place!"

He stepped toward her again. "I think you're the prettiest girl -" he stopped, considering. He spread his arms and turned in a circle. "- EVER!" he finished, looking proud.

Margot giggled. "That's ridiculous," she said, her tears already fading.

"Maybe, but it's true, too. And I want you to know that I feel lucky just to talk to you." He smiled down at her. "To explore this place with you." He gestured around them again. "To hold your hand." He took her hands gently in his own.

Butterflies filled Margot's stomach again. She took a step back, Chris's hands falling.

His face fell, too.

Now she had her palms out. "No, please don't take that wrong. I'm sorry. I just – I want to be honest with you!"

Chris looked down at his feet.

She rushed to continue, "I – what you just said – well I think you're so sweet, Chris. And handsome, and frankly I feel lucky to have a good person like you admiring me."

He looked up at her now. "But?"

"But, you should be aware of some things," Margot said, feeling shaky.

"Margot, people talk. Not in a bad way," he added when Margot looked worried at his words. He sighed. "The truth is, I asked about you after that first time we met."

"Asked who?" Margot interjected.

"Umm...everyone?" Chris said honestly, squinting at her with a modicum of guilt.

Margot laughed. "At least you're honest."

"I know you've never had a boyfriend, despite having plenty of opportunity," he said, and she motioned for him to continue. "And the fact that you're homeschooled has caused people to speculate on your family's -" he paused.

"What? Finances? Parenting methodologies in general? Sanity?" she listed. "None of this is news to me, Chris."

"It's not all bad, Margot. Every single person I talked to said you're the smartest kid around. And that you're cool – you're a great person."

Margot looked at her feet again, rolling a bit of gravel beneath her shoe. "We have to get going," she said.

"I didn't mean to get into this conversation now," he said.

They were quiet for a minute. Margot finally looked up. "All I wanted to do was make sure you know that I've never had a boyfriend, nor have I ever felt the need to get into a relationship at my age. The fact that others feel differently doesn't do much to sway me. But I like you, Chris. I think about you a lot. I look forward to seeing you. The things you do and say make me feel – weird."

Chris burst out laughing.

"I'm trying to say that I don't know what I'm ready for, here."

Chris nodded. "If I said that's totally fine with me, would you believe me?"

Margot thought about the boys his age she knew. She looked at him doubtfully.

"Right now, Margot, the fact that you talk to me just like you are is enough. I've never been so – fulfilled – just having a conversation with some-one."

"Hmm," Margot said, still dubious.

"Tell you what. I'm going to hang out with you as much as you let me, but I'm not ever going to push you. I just hope we both can enjoy each other, and see where things go."

Margot looked at the trees, her heart feeling large in her chest. "That's very mature of you," she admitted.

He pulled her gaze back to him gently, his fingertips soft on her chin. "There's no rush. I promise."

She smiled now, but didn't say anything for fear she'd cry again. They continued down the hill, she taking his hand this time.

"This is OK?" he asked.

She nodded. "You know, I was your age when my mother died," he said casually.

Margot looked up at him as they walked. "And before that, she was sick for a really long time. After she died, all I wanted was to be alone. Then when Dad – well, you know. When *that* happened, I kind of retreated into myself even more."

"Oh, Chris," Margot said, resting her head on his shoulder. A kind of walking hug.

"I don't want you to feel bad for me. What I'm trying to say is that because of all that, I probably have about as much experience with relationships as you."

Margot's eyes widened. "Huh!" she said, unexpectedly surprised.

"So maybe we just figure this out together, taking our time?" he suggested.

"Yeah," she answered, "That sounds perfect."

"Funny about timing, huh?" he said, and Margot nodded.

They walked the rest of the way in silence.

CHAPTER 14 - MESSAGE: DELIVERED

Dinner was – comfortable. Margot was relieved at the casual atmosphere and the friendly efforts of both Harris and Nancy to make her feel welcome.

They ate barbequed hamburgers and a salad, Chris's father saying he'd barbeque every night of the year if he could.

Nancy had rolled her eyes and shot a look to Margot. "It's true," she said.

"Vegetarians wouldn't stand a chance around here!" Harris had said, beating his chest and making monkey noises. Nancy had collapsed into a fit of giggles at his antics, but Chris only hid his face. "What's wrong, Chrissy? Your caveman of a dad embarrassing you?" his father had prodded, and even Margot had to laugh.

Nancy sighed. "You think we're nuts, don't you?" she asked.

Margot shook her head. "No! Actually, I'm relieved. My mom invited Chris to dinner on Sunday and now that I know you guys are so -"

"Weird?" Chris offered.

Margot laughed. "Well, let's just say I'm not as worried about my family scaring Chris away!" she finished, and Harris smiled. Margot looked at Nancy. "I have seven-year-old twin brothers," she explained.

Margot's nerves kicked up a few notches as they finished their relaxed meal. Harris started to stand, holding his hand out for Margot's plate, but Chris stopped him.

"Dad – if you don't mind, can we just hang out for a bit? There's something I – Margot and I – want to talk to you about. You too, Nance," he added as Nancy bounced in her seat.

She deflated, sighing.

"It's important, sis."

Harris looked concerned. He looked at Margot and then back at Chris. "Everything OK?"

Chris glanced at Margot and she gave him a subtle nod.

"Well, not really."

Harris folded his arms and sat back in his chair. He looked like he was arming himself for bad news.

Margot's stomach flipped as she realized she

would have to step in before long.

Chris continued. "Dad, you know things have been really rough – for all of us! – since Mom died. And I think they were rough for you even longer."

Harris scratched at his stubble. Margot imagined he'd shave the weekend beard off before school. He motioned toward Margot, saying, "Chris, maybe this isn't the right time to bring this up?"

Chris floundered for a moment, and Margot took a breath.

"Actually, sir, with all due respect, Chris is bringing this up because of something that's been happening with me."

Harris looked confused again. "You have a sick family member, or something?" he asked, knotting his eyebrows over the pain in his eyes.

Margot shook her head.

"Dad, this is about the reason we moved here – moved back here, in your case," Chris continued, and Margot felt comforted. He was really trying to approach this carefully. She resolved to take her cues from him.

"OK?" Harris asked, almost confrontationally.

"It's about Wren," said Chris, and paused, looking intently at his father.

"Well, given that's one of the reasons I came back here, I figured you meant that," Harris said.

Everyone around the table was silent.

Margot met Nancy's confused eyes before she cut into the quiet. "Well, it turns out Wren has affected my life, too."

Harris frowned at her. "How's that?"

"Oh!" Nancy sat up straight in her seat. "Is he, like, one of your an-spectres?"

Margot couldn't help it - a laugh escaped her. Nancy's mispronunciation of "ancestors" hit the nail right on the head. She took a gulp of water and got hold of herself. "No, Nancy, I'm not related to him." Margot looked at Harris and continued, clenching her fists with the effort it took, "But he is a friend."

"What?" Harris asked, anger mixing with confusion on his face.

"I'm so sorry to spring it on you like this, Mr. Chalk," Margot began, but Harris wasn't finished.

He looked at Chris. "What is she saying?"

"Dad, calm down," Chris said, and Harris stood, his chair falling backward as his legs knocked it off balance.

Nancy let out a little squeal as it banged against the floor.

211

Margot gathered her courage and stood, too. "Mr. Chalk, I met Wren before I even met Chris and Nancy," she said, and continued hastily as he raised his hand and opened his mouth to speak. "And he told me your name before I knew anything about you."

Harris's hand lowered, his face going blank. "Wren is dead, Margot," he said.

"I know that now," she replied. "But at first, I thought I'd just made a new, and honestly kind of strange, friend." She heard the conviction in her voice and hugged herself reassuringly.

"You're saying you've been talking to the *ghost* of my best friend?" Harris asked.

Margot could see Chris and Nancy's heads going back and forth with the conversation, just as Mason's had only days before when Margot had been talking with Mom. She faltered.

"My best friend who got HIT BY A TRAIN?" Harris's voice had raised to a shout, and he banged his fist on the table, making everybody jump.

Margot didn't miss a beat. "YES!" she shouted back. "And it hasn't been easy!"

"How do you expect me to believe that?" the man asked, beads of sweat on his forehead.

"I'm asking you to try, because he's asking for you," she said quietly. "Because he's *here* for you."

Harris rested his hands on the table, palms down. He let his head hang between them, his shoulders shaking with emotion.

"Dad," Chris said, "I've been there when he's speaking to Margot."

Harris looked up at his son, his cheeks streaked with tears.

"It's for real, Dad. I promise." "Oh, my GOD!" Nancy said, making Margot jump.

She sounded just like Kim.

Margot smiled.

"I wanna meet him, too!" she yelled now, bouncing again in her seat.

Harris held a hand up to her. "Now just a minute, here. Nobody is going to get all excited about talking to any ghost," he said, then looked back at Margot. "Do you realize what you're bringing into this family?" he asked.

Margot nodded. "I do. But I don't feel like I have a choice. Wren is my friend. I care about him. And I care about Chris, too. And Nancy -" she looked at Nancy with a smile. "And you," she finished, looking back at Mr. Chalk.

"And just what do you expect me to do?" Harris raised his hands in defeat, then let them fall.

Chris stood. "We just want you – you and

Nancy – to take a walk with us."

Nancy jumped up, yelling, "Yay!!!"

Harris didn't share her enthusiasm. "I'm not going on those tracks," he said, and Margot felt panic stirring up her insides.

"Dad, I know this is hard -"

"The truth is, Christopher, you don't know SHIT!" Mr. Chalk yelled again, but there was fear in his voice. He looked at Margot, his expression hardening. "I can't go back to those tracks. I'll walk anywhere else."

Margot sat down. The other three looked at her with confusion.

"What?" Harris asked.

"I can't take you to Wren if you won't go to the tracks," she said. "Wren is only able to appear there; he's bound to them. That's all there is to it."

Harris looked dumbfounded, now. He went to sit, too, but ended up falling awkwardly, his chair still on the floor where it had landed earlier.

Chris and Nancy rushed to him and Margot stood, craning her neck to see past the table. She heard him before she saw him. He was laughing. Margot relaxed back down. *This was either really good, or really bad.* She tensed her "flight" muscles, just in case. Harris let his children help him up, still laughing as he stood.

Chris looked at Margot's questioning face and shrugged.

"Alright," Harris said, finally. "Let's go."

"But Dad -" Chris started.

"No. I've spent my whole life avoiding this. Too much has happened to walk away from it now." He looked at Nancy, cupping her face in his hand, then at Chris. "I owe it to you both to try."

Chris collapsed into his father's arms, and Nancy joined in, crying.

Margot felt awkward, so she hugged herself again.

Harris looked at her as they went to get their shoes on. "I'm sorry I yelled. Things have been -"

"It's OK," Margot said, relieving him of the explanation.

They were on the street in minutes. Nancy skipped up the hill ahead of them.

"Is she always this happy?" Margot asked.

Chris shook his head. "Her exuberance transfers across the entire spectrum of emotion," he said, making an arc like a rainbow to illustrate.

Margot laughed. She glanced at Harris, who walked between them, a look of determination on his face.

Chris nodded to her. "It's OK," his eyes seemed to say.

She took a deep breath. They walked by Margot's house and she was relieved nobody was outside. She didn't want any other distractions.

This was it.

Chris stopped by the field that separated them from the dump, and the tracks beyond.

"Not here," Harris said stubbornly.

"If we don't go across here," Margot said, "we'll have to go to the gate at the top of the hill and cut across the field there, eventually bringing us back to the same spot on the tracks that this field leads us to."

"Isn't there another way?" Harris asked. He looked at Margot. "This is where it happened."

She nodded. "I know. That's probably why it's where I've often found him."

"Where else have you found him?" he asked quietly.

"The willow by the river," she answered, and his face contorted, remembering. "There *is* another way," she said. "We can go through the woods by the bridge. The trail isn't as nice, but -"

Harris shook his head. "We'd have to go all the way back down and around," he said.

Margot confirmed with a nod.

"OK," he said. "Looks like I don't have a choice." Before anyone could respond, he'd started across the field. Margot and Chris followed, but Nancy took some coaxing, having heard about the snakes.

Margot made a sound of annoyance. "I wonder who told her that?" she said sarcastically, thinking of Kim. One glance at Chris told her differently. "Chris!" she exclaimed.

"I ran out of made-up stories," he said, turning around. "Come on, kiddo! You get a piggy back!" he said, turning so Nancy could jump up.

Margot melted just a little more as she watched Chris take care of his sister. Nancy hooted and hollered excitedly as he ran, her sandaled feet dragging through the tall grasses.

When the three of them caught up with Harris, he was standing at the top of the trail, looking down at the tracks. He looked at Margot. "Well?" he asked, and Margot realized he was waiting for her to tell him what to do.

She pointed at the trail and they carried on. She didn't have to mindfully reach out to Wren this time. As soon as they started down the hill, he was there, standing on the tracks with his hands in his pockets. "He's there!" Margot announced, realizing too late that her excitement might not be appropriate for the situation. She ran ahead anyway when Wren smiled at her and held out his arms. They shared a happy hug and then he held her arms, looking down at her.

"You did it," he said.

Margot nodded. She looked back at the Chalks. They'd slowed down and their faces showed a myriad of emotions.

Wren moved to stand next to her as they approached. "He's fat!" he said when they stopped in front of them.

"Wren!" Margot admonished. "That's rude... and he is not!"

"Tell me what's happening," Harris said.

Margot's smile slid away. "I'm sorry. I forget nobody else can see him," she said.

"I can," said Nancy. Everyone turned to her. She pointed at Wren, squinting up at him in the waning sunlight. "What's the big deal?" she asked.

"What does he look like?" Harris asked. Nancy cupped her hand in front of her mouth, loudly whispering, "He's gorgeous!" to her father.

Chris laughed.

Wren bent down to look Nancy in the eye. "Hi," he said.

She blushed, raising a hand in response.

"She can see me," he said, rising.

"Told ya," Nancy said.

"She can hear me, too," Wren said, and Nancy giggled.

Margot looked at Harris, who looked overwhelmed. "Where is he?" he asked.

Wren moved to stand between Margot and Harris, and Margot took a few steps back.

Chris came to stand beside her. "How come she gets to see him?" he whispered, and Margot laughed.

Harris looked at her.

"He's in front of you," she said.

Harris studied the air immediately in front of himself. "Wren?" he asked, his voice shaky.

Wren looked back at Margot. "He can't see me."

"Wren?" Harris said again.

"He can't hear me either," Wren said.

Margot had to laugh. Harris looked at her again. Margot shook her head. "He's joking around."

Wren raised a finger. "Margot, tell him I'm going to put my hand on his shoulder."

"He says he's going to put his hand on your

shoulder," Nancy cut in, giggling.

"He said Margot, silly!" Margot said, but Wren was already reaching out for Harris.

Harris seemed to brace himself, and when Wren touched him, he said, "Whoa!" and looked over to Margot and Chris, his eyes wide.

"I felt him the other day!" Chris said.

"OK, lemme do a test," Harris said, and Wren sent a look to Margot.

"I can't stay forever!" he said.

"Dad, he says he doesn't have much time," Nancy said before Margot could even take a breath.

She watched Harris look at his daughter in awe. *This is good,* she realized.

"Just ask him to touch the tip of my nose," Harris said, his voice quietly reverent.

Nancy laughed, "You just did!"

Wren shot Margot a wicked grin, then leaned forward, kissing Harris on the nose.

Harris stumbled back, falling into the grass.

"You sure know how to shock the Hell out of people," she muttered, and Wren clasped his fists together, raising them first to one side, and then the other.

"You win!" Nancy giggled.

"I like you," Wren smiled down at Nancy.

"You have the prettiest eyes I've ever seen," she said. "Is that because you're a ghost?"

Harris, still on his back in the grass, was listening to Nancy's side of the conversation, a look of amazement on his face.

"Are you OK, Daddy?" Nancy asked.

Harris stood, looking at his daughter. "He had those eyes in life, too, baby."

Nancy looked admiringly up at Wren again.

Margot whispered, "He really does have a way about him."

"OK, I get it," Chris said, and she linked her arm with his, laughing.

"I've gotta sit," Harris said, walking to the tracks and sitting on a rail. Wren sat beside him. "Is he here?" Harris asked.

Margot nodded. Harris pointed to the side Wren was on, eyebrows raised.

She nodded again.

"This is all cool," Wren said. "But we have to get down to business."

Margot nodded. Nancy sat across from the two. "Wren needs to talk to you," Margot said to Harris.

He looked to his right, where Wren sat. "Talk, then," he said.

Wren looked at Margot. "Tell him I know how things were after the accident."

Margot repeated Wren's words, and Harris's tears were quickly renewed. He put his face in his hands. Margot looked at Wren as she sat down beside Nancy.

Chris lowered himself to sit on one of the wood ties.

"He wants you to know, once and for all, that it was an accident." Margot conveyed Wren's messages quickly as he spoke. "His shoe got stuck. Remember the way he used to stuff his foot between the rail and the tie?"

Harris nodded, unable to speak.

Margot lowered herself to a tie, demonstrating, her foot wedged sideways under the rail.

"My God," Harris said, shaking his head.

"That last time, it was too tight," she said, pretending she couldn't pull her shoe out.

"Margot, you're seriously freaking me out with this little re-enactment," Chris cut in, his face concerned as he stared at her foot.

"Just a sec," she whispered. "He got his foot out of his shoe at the last second," she said, yanking her foot out from her own shoe as she flipped to her front and started crawling over the rail, stopping when just her left leg was left over it. "Oh, Wren," she cried now, overcome as she watched Wren go through the motions of the event that had killed him.

Wren squatted beside her and put his arm around her.

"Aw, he's really sweet," Nancy said, tears in her eyes, too. "He's hugging her," she said to her father and Chris.

Everyone was quiet, Harris and Chris watching Margot nod before saying, "The train hit his left leg, and he was dragged -" she broke down again, this time turning to sit, her legs bent over the rail. She nodded again. Margot met Harris's eyes. "There was nothing you – or anybody else – could have done to save him." She leaned to her left, resting her head on Wren's shoulder.

"Why does he look like that?" Nancy said, standing quickly.

Margot saw the fear in her eyes and knew Wren was changing. She pulled away. Indeed, he was filthier than she'd ever seen him, grease and blood mingling with the torn flesh of his leg.

"Wren! It's happening!" she said, her pitch escalating with her anxiety.

Wren shook his head, shouting, "NO!" and Nancy squealed, jumping into her father's lap.

"What is it?" Harris asked.

Margot was fixated on Wren as he changed, his face a mask of determination. "He's getting better!" she breathed, looking first to Chris and then to Nancy. "Nancy, look!"

Wren had cleaned up, it seemed, by the sheer force of his will, but he still wasn't the same as they'd found him.

He looked at Margot. "I don't know if I can do this," he said, his face crumpling with his effort.

"Wren! Of course you can – you've waited this long, you've worked so hard!"

He held out his hand and Margot helped him stand.

"This is the most important part," Wren said, this time talking to Nancy as he put his arm over Margot's shoulder, his weight resting on her.

Nancy nodded, her tear-streaked face brave, as she listened. She cried when he was done, but nodded. She'd gotten the message.

Wren turned to Margot now. "I don't know if we'll see each other again," he said. "I want to thank you. You've been an incredible friend and ally."

Margot hugged him. "We will, someday."

Wren smiled. "I just meant -"

"I know," Margot whispered.

Wren backed away. "I love you, Margot. Thank you."

"I love you too," Margot choked a little on her tears as she said it, wondering at the many faces of that word: love.

And he was gone.

"What did he say, Nancy? Am I allowed to know?" Harris asked.

"You *have* to know," Nancy said, getting off her father's knee, turning to face him. She looked at Margot.

"Go on," Margot said. This was her message to give.

"Wren said that Mom loves us all, and that she's always around."

Harris bowed his head as the tears flowed again.

Chris reached for Margot, and she joined him on the tracks, taking his hand in hers as she sat. It was trembling.

Harris sobbed unabashedly, and Chris cried too, his tears rolling down his cheeks as he looked at his father and sister.

"I saw her, Daddy. She was with Wren. She smiled at me and waved. She promised we'd all be together again, but said it wasn't up to us to decide when. You can't try too early again, Daddy. You won't find her – not like you want to."

Margot made a shocked noise.

Chris looked at her. "What?"

"I didn't see her!" Margot said. "I only saw Wren!"

Nancy looked at her. "It's OK. She said it needed to be me."

Chris crawled to his sister and father and the three of them embraced while Margot looked down the tracks, feeling more peaceful and content than she had in weeks.

"Goodbye, Wren," she whispered.

CHAPTER 15 - ONE LAST MESSAGE

Margot raced through the trees, the early morning sun making no dent in the chill of the trail to the orchard. Birdsong filled her ears, somehow beautiful and cacophonous at once.

She burst into the orchard as she always did, and was relieved to find it deserted, despite the fact that it was Saturday.

So much had happened, so much had changed. Margot craved some quiet moments to herself in her favorite spot before facing the rest of the day. She and Chris were bringing a picnic lunch to the abandoned house by the gate, both of them amused at the seemingly contradictory qualities of the two activities.

Margot stepped past the willow to the spot by the river where Wren had cast his line. She touched the boulders where he'd balanced his rod with the toe of her sneaker, smiling. She sat on one of them for a while, just watching the water go by.

She turned back toward the slope to the orchard, no longer wanting to sit by the willow. It felt empty here now that there was no chance of Wren showing up. She was walking past the trunk of it when it caught her eye: a deep carving in the woven bark of the tree:

Wren Loves Margot

Margot's hands flew to her mouth, tears springing to her eyes. She didn't know how or when he did it, but this was the best farewell gift Wren could ever have given her.

Chris is gonna love this, she thought, smiling. She knew he wouldn't mind. Chris loved Wren too, after all.

She hugged herself, barely able to contain her joy. She was still studying the sweet sentiment when she heard someone approaching. Looking toward the slope, she hurriedly wiped her tears away.

"Hi Margot," Ella said, looking sheepish.

Margot didn't say anything.

"Are you crying?" Ella asked, then gestured at the carving behind Margot. "Oh, you're just finding this, I guess?"

Margot frowned as her stomach plummeted to her feet. If Ella knew about this already - was this some kind of joke? Had one of the boys done it to make fun of her?

"The boys saw him doing it," Ella said, looking concerned at Margot's devastated expression.

Margot shook her head. "Who?" she asked.

Ella rolled her eyes, and the familiarity of it was somehow comforting. She pointed at Wren's name. "Wren, of course!"

Margot gasped. "Who saw him?"

"Adam and Jack. They thought it was Chris, at first, but they got closer and realized they'd never seen him before. They said he was wearing – ugh, what was it?" Ella trailed of, looking toward the water as she tried to remember.

"A Dukes of Hazzard t-shirt?" Margot asked.

Ella brightened. "Yeah!"

Margot looked back at the carving and ran her fingertips over it, her heart as full as it could be.

"And you thought he was a ghost!" Ella laughed.

Margot couldn't answer; she was too overcome with emotion.

"Anyway - he probably won't be around as much now that you and Chris are sort of together?" Ella fished, and Margot looked at her.

"I wish he could be," she said.

Ella nodded, but Margot could see the confusion in her eyes. There'd be questions later. That was OK. For now, Margot had her thoughts to herself.

"Listen," Ella said, "I'm really sorry about the way I've been acting."

Margot shook her head. "Let's just forget it, OK?"

Ella smiled. "I wasn't even finished apologizing!"

Margot laughed and hugged her friend.

Ella's eyes brimmed with tears when Margot stepped back. "I missed you, Margot. I guess she looked at the river. "I guess I - got jealous. You seemed to have so much going on – even the new boy was head over heels about you! And all I had was – Adam." She rolled her eyes and Margot linked her arm with her friend, steering her toward the slope to the orchard.

"Ella, I've been jealous of you for years. Trust me, I understand," she said, and Ella laughed.

"I think things will be different now," Ella said quietly.

"That's OK, right?" Margot asked.

Ella looked at her thoughtfully before nodding. They reached the orchard and Margot turned around and looked down at her willow – she and Wren's willow – once more. And this time, she was able to walk away from this place with happiness in her heart.

"Thank you, Wren," she whispered.

"Did you ever figure out his story - Wren's?" Ella asked.

Margot shrugged. "Some of it," she said. "But I guess there are some things about Wren that will always be a mystery."

The End

THAT SUMMER

First published in April, 2019 by
Paper Doll Publishing.

This is a work of fiction. Any similarities
between real life and the characters and/
or events within is purely coincidental.

ISBN: 978-1999277307 ISBN:
978-1999277338 (eBook)

For Chad, Caleb, Kalei, Cora, Aidan, Declan and especially Liam, who is my most enthusiastic reader.

CHAPTER 1 – PEYTON ARRIVES

The trees whizzed by. Blurred shades of brown, green and yellow. If she let her eyes relax, just so, it was like one of those dreamy Monet landscapes she'd seen at the art museum with Mom.

She'd wondered many times since then what she'd be able to create with paints and canvas. She went through the motions: choosing the subject, then the medium, then spending hours bringing her ideas to life, if only in her mind.

"OK, Peyton?" her mother asked from the front passenger seat, and Dad's frowning eyes found Peyton's own in the rear-view mirror.

"I'm thinking about paint," she answered, turning her gaze back to the window.

"Paint again, huh?" Mom looked at Dad, who shrugged. "Hey - you know that while you're here you can talk to us anytime you want," Mom prodded again. "Gram and Grandad said you can use the phone whenever you want to!" When Peyton maintained her silence, she added, "You know, if you let it, this could be really fun."

"I know, Mom," Peyton said with a sigh, her eyes steadfastly on the scenery as it flew by.

"I hope there are some kids nearby," Dad grumbled.

Peyton could see Mom's gaze turn to her father in her peripheral vision. "Of course there are. They're just a few streets over from the Elementary school, aren't they?"

Her father grunted. "You agreed to this, Charlie," Mom said then, and Dad patted her knee, leaving his hand there for good measure.

It didn't really matter to Peyton if there were kids nearby. Her grandparents lived in a huge old house, with nooks and crannies galore. Whenever they'd visit, Peyton would spend hours exploring, picturing her aunts and uncles as children in the many rooms, or opening mothball-scented drawers and searching for treasure. She always found it, whether it was in the form of an old chess set, a velvet bag filled with marbles or a wispy, flower-patterned scarf left behind by an aunt.

Peyton had loved those parts of her childhood. And now that she was older, her parents allowed her to turn the television on and watch the soap operas while they were at Gram and Grandad's, a glass of Ovaltine unfailingly provided by her grandmother sweating on the cork coaster beneath it.

And outside – outside was even better! The side yard alone provided endless possibilities. A vast vegetable garden, its well-kept rows piled high on either side with rich soil and various buds of leaf and fruit both, occupied half of it. The focal point of the other half was a firepit and grill surrounded by mismatched lawn chairs and the occasional tree stump or overturned milk crate to rest your plate or drink on. Much of the family lived nearby, which meant frequent family gatherings.

Peyton had spent many an evening here with her cousins, running between the chairs as the adults drank beer and laughed about adult things. A shallow copse of trees lined the far end of the yard, separating the property from the next one over. Grandad called their neighbor's yard a 'car graveyard,' and it was an appropriate name; the neighbors were a family of car mechanics that collected junked cars and used their parts to fix broken ones. They were quite successful, apparently, eventually adding their mobile home to the lot of cars when they were able to build a larger house to replace it. The length of it directly behind the trees, it was an effective, if not unexpected, barrier between the two properties - one which Peyton's family had been glad for.

"It's just two months," Mom said quietly now, adding, "It'll be good for all of us."

Peyton lowered her eyes, watching her fingers as they toyed with one of the knitted straps of the bag she wore across her body. She knew it was her fault she'd be spending the summer apart from her parents. Things hadn't gone so well that year - in school, or at home. Any year, really, but the last was the toughest. Peyton had skipped Grade 6, the school and her parents convinced that her behavioral issues stemmed from boredom. Her grades were excellent, but other things – were not.

Peyton drew pictures while her teachers talked. She wrote stories instead of doing her work, stared out the window when asked to answer a question. Yet somehow, she could zip through her homework and tests without batting an eyelash. They reasoned that skipping a grade would challenge her, force her to engage. But it wasn't just a grade she missed; Grade 7 had meant junior high, which was in another school altogether. That meant new people and a new, larger building to navigate on top of the same problems she's always had in school – which, of course, had followed her. She'd continued to be preoccupied, her inability to focus on the task at hand intensifying, unless it was something she was particularly interested in.

And her behaviour at home had become cause for concern, too. It wasn't that she was suddenly different; it was that the contrast between she and her classmates had become strikingly apparent.

Her parents and teachers alike had always

written off her behaviour as childishness or introversion. Later, they explained it away using her grades. She was gifted. She was different. They'd seemed proud, then.

But her differences didn't seem as easy to explain when she was compared with her new peers. It wasn't just that she was the youngest. It wasn't even that she didn't belong. It was that she hadn't the slightest desire to. Instead of inviting friends over after school, she would rush home alone to spend hours on whatever her latest obsession was – Lego, dinosaurs, physics. Whatever it was, it would consume her like an addiction. She would learn as much about it as she could, transforming her whole room with pictures, posters, notes and models. Until she was done with it, and on to the next thing.

Which, in and of itself, would not have been troubling.

Except that if you asked Peyton, she wasn't alone. When she'd been very young, her mother had talked about Peyton's "imaginary friends" as though it were a normal phase for bright children to go through. But to Peyton, her friends were as real as any other kid at school. And she didn't know why nobody else could see them – that discovery had come as a confusing shock. Still, how did that make her the one with the problem?

At the end of the year, there'd been a meeting between Peyton, her teachers, her principal, and her parents. Much of it had been spent trying to convince Peyton that it was time for her to act her age; make some real friends and participate in real life with her classmates. And a tiny little bit of it had been an agreement between the guidance counselor and her parents to put Peyton through a series of tests with a specialist to determine whether there was something else going on.

None of it had interested Peyton much, but her parents had been consumed by it. As soon as school was out, they'd begun the appointments. Peyton acquired a team of specialists, in fact, that were going to take turns spending time with her, asking questions and filling out forms.

Peyton had endured it all with passive indifference. She was cooperative enough – she answered questions and completed tasks dutifully, but she was invested in it all only as a measure to comfort her parents.

On her twelfth birthday, they'd asked her what she wanted and she'd asked to stop the tests, just so she could have some fun over the summer. Her parents had agreed. But then there'd been the second meeting. The team of specialists met with Peyton and her parents to discuss the results up to that point as well as next steps. Peyton had watched her mother react to words like "Asperger's" and "high-functioning," with interest. Her father had laughed, waving the notion away, but her mother had gasped, her eyes filling with tears.

"How can she have autism?" she'd asked.

"I'm OK, Mom," she'd said, and her mother had taken her hand, looking at her with fresh eyes. As though Peyton had been transformed in the few moments it had taken for the specialists to say those words.

"Of course you are!" her mother had said, and then repeated herself. "Of course you are." Then she'd hugged her, and Peyton had felt her mother's fear as though it were its own heat source, taking over as it transferred to Peyton and burned through her.

What happened next was fuzzy to Peyton; she hadn't been involved in the decision to go ahead with the break. She'd been told she'd be going through more tests before school started, and that her parents were going on vacation in the meantime, while she stayed with her grandparents.

She also knew that Mom needed the vacation very much because she was pregnant – finally, after ten years of trying - with Peyton's brother or sister. So, she went along with it, uncomplaining.

A summer in Kingston would be great; Gram and Grandad pretty much let her do her own thing when she was with them, and now that she was twelve, she was sure to be given free reign over the house and surrounding neighborhood.

But then, her friends hadn't been able to come. Lottie had explained that she belonged to Peyton's house and Quiz had looked confused, saying he didn't even know how he could come with her. And despite Peyton's ideas and arguments, they'd remained resolute, and Peyton realized she'd really be alone.

As alone, truly, as everyone thought she always was.

CHAPTER 2 – AN INTRODUCTION TO LEX

Lex was there as soon as they parked the car at the head of the long driveway. He appeared as a rabbit first.

Peyton brightened as she exited the car. "A rabbit!" she'd exclaimed, jogging toward the trees it had scampered into.

"What?" she heard her father say behind her.

"A rabbit?" Mom questioned.

"We see a few now and then," Peyton heard Gram answer and she turned, rushing back to the driveway and into her arms.

"What did you find?" Gram asked, her hands holding Peyton's cheeks between them and gazing into her face as though she were made of glittering jewels.

"There was a rabbit," Peyton replied, and Gram's eyes sparkled. "Can I go find it?"

Gram nodded. Peyton was off, the rabbit nowhere in sight.

Her Gram was saying "They've got them next door," to which Peyton's mother made a sound of annoyance.

The adults continued to converse behind her. Those words again, the ones that had so bothered her mother. Gram said, "Just like Barry," making Peyton think of her uncle with curiosity. He was notoriously clumsy, scatterbrained, quiet - he kept to himself for the most part, but seemed to be a wonderful father to Peyton's cousins.

How am I like him?

Two slanted eyes peered at Peyton as the rabbit poked its head out of a well-concealed hole beneath a tree root.

"Hello," Peyton said.

His nose wiggled. He blinked several times, his eyes turning large and human-like in his tiny bunny head.

Peyton gasped, then giggled. He looked ridiculous.

The bunny popped back into the hole and Peyton looked around. These trees led to the ones at the side yard, where the trailer was. Thinking of her parents, Peyton turned, walking back to the driveway.

"Did you find him?" Gram asked, smiling.

Dad was disappearing into the house with

Peyton's suitcases, and Mom was leaning against the car, regarding her with strange eyes.

Peyton's stomach fell. All this mystery and worry, just because she was different. It had been wonderful when her differences had seemed to point to her being gifted, but now those very same things that made her, her, had somehow twisted into something bad. Something that made her mother look at her as though she didn't know her.

Peyton nodded to answer Gram's question, but went to her mother. "Don't worry, Mom," she whispered, hugging her. Her mother rested her chin on Peyton's forehead as she returned the hug, her firm little belly against Peyton's stomach. "Hello," she whispered, feeling the baby's energy. "Oh!" she exclaimed without thinking.

"What?" Mom asked, looking down at her.

"A boy," Peyton replied, but she'd said it absently, noticing a teenager leaning on the truck of the tree the rabbit had disappeared beneath. He was dripping wet, oddly enough. His leather jacket looked heavy and shone with water. The arm whose shoulder leaned against the tree hung limply beside him, while the other brought a cigarette to his mouth. He squinted at Peyton as he took a long drag.

Mom whirled around, her eyes going to the trees, then looked questioningly back at Peyton.

"Where?"

Peyton shook her head, tearing her eyes from the boy. She laid her palm on the little bump in her mother's abdomen. "Sorry; I didn't mean to tell you."

Mom looked at Gram, saying, "See?"

Only last year, Peyton would have pointed to the boy in the trees, announcing his presence to whomever was listening, but she'd since learned how to wait, observing until she could tell when they were visible to others.

The boy in the trees motioned for Peyton to come closer. She shook her head no, her arms around her mother again. Her Grandmother was muttering something comforting to her mother.

Dad appeared in the doorway of the house, holding a glass half full of water. Peyton went to hug him, now. The sooner they got their goodbyes out of the way, the sooner she could go exploring.

Dad kissed the top of her head, inhaling. "Strawberry," he said.

Peyton nodded. "I used the one Mom got me for Christmas."

Her father nodded perceptively against her head. "I love you, Pey," he whispered.

Peyton pulled away slightly. "It's not like you're never going to see me again!"

He smiled. "No, but we've never been apart this long." Despite the smile, his eyes betrayed any efforts to hide his regret.

Peyton hugged him again. "I have a plan," she said.

"What's that?" he asked into her hair.

"I'm going to learn to be just like everyone else this summer so you and Mom don't have to worry. And I'm going to be the best big sister, too. Just wait and see." She said it all while her left ear pressed against his chest, so it sounded faraway to her.

A train sounded its warning in the distance.

Dad hadn't replied; only kissed her head again.

"Which room am I staying in?" Peyton asked, trying to pull away, but Dad held her tight.

"I put your suitcases in the one that overlooks the street," he said, his voice breaking.

"The one with the tree outside?" Peyton asked. He nodded into her hair. "Yes!" she replied. She loved that tree. "Daddy, don't you guys have a plane to catch?" she asked, feeling moderately constricted by their ongoing embrace. He released her and she took a deep breath, relieved.

"Sorry," he said. "I'm just going to miss you."

"I'll miss you, too!" Peyton said, but her thoughts were on other things. She wanted to check out her room and unpack. She looked at Gram. "Can I use the dresser drawers?"

"Of course!" Gram said. Then she looked at Peyton's mother. "Go on, then, Celia! Have a wonderful time."

Hugs were exchanged all around and her parents got into the car, Mom waving at Peyton, then searching the trees beside the driveway again. Peyton followed her gaze. The boy was gone. When Mom looked back at her, Peyton was holding her hands like droopy front paws in front of her chest, her teeth protruding over her lower lip. She scrunched up her nose for effect.

Mom laughed. "I love you," she mouthed, and Peyton smiled, waving as the car began to back out of the driveway.

Gram turned to her. "Let's go get you settled, hm?"

Peyton looked levelly at her grandmother, who was exactly her height. "Where's Grandad?"

"Oh, he's over at the Canadian Tire," she replied, putting her arm around Peyton's shoulders as they started toward the side door. "He'll be back soon, and he'll be sad to have missed your mother," she added, tut-tutting to emphasize her point. "I told him when their flight was!" she muttered.

Peyton giggled. Adult concerns seemed so strange, sometimes. She glanced back at the trees as they went through the door, Peyton letting Gram go first. The fluffy little bunny sat at the edge of the trees now, wrinkling its nose at her.

"I'll be back," she said aloud, giving it a little wave.

"What?" asked Gram from the entryway.

"Nothing," Peyton said, remembering her promise. Even if she wasn't like everyone else, she'd learn to act as though she was.

CHAPTER 3 – SETTLING IN

Peyton finished putting her clothes into the dresser, the sound of Gram's footsteps fading on the stairs as she went to start dinner. She zipped up her empty suitcases and put them into the closet as Gram had asked.

She took a look around the room, satisfied, and then crossed to the window. She smiled as she caught sight of the large oak on the corner of the property, its long arms reaching her window with ease. It was a quiet view, making Peyton ache with melancholy.

The house and its yard were on the 90-degree turn of the road, one which drivers avoided if at all possible. Too many near accidents haunted the place, its near-zero visibility rendering any walker or bike-rider – not to mention the drivers – under-confident and nervous. This resulted in two things: first, traffic was low. There were other ways to get to the small town's Main Street, all of them faster than the curvy street beside her grandparents' house. Secondly, the folk that did travel this road were either experienced locals who drove cautiously out of habit and experience, or they were new to the area, unfamiliar with the treacherous corner and therefore taking it far too fast.

The little corner was always dark, too, perpetually shaded by the oak and the house, its shadows waxing and waning as the sun travelled across the sky, but always there.

Peyton leaned toward the window, craning her neck to the right, the left side of her forehead pressed against the chilly glass. No-one. She wandered from the room now, headed for the stairs, but changed her mind at the last second, continuing past the stairs to the bedroom at the end of the hallway. She knew the window overlooked the driveway, and she crossed to it, thinking of the teenaged boy she'd seen.

The rabbit was still there, in the grass. Peyton sighed. *How am I going to act normal when they're everywhere I go?*

She backtracked to the stairs, skipping down them as they twisted, her reflection skipping too, in the tall mirror on the wall opposite the stairs.

"Gram, I'm going outside!" Peyton called through the kitchen. Gram answered from the living room.

"Don't go far, love! Your cousins are coming for dinner! Oh!" Peyton could hear slippered footsteps now, her Gram hurrying toward the kitchen. "Go take a look in the garden; see if there's anything we could have with dinner," she said a bit breathlessly when she caught sight of Peyton. She motioned to a basket on the table.

"Isn't it early in the season for that?" Peyton asked, though she grabbed the basket anyway.

"Yes; don't try to pull anything from the ground – the carrots and beets won't be ready for another month, at least. But the lettuce and peas are crazy this year; you should find enough of those."

Peyton nodded, then gave her grandmother a little wave as she went to the door. Her eyes found the trees as soon as she exited the house, but Grandad's car was blocking the view, now. Peyton looked around; he wasn't anywhere she could see, which meant he was in the garage, most likely. Her grandparents had a detached garage, which also served as her grandfather's studio. He created folk art, his pieces in demand at the local flea markets.

Peyton went around the car, finding nothing in the trees, then carried on toward the garden.

"There she is!" a booming voice said from behind her, and Peyton jumped, nearly dropping her basket.

"Grandad!" she squealed as she spun and ran toward the garage, where he stood in the doorway.

He bent low, enveloping her in his massive arms, saying, "Oooh!" as Peyton ran to him. He lifted her, which, given his six-foot-five height, meant a new point of view for Peyton. "You've grown," he said, like always.

"I saw you a week ago, Grandad," Peyton said as she rolled her eyes.

"I know, but I think you stretch every time you leave, like part of you is trying to stay right here with us!" Grandad joked.

Peyton giggled to please him. This joke was an old one, and she heard it almost weekly. While Peyton's parents would be thousands of kilometers away for the next eight weeks, Peyton's own house was only a half-hour drive away. "Kingston to Kentville isn't that much of a stretch," she said, finishing the joke, and Grandad lowered her feet to the ground and released her, chuckling.

"Where are you off to?" he asked, pointing to the basket.

"Pickin' veggies," she answered, already turning toward the garden.

"Did Gram tell you your cousins are coming?" he asked after her, and she turned, nodding.

"Yeah, but not which ones."

"Shawna and uh, Jackson, Barry's kids. They're all coming for dinner, Lois too," Grandad said, stumbling over the names. There were so many relatives nearby it was all too easy to get them mixed up.

"OK," Peyton said, turning again. Shawna and Jackson were just kids. She'd be stuck with them all night.

She quickly lost herself in the rows of the garden, examining each group of plants to see how they were coming along. Most were just babies, their leaves still a brand new and bright green. But Gram hadn't lied; the lettuce was bordering on bushy with plentiful leaves. Peyton paused, looking back toward the peas, which were easy to pick out, delicate vines twisting around and grasping the tall stakes and the mesh in between with curling tendrils. Starting toward them, she thought, *I'll get the lettuce after the peas; the leaves won't wilt as much that way.* She grinned, impressed with her own forward thinking.

She delighted in choosing which peas to pick, running her fingers along the pods, feeling for size and shape. The pods were in all stages of growth, the largest of them boasting thick pods, slightly prickly with their tiny white hairs.

She'd chosen several handfuls-worth and was ready to turn back for the lettuce when she heard a sound from the direction of the trees at the edge of the property. Squinting, she brought a hand up to shield her eyes from the waning sunlight and looked toward the trees. Though she expected the rabbit at the very least, she could see nothing out of the ordinary. She turned back toward the lettuce, but within the first two steps it came again. She spun once more, shielding her eyes.

There he was. The boy. Peyton jumped when her eyes made out the outline of him. He was in shadow, but Peyton recognized his lean, tall figure and the way he leaned against the trunk of a tree. Now he stood straight and motioned for her to come closer.

She started, but paused, looking back toward the house. Conflicted, she looked back toward the boy, whose hands appeared to be in his pockets, now.

What am I supposed to do? She grimaced. She had promised her father she'd figure out how to be "normal". But did that have to mean all the time? What about when she was alone and nobody could see her? Could she be herself then?

That noise again. *What is that?* Her feet started moving toward the trees before she had finished turning back around. *Guess I'm going to find out,* she resolved, partially thankful her body had made the decision for her.

The boy seemed anxious, hopping from one foot to the other. Peyton noted inwardly that he was dry, his blonde hair feathered dramatically away from his face. She was still studying his hair as she approached him. She pointed, asking, "How do you get it to stay like that?"

He rolled his rather large eyes, then raised his eyebrows at her. He opened his mouth to reply, but water gushed out instead of words, Peyton dodging to the side with a squeal. She checked the basket. The peas were dry. *Good.* She ruminated on them, though, considering the guilt of bringing peas that had in any way been contaminated by the vomited water of a – friend – of Peyton's, to the table.

A sound from beside her made her jump. It was the same sound she'd heard when she was in the garden. Her head jerked up from the peas to his mouth, which was still trying to work around the words it wished to say. Peyton went closer; perhaps he was whispering. But it didn't sound like a whisper. It sounded like gurgling.

She remembered being at the indoor pool with her classmates on one of their school outings. Peyton had become obsessed with staying under the water for as long as she could, and her classmates were cheering her on. Some attempted it with her, and they'd gotten into a rhythm of taking long, deep breaths before ducking gently beneath the water, pressing firmly upward on the lip of the pool as they did. Peyton did the whole thing blind. She kept her eyes closed, even as she inhaled, focusing on her breath only. On her lungs opening up. She was like a machine rising slowly, slowly, then surfacing to gasp quietly, controlled, then starting over again. Her classmates had mostly grown bored and wandered, but Peyton had opened her eyes as she surfaced once more, and was surprised at the little group around her, entranced by her movements. She'd stopped and within moments, it was like they woke up, a couple of them looking around with goofy smiles on their faces.

"I'm dizzy," one of the girls had said, then laughed like a drunk.

"OK next time we go under, let's talk to each other," one of the boys suggested, and everyone was smiling in agreement, except Peyton, who was frozen on the spot, her heart still racing from finding herself to be the centre of attention.

It wasn't until one of the girls motioned for her to join them, saying, "Come on, Peyton," that she snapped out of it and moved forward. She wasn't included often, and wasn't sure how to act. So, she smiled. The girl – Paula? – had smiled back, and Peyton had felt a little seed of joy take root in her belly. The group made a circle, joining their hands, and had counted to three before plunging beneath the water as a group. That first time, Peyton forgot to open her eyes until just before they resurfaced, but when she did, it had been like magic. She saw them all holding hands, looking around at each other, their hair floating around their heads like sea grass in the deep waves of the ocean.

When they stood up again, they were all

laughing, except the boy that had made the suggestion. "You idiots! Nobody said a word!" he shouted.

The boy next to him hit him on the shoulder, "Didn't hear anything from you either, douchebag!" he retorted, and both boys laughed. Then, they had all joined hands again. Douchebag counted them down, and they collectively breathed in, then sunk underwater. That time, they started shouting as soon as they were submerged.

Peyton had looked around in awe as her classmates screamed, bubbles trailing from their mouths and rushing to the surface. Most of the kids rose quickly, having expelled their lungfuls of air too fast. But some remained - Peyton and three others. Paula was one. The other two were Douchebag and the boy who'd dubbed him as such. They looked around at each other, smiling. Douchebag looked at Paula and talked in a normal tone of voice. Peyton thought he said, "Hi, Paula."

Paula had replied, "Hi, whateverhisname-was." Their voices had been muffled, reaching Peyton's ears quickly via the liquid between them. Then she remembered to speak, and her own voice had been loud in her head and distant at the same time as it had traveled to the others. At a loss as far as content went, she'd simply allowed her mind to decide what she'd say, the word, "douchebag" coming slowly from her mouth as she dragged out the vowels. Her classmates watched as her eyes crossed, focusing on the bubbles escaping her with the elongated, "a" sound. They'd all surfaced right away, all of them gasping as they laughed at Peyton's one spoken word. Peyton had laughed, too, but soon sunk beneath the water again to keep going, fascinated by the dual inner and outer qualities of her underwater voice.

And that was what the boy in front of her sounded like. Like the screaming at first, and now like he was talking underwater, but in Peyton's head at the same time. She wasn't sure if she liked it. Her heart sped to a gallop as he tried to speak again.

Peyton leaned forward, holding her breath. They often had strange smells about them, these friends. She'd learned to hold her breath when she was near them.

"Aqua net," he said, enunciating each syllable carefully.

Peyton backed up. "What the heck is aqua... net?" she asked, her eyes back on his perfectly feathered hair.

"Hair spray?" he answered, his disdain perceptible even with all the underwater sounds that came with it.

Peyton shook her head. It felt like a bit like she was beneath water – her ears even seemed to register a certain pressure.

He must have noticed her discomfort, for he backed up a step and mumbled something too low for Peyton to hear.

"What?" she asked.

He only shook his head. He looked at his dirty high tops as they shuffled in the leaves.

Peyton had that familiar awkward feeling – the one where you know you should say something but you have no idea what the other person would like to hear so you take so long trying to figure out what to say that the other person finally says something and you lose your train of thought entirely.

He raised his head once more. Peyton got a whiff of him as he moved – hair spray indeed, and soap. And wet leather, though he appeared dry. And underneath it – rot. Still, she'd practically had to search for the underneath smell. She'd experienced much worse.

He pointed to himself, raising his eyebrows and saying what Peyton could only assume was his name. She got an "eh" sound, but that was it.

"Say it again," she asked, yelling as though the strength of her own voice would buoy his.

He glanced to the side, looking frustrated, and Peyton bit the insides of her cheek to ground herself. She knew he wasn't going to hurt her. They almost never did. She simply waited.

He tried his name unsuccessfully again, then scanned the branches all around them before reaching out to snap a long, dead one off an old maple. His eyes lighting up, he cleared dead leaves and pine needles from a small patch of ground, the dirt below revealed. He wrote, 'LEX' in the dirt with the stick, then pointed to himself again.

Peyton nodded. "Nice to meet you, Lex. I'm Peyton."

He nodded as he stood.

"I have to get back inside," Peyton said, and she recognized the look of urgency that flickered in his strange dark eyes. "I'll be back tomorrow," she added, backing up slightly.

They rarely understood timelines or schedules, but she'd learned to stick to hers as much as possible, despite their boundless needs and wants.

He raised a finger. "Wait," he said, and Peyton was able to make the word out as she watched his mouth.

She waited, her eyes still on his thin lips. But he didn't say anything else; just pointed behind himself at the trailer that separated the two properties.

Peyton squinted, trying to study the wall of the junked mobile home that lined the back of the trees, but struggling with the shadows it sat in.

She looked at Lex, shrugging. "What?"

He moved to the trailer, looking back at her as he pointed to one of the boarded windows.

Peyton frowned. "I have to go," she said again.

He was suddenly in front of her, and she was enveloped in his energy – damp, desperate, determined.

She stepped back, gasping. Willing herself not to panic. She spoke quietly. "I won't talk to you at all if you keep trying to scare me."

He recoiled slightly. Peyton noted he was dripping wet again.

"I'm sorry for whatever happened to you, but you have no right to scare me just because you can," she said, then turned again for the garden.

"I'm sorry," came the watery voice from behind her.

She sighed, then turned, intent on telling him she'd be back, but he was gone. She saw the rabbit then, his white tail flashing at her as it rounded the mobile home. Shaking her head, she turned again toward the garden.

Grandad was standing on the driveway on the other side of the yard. He raised a hand slowly. He'd seen everything. Peyton bowed her head, cursing herself, but quickly raised it again at the sound of her uncle's car turning into the driveway.

Grandad walked to the passenger side to open the door for Aunt Lois, any chance Peyton had of smoothing things over vanishing. *Their first report back to Mom and Dad won't be a good one if I keep this up,* she thought, resolving again to try to at least act like a normal person. Taking a deep breath, she skipped through the garden, bypassing the lettuce without a thought, to greet her cousins, and then her aunt and uncle.

Gram appeared at the side door. "Hey, there they all are!" she exclaimed, holding her arms out for Shawna and Jackson. She looked at Peyton. "What'd you get from the garden?"

"Oh!" Peyton startled, then peered into the basket. "Peas! And I'm going to get the lettuce now!" she called, running back to the garden.

"How's she doing?" she heard Aunt Lois ask.

Peyton glanced back reflexively, Uncle Barry catching her eye and giving her a wink. *The hardest part of trying to be normal is that people are already making assumptions about me,* she thought.

Maybe the best thing would be not to draw any attention to myself at all, her inner voice continued, rather pitifully. *A whole summer of pretending. Yay.*

CHAPTER 4 – JADE

Peyton stopped, pressing the crosswalk button as she reached the intersection. She glanced back, fiddling with the coins in her pocket. She couldn't see her grandparents' house anymore.

A little thrill went through her. She'd been through Kingston more times than she could count, but she'd never been allowed to walk to Wilton's Farmer's Market alone before. Gram had folded the coins into her hand, telling her to get herself an ice cream.

"Remember," she'd called out the door as Peyton left, "It's just a straight shot to the right!"

Peyton had nodded excitedly, skipping backwards and waving at Gram.

"Watch where you're going, Peyton!" Gram had warned, her voice shrill.

Peyton froze, a car whizzing by behind her. Adrenaline surged through her as she looked at Gram with wide eyes.

"That's it; I'm coming!" Gram had said, disappearing into the house.

Peyton had rushed back to the door, feigning a laugh. "Don't worry, Gram; I'll walk forward the whole way," she'd said, beginning to call after her grandmother before she'd even reached the door. When she did, she saw her Gram, one foot poised in the air, a shoe in her hand.

"That's not enough, Peyton; you have to be alert! You have to pay attention to everything going on around you!"

Peyton saw real fear on Gram's face and softened. "I'm sorry. I really am ready for this, Gram. I just got excited. Let me prove it?"

Gram sighed. "If your mother knew -"

"Mom's always saying I need to learn to be more aware of my surroundings. I know I can do it if I focus!" Peyton tried again, inwardly rejoicing as Gram let her foot drop. "You won't regret it!"

Gram shook her head, pointing at Peyton with her shoe. "Your mother is calling me tonight, Peyton. I don't want to have to give her bad news of any kind. Got it?"

Peyton gave Gram two thumbs up. "I'll make you proud!"

Gram glanced at the clock in the hallway. "It's two-thirty...no doubt you'll get distracted on the tracks, but it's the easiest way there..." she mumbled, her fingers tapping on her chin.

Peyton danced between her feet impatiently.

"Be back at four-thirty," Gram said, finally.

"OK!" Peyton answered, starting at a run off the step, then stopping as a thought occurred to her. "Oh! I don't have a watch!" she exclaimed, and Gram tut-tutted as she opened the screen, taking her own watch off as she did.

"Take good care of this," she said, clicking it together around Peyton's tiny wrist. "Just like a bird, you are," she muttered.

Peyton shuddered involuntarily as Gram grazed the tiny hairs on her arm.

"OK?" Gram looked at her.

Peyton smiled and nodded.

"It's too big, but shouldn't slip off," Gram said, giving her hand a pat before releasing her.

Peyton exhaled.

She'd dutifully turned to the right when she reached Main Street, and now waited at the largest intersection of the road so she could cross and get back to the tracks.

She'd learned to listen for trains, her older cousins showing her how to feel the rails and gage the distance of an oncoming train by the sound of its whistle. Mom and Dad had simply said to get off the tracks as soon as you hear that whistle, whether it sounded dangerously close or hauntingly distant. Peyton tended to err on the side of caution, remembering stories the kids told about accidents on the tracks.

The "walk" signal flashed on the other side of the street and Peyton started across, then stopped, remembering to look both ways. She ran the rest of the way, across, feeling free, and didn't stop until she'd sprinted through the long grass and onto the tracks.

She looked as far as she could see in both directions. Nothing, nobody. Pleased, she skipped along the ties, counting as she went. She picked a tie well ahead of herself and fixed her gaze on it, guessing the distance. Thirty-two ties away, and she'd step onto it with her left foot. She counted as she went along, keeping the tie in her sights. Thirty-one, right foot. *Just one off, really,* she thought. She could do that off the tracks, too. She'd pick a locker in a hallway or a tree that stood to the side of a sidewalk and know how many steps it would take to get to it, with which foot.

She played the game twice more, then realized she was nearly past Wilton's. She jumped over the rail and skidded down the gravelly decline, slowing when she reached the parking lot. It seemed busy. Her head started to hurt. She'd never ordered her own ice cream before, either.

Thinking, she walked around to the front lot.

She supposed she'd just wait at the counter for someone to help her and then point at the type of ice cream she wanted. She jingled the change in her pocket again, looking further up the street. After the large graveyard at the next set of lights, the buildings thinned considerably, the sidewalks ending and the trees growing thicker beside the road through Tremont and on the way to Middleton.

Part of her wanted to forget the Farmer's Market and detour to the graveyard, instead. It had been years. She used to play with the little girl that lived beside it, Mom and Dad dropping her off for an hour or two when she was really little.

It had been years since they'd moved away. Peyton squinted to see the house, but she was too far away to see any details. She hung her head, indecisive. She glanced again toward the entrance of Wilton's. It was a long, low, cabin-style building. There was a steady stream of customers flowing in and out. Her stomach did a nervous flip.

This should be easy, she thought. But when it came down to it, it wasn't. Not for her, not right now. So, she made up her mind and walked toward the graveyard, feeling defeated and a little ashamed.

She felt better by the time she reached it, peering through the cedar bushes that lined it whenever they grew thin enough to let her. She found the arched entrance and entered, instantly feeling the air change. You'd think the location of the yard on the corner of the street would render it loud and vulnerable, but the cover of the cedars provided not only a visual barrier between visitors (or residents!) and the traffic, but proved an effective sound barrier as well.

Tall maple trees further sheltered the yard, their leaves making a *shushhhh* sound in the breeze. Peyton felt instantly sleepy. She walked the rows, asking permission when she crossed over plots and saying thank you as she read names and epitaphs.

She nearly jumped out of her skin when she turned the corner of one row and started down another, spotting a small figure crouching in front of a gravestone. A short scream escaped her, her hand flying to her mouth.

The small figure jumped, too, looking toward Peyton, then freezing in her crouch as though her stillness could render her invisible.

A little girl. Her lavender silk dress was gorgeous against her dark skin, her hair intricately braided around her head and fastened at the end with clear spheres. Peyton loved those hair elastics with colourful baubles on the end and was instantly charmed.

Little kids didn't intimidate her as much as kids her age and adults did. She took a couple more steps, her heart hammering in her chest. "You scared me!" she said, and the little girl raised her eyebrows at her, disbelief lining her pretty features. "I guess I scared you, too. I'm sorry," Peyton continued, then stopped abruptly, two plots away from the girl.

She looked terrified. "I'm not going to hurt you," Peyton continued, and noticed something else. The little girl was flickering, parts of her fading in and out like a static-riddled tv station. "Oh," she said aloud, all at once realizing she was one of *them*. "I'm sorry; I didn't know."

The girl's eyes widened and she flickered again.

There was a buzzing sound coming from her. "What's happening?" Peyton asked, feeling a little like she should run. She backed up a couple steps, unwilling to turn her back on the strange girl.

"Are you – talking to me?" the girl asked, one of her hands splaying out on her chest.

Peyton stopped her backward steps, remembering her promise to Gram to walk forward only. *Figures something would happen to prevent me from keeping one tiny promise*, she thought. "I have to go," she said, but didn't turn, or backstep. Hating how every decision, large or insignificant, seemed so fraught with dire consequences since that stupid meeting with all the doctors. Every action risky with all eyes on her. "Ugh," she said, frustrated, and turned, the energy of her little girl hot on her back as she did.

"Wait!" she called, and Peyton turned. The girl was standing now, her hands hanging at her sides. The purple dress was edged with white lace, and the girl's skinny legs ended in matching white lace socks, folded over. Shiny white patent leather shoes adorned her feet.

"I love your dress," Peyton offered awkwardly. "And your socks, and your shoes, too. And your hair baubles." She bit her own lip, desperate to stop talking.

The little girl looked down at herself, then back at Peyton. "You really can see me, can't you?"

"Of course," Peyton answered.

"Come here," the girl said, beckoning Peyton forward.

Peyton considered the girl. The top of her head probably came to her own shoulder. "How old are you?"

The little girl shrugged, then pointed to the gravestone beside her. "This could help, maybe?"

Peyton nodded, walking forward. The buzzing sound got louder as she approached the little girl, making the hair on the back of her neck stand up. "Our baby girl," she read aloud. "Nineteen seventy-eight to nineteen eighty-five. So, you were seven." She looked at the girl, whose dark brown eyes were regarding her in awe. "But it's nineteen eighty-seven now, so you'd be -"

The girl shook her head, cutting Peyton off. "It doesn't work like that. I haven't changed at all since – since I came here.

Peyton frowned. "I'm sorry," she said, then brightened. "You know, you don't have to stay here..."

The girl looked disbelieving again.

"You can go, you know?"

The girl shook her head, her braids moving back and forth on her shoulders.

Peyton continued, "There should be, like, a light or something. Just a pull, sometimes. Others have told me..."

She shook her head again. "I don't want to go. My parents come here. I wait for them. I don't feel like I can leave them yet."

Peyton nodded. "That's OK." She wasn't really sure that it was, but the girl's eyes were wide and glistening with tears, so she went with it.

"They aren't doing very well," the girl said, a tear falling to her cheek.

Peyton squirmed uncomfortably. "Don't cry, um...what's your name?"

"Jade," the girl sobbed, her tears really flowing

now.

"Jade. I'm Peyton. I'm so sorry you're sad," Peyton said, wanting so badly to comfort the girl but feeling vastly under-equipped for it. Her stomach clenched. "Don't cry," she said again, her own eyes welling with tears.

Jade's head dropped as she wept. Peyton's feet carried her forward so she stood very close to Jade, allowing the little girl to put her arms around her as she cried. Peyton patted her back, hoping she was doing it right.

Jade pulled away from her. "You're weird," she giggled through her tears.

"I know," Peyton replied. "I'm not very good with people and – feelings…"

"Sure, you are. You have to be, don't you? To be able to see ghosts?"

Peyton burst out laughing. "What?"

Jade shook her head and frowned at Peyton, her hands on her hips. It was adorable. "What do you think I am?" she shot, her eyes dark.

Peyton paused. "Well, not a ghost. Ghosts aren't real. And they don't look like people!" she explained, still giggling.

"So, answer my question. What am I?"

Peyton frowned. She'd often wondered that,

herself. She knew they were...not like everyone else. But nothing she'd learned about "ghosts" fit with what she saw. "I don't know. An alien?" she tried, and now Jade burst out laughing.

"You'd believe I was an alien before you'd believe I was a ghost?" she asked, her voice high.

Peyton considered the question. She thought of Lottie and Quiz back home. "You don't always look like people," she challenged.

"You mean you see other stuff, too?" Jade asked, scrunching up her nose.

"Sure," Peyton answered. "I think it's because I'm on the spectrum," she explained.

"What's that?" Jade asked, squatting again on the grass in front of her gravestone and running her splayed fingers through the grass. Peyton shrugged.

"I'm not exactly sure. I think it's something bad, though. My mother's pretty upset."

"How can you not even know what's wrong with you?" Jade asked, squinting up at her.

Peyton felt stupid. "I don't talk to them about it because it gets them all worked up," she muttered.

Jade seemed to understand that. She nodded, then sat, folding her legs in front of her. Peyton sat, too. The little girl smelled like burning. Like when their toaster had broken at home. The kitchen had reeked of the smell for days. This was more subtle, though.

Jade looked at her. "Well, since it's pretty cool to be able to talk to somebody, I'll explain something to you. I? Am a ghost," she said, her hand to her heart again. "All that means is that I was alive, and then I died, and my body got buried." She looked at her gravestone. "But I didn't…go, like you said."

"OK," Peyton offered lamely, her mind racing. How had she not known this? *Why else would she have a grave, dummy?* Her inner voice mocked her. "I just - my – everyone at school uses sheets when they pretend to be ghosts. On Halloween, you know?" she said, remembering. "And ghosts are scary…" Peyton thought about Lex. How she'd felt as he'd surrounded her. Then she thought of the soft bunny Lex also was. "I'm more scared of normal people than -" Peyton started, but stopped as her forehead creased.

"You don't have a lot of…people skills, do you? Jade asked. She leaned back, her arms stretched behind her, her hands taking her weight. She straightened her legs too, then raised her hips, flattening her body from feet to crown, her hands turning pale as they supported her upper body.

Peyton unintentionally caught sight of Jade's yellow underpants and looked away, blushing. "You shouldn't do that in a dress," she said.

Jade sat back down, sighing. "Whatever," she said, looking to the side.

Peyton's breath caught in her throat. She recognized when someone had grown bored or exasperated by her. She stood.

"Where you going?" Jade asked, her head tilted back to look at Peyton.

"I'm going to get some ice cream," she said, but it sounded weak.

"Sure, you are," Jade said, and she flickered again, the buzzing sound reminding Peyton of how it sounded when a bee was nearby. She turned and started walking.

"Wait! Are you coming back?" Jade called out behind her, her voice suddenly laced with anxiety.

"Why should I?" Peyton asked, without turning.

"Because I can help you!" Jade called.

Peyton did turn, now. "With what?" she asked, folding her arms across her chest.

"With – with learning about ghosts! How to tell when the person you're talking to is dead!" Jade yelled, her words tumbling out in her effort to keep Peyton from leaving.

"Actually," Peyton started, looking thoughtful. "That would be really helpful."

Jade jumped a little on the spot, her hands finding each other under her chin. She really was cute.

"I need to learn how to be "normal" before the end of the summer," Peyton said.

Jade laughed. "I don't know if I can help you with that," she joked, and Peyton rolled her eyes. "Just kidding, just kidding!" Jade said, holding a hand up in surrender even as she bent over laughing.

"I don't need to be made fun of," Peyton said, and was surprised by the strength in her voice. It was true. Jade seemed bound to the graveyard – to her own plot, even. Peyton never had to see her again, if she didn't want to. "Trust me, I hear enough of that at school. And I know I'm weird."

Jade straightened up, breathless.

"But that doesn't give anyone license to make me feel even worse about myself, even a ghost!" she cried, then thought better of it, adding, "ESPE-CIALLY a ghost!"

"I'm sorry, I'm sorry, Peyton!" Jade said, smiling. I'm used to my brothers giving as good as they got!"

"You sure you're only seven?" Peyton asked.

Jade shrugged. "I dunno how it works. I said I haven't changed at all since -" she gestured toward her stone again. "But that's not entirely true.

I haven't grown – haven't even changed my clothes. Half the time, I'm not even here. More than half the time -" she looked across the graveyard, her eyes more distant than the cedar barriers should have allowed for. Looking back at Peyton, she shook her head, her bold confidence vanishing for the time being. "I shouldn't have made fun of you. There's a lot I don't understand, too."

"You don't talk like a seven-year-old, or even a nine-year-old, which is how old you'd be, you know -"

"If I wasn't dead?" Jade finished.

"Yeah, I guess."

"You scared, now?" Jade asked, her voice very quiet.

Peyton shook her head no. "You're no scarier than before you told me...more about yourself," she said. "Besides, I'm scared of everyone, so that's a tough question. For me. Because of...anyway, you were saying?"

Jade paused, giving Peyton another look. "Uh – yeah, like I was saying, I hear people talking. I practice a lot. I like words. I like how different people put them together. So many ways to say one thing, so many interpretations of one word..." she looked out into the cedars again. "It fills up the loneliness."

Peyton stepped toward Jade again, softening

at the girl's vulnerability. "I have to go, but I'll come back, OK?"

Jade nodded, her eyes on her shiny shoes.

"I promise," Peyton said, meaning it, then turned again.

"Try the black raspberry cheesecake!" Jade called.

Peyton gave her a thumbs-up but kept going. Jade would keep her here forever if she let her. But now she had a new perspective – she knew why they always wanted something from her. They were spirits, all of them. Ghosts. She resolved to look at Gram's dictionary when she got home. Her definition of "ghost" had in no way resembled her friends. Still, it explained a lot.

She brought her left wrist in front of her, suddenly aware of the passage of time as she stepped through the cedar archway and onto the sidewalk. 3:45. She'd need to hurry if she wanted to get her ice cream and get home on time to prove her trustworthiness to Gram. She took just a moment to glance back into the graveyard, thinking of waving to Jade, but she was gone. She wondered briefly to where. Then, she wondered if Lex and Jade knew each other in that – other place.

Then she thought of the many others from over the years, and of her friends at home. All – ghosts. But, why? The new label didn't solve much.

It was still strange for her to be seeing stuff others couldn't, regardless of what you called it. She wished for just a moment that she could talk to someone about it, but that had only caused trouble and worry in the past. Her resolution to hide all the weird stuff in her bid to act normal made more sense.

She was inside the Farmer's Market before she snapped back to the present, her mind racing as she contemplated the new information she'd gleaned from Jade.

"Can I help you?" a pimply boy asked from behind the ice cream counter. Peyton surveyed her choices, panic descending on her swiftly. She hadn't even planned what she'd say. Her eyes spied a label that looked familiar. "One scoop of black raspberry cheesecake," she blurted, relieved.

"Bowl or cone?" the boy asked, his voice cracking dramatically. He shook his head, his cheeks reddening, and Peyton smiled in recognition of his self-conscious response.

"Cone," she replied, offering the boy her smile, and then frowning, realizing he could misconstrue the gesture as Peyton laughing at him. She cursed herself for never knowing what to do with people, especially new ones.

She accepted her cone and paid, all the while avoiding the boy's eyes.

"Have a nice day," he said, his voice intentionally low. Peyton smiled, but kept her eyes on the ice cream as she fought the urge to giggle.

She took her first bite when she was back on the tracks, moaning with pleasure at the surprising taste. "Thank you, Jade!" she said aloud. The stuff was delicious. She finished it in minutes, still standing in the same spot as she licked her fingers.

"Crap!" she said, looking at her watch again.

It was late.

CHAPTER 5 –
PEYTON'S DREAM

She needed to run. Her mind was blissfully focused as she did, the one goal of reaching Gram on time eclipsing the rest of her thoughts. Eyes ahead of her, aware of the cars at the intersection and the 'walk' signal flashing ahead of her. Pushed by necessity, she managed to keep her thoughts in a straight line, undiverted by even the most tempting of distractions as she reached the house and noticed Lex – the rabbit - twitching his nose at the edge of the trees by the driveway.

"Sorry, Lex! I can't be late!" she said aloud, then dashed inside, nearly smashing into Uncle Barry, who was removing his shoes in the entryway.

"Whoa!" he exclaimed, his hands flying over his head as he lost his balance. He caught himself, pressing against the wall to get himself upright.

"I'm sorry, Uncle Barry!" Peyton said breathlessly, her hands reaching toward him in an impotent gesture to help him steady himself.

He looked at her for a moment, then smiled. "Not a problem, Peyton! I'm as clumsy as they come."

Peyton was relieved. "I was rushing to get back on time," she admitted, and her uncle leaned conspiratorially close.

"The trick is to be mindful of distractions," he whispered, then patted her head awkwardly. "I'm just dropping a cabbage off from our garden," he added, pointing at a large cabbage which looked out of place on the floor, amongst the shoes. "Hmm. I should have brought it in a bag," he said, and Peyton giggled.

She kicked off her shoes and ran toward the kitchen, scooping the cabbage up as she passed it. Gram was at the stove, stirring something that smelled heavenly. "Cabbage!" Peyton announced, making Gram jump. "Sorry. But look, Gram!" she said, pointing at the clock. "I'm back on time! Alive!" she said, her cheeks aching as she smiled her biggest smile.

"Jesus Murphy, girl, your face is going to crack in half if you keep that up!"

"What?" Peyton asked, her cheeks tingling slightly as she let her smile drop.

Gram laughed, kissing her on the forehead. She took the cabbage, calling, "Thank you, Barry!" toward the entryway.

He appeared in the hallway, hopping as he

pulled up a sock. "No problem; we need to get rid of some," he said, finishing his statement as he straightened and pulled his pants up. "The whole family is gassy as Hell."

Gram tut-tutted while Peyton laughed. "Guess you won't stay for supper, then?"

"Oh! Yeah, I'll stay!" Barry replied, looking grateful.

"What about Lois and the kids?" Gram asked. Barry frowned. "Oh, yeah. They won't mind. Oh, actually," he glanced back toward the entryway, "I have ice cream in the car for after dinner. The kids are expecting it. I'm sorry, Mom," he said, turning a worried face back to Gram.

Peyton shook her head. Her family was comparing her to – this? Barry was so scatterbrained he bordered on seeming dumb. She only knew he was actually quite smart because her mother talked about his grades as they'd gone though school together with such reverence. It was of little comfort now, though.

"Uncle Barry, what's your job, again?" she piped up.

Barry's head whipped in her direction. "I work for the Government," he said absently, then looked back at Gram. "Sorry again, Mom, I wasn't thinking."

Gram shooed his concerns away, putting the cabbage on the cutting board. "It's fine, Barry! Just go back to Lois and the kids. I'm sure she's got something cooking." She winked in Peyton's direction. "I was just asking to be polite, anyway, she joked, her palms going to her son's cheeks as he laughed.

"Well, then!" he said, his eyes sparkling. "I see how it is!"

Peyton shook her head again, embarrassed on her uncle's behalf. Barry turned to go. Peyton straightened, calling, "Uncle Barry!" as a thought occurred to her. There was one way to figure out if she and Barry were alike. "Have you ever seen a ghost?" she asked casually as he looked at her.

He made a face. "What?" he asked. "Like, a real one?"

Peyton caught her breath. She really needed to reel her stupid mouth in. *Too late, now.* She nodded.

Barry shrugged. "Don't think so, though some of the guys I work with seem dead," he replied, smiling. "Seriously, this guy farted in a meeting the other day, Mom, and *nobody laughed*. We all knew it happened, but I was the only one who was trying not to lose my shi – whoops!" he said, putting his hand over his mouth and looking back at Peyton. "Sorry, kiddo," he apologized.

Gram smacked him on the arm. "Watch your mouth, son," she said. She looked at Peyton. "Why don't you go turn the tv on, dear? I'll let you know when supper's ready."

Grateful for the opportunity to escape, Peyton climbed the stairs in twos, then avoided the window that overlooked the driveway and trees, turning straight to the left as she arrived on the landing.

She spent an hour watching the television, goosebumps breaking out all over her skin when she turned it off to go for supper. The flash of static, accompanied by that buzzing sound, brought her thoughts back to Jade.

Jade was still on her mind when she went to bed that night, which, she reasoned the next morning, probably explained why she dreamt the way she did. She must have fallen asleep as soon as her head hit the pillow, for it seemed to her that there'd been no transition at all between being awake and asleep. One minute she was sinking down into her pillow and the next, she was standing outside of the fenced yard on the corner of the property, the shadows around her strange purple and green shades in the fading light of the day.

She looked at the sky through the oak branches above her and gasped. She'd never seen such a sunset; the sky more like the scenery that had flashed past her eyes as she'd traveled here with her parents. "Like Monet," she whispered.

"Peyton," a voice said to her right. Her head jerked toward it.

Lex was standing at the ninety-degree turn. "Come on," he said, tilting his head, then indicating the direction of the side yard around the house.

Peyton walked toward him, saying, "How come you can talk now?"

He backed away as she got closer, finally turning his back to her when she reached the corner. He led her around the house and across the driveway without a word.

Peyton looked at the sky again; it was darkening quickly. "I should get inside," she said to Lex's back.

He didn't turn.

They passed the garden on the left. "Why are we going back here again?" Peyton asked. "Hey, Lex," she said, louder this time. When he still didn't turn, she stopped, her hands on her hips as Jade's had been, earlier. "I don't want to go into the trees."

But she was suddenly there. She and Lex stood at the back of the trees, the trailer wall in front of them. "What -" she began, but closed her mouth as Lex stepped toward the wall. He was soaked again. She was sure he'd just been dry. "Are you in the water?" she asked, not sure she could articulate her meaning, had she been asked.

He finally looked at her, his large eyes intense. "This isn't about me," he said, raising his arm to point at one of the boarded windows.

There was a thud inside the trailer, and Peyton jumped back with a scream. She squeezed her eyes shut as she stumbled backward, anticipating the impact. But it was soft. She landed on her mattress, instantly opening her eyes and sitting up, gasping.

The digital clock on the bedside table glowed, its green numbers reading 3:03. She looked toward the window, silently willing her heart to slow down. Then she stood, looking past the glass and down to the street as she did. It was lit dimly by an old streetlight, which flickered every few seconds. Her breath caught. Lex was on the corner, his hands in his pockets as he looked up at Peyton.

She opened the inside window, propping it up with a long chunk of wood cut just for that purpose. She pressed her forehead against the screen, her eyes on Lex. She breathed in the cool air. Lex opened his mouth to say something, but water gushed to the ground, as it had in the woods before. He coughed and sputtered, then pulled what Peyton could only assume was a pack of cigarettes from his jacket pocket. He yelled in frustration as he tried in vain to light it, having pulled a lighter from the same pocket. It sounded like the same word Uncle Barry had said, but was garbled with that underwater quality again. He looked up at her.

"I have to go," she whispered. He swore again, water spilling over his chin, then turned and walked around the house, as he had in her dream. But he hadn't been angry in her dream, and she hadn't been on the second floor inside the house, either. She backed away from the window, shivering. She didn't have to follow him or even acknowledge him. That garbled water sound came again, and Peyton sprung forward, grabbing the wooden prop and closing the window without hesitation.

She leapt into bed, pulling her covers up to her chin. Basking in the silence, she willed herself to sleep, hoping she'd awake in the morning having forgotten both the dream and what had happened afterward.

What does he want? And why does he want it from me?

She thought of Jade again. She knew far more about ghosts than Peyton did – in fact, she seemed to know more about everything than Peyton did.

She needed to talk to her.

CHAPTER 6 – SICK

"Honey?" Peyton stirred, groaning. Her head felt like it was bound in cement.

"Peyton? It's late, honey. Time to wake up," Gram's voice again, but gentle.

Peyton felt Gram sit on the bed. "Something's wrong," she croaked, but was still unmotivated to open her eyes. Even the light that lit up her eyelids hurt.

"What is it, darling?" Gram said now as she placed a soft hand on Peyton's forehead. "Oh, you're burning," she whispered, and though her voice was barely audible, Peyton caught the new urgency in it with ease.

Gram's weight was gone from the bed in an instant, her feet stepping softly on the carpet and out of the room. Peyton turned onto her side and pulled the comforter over her face. It became mercifully dark.

Suddenly, Gram was back, pulling the comforter down. Peyton groaned again.

"I know, dear, but this is good for you," Gram

said as she helped Peyton sit up. "Here, open your mouth." Peyton did as she was told, her only desire being to do whatever she needed to do so she could sleep some more. Two pills were placed on her tongue and she reflexively gagged, both of them tumbling out.

She opened her eyes without thinking and the light sliced through them. "Ah," she muttered, bringing her arm up to block her eyes.

Gram was fumbling around on the comforter. "Sorry dear; I should have warned you," she was saying.

Peyton let herself ease back down to the pillow.

"No, sweetheart, sit up. You need to take these pills."

Peyton started to cry. Gram slid her hands under Peyton's armpits and pulled her upright with a grunt. "I know, baby," she said. "Open your mouth and we'll get this over with, alright? Then you can lie down some more."

Peyton opened her mouth. Her tears felt hot on her cheeks.

"I'm going to put the pills on your tongue. Ready?"

Peyton nodded, wincing as her brain moved in her skull. This time she was ready. She closed her mouth over the pills, reaching for water blindly.

Gram placed a cold glass in her hands. "Take a good drink, dear," she whispered.

Peyton let Gram's voice wrap around her like a blanket. "Thank you, Grammy," she said, lowering herself again. She heard the sound of the glass being placed on the bedside table.

"I want you to take sips of this when you wake up again. I'll check on you in an hour, alright?"

"Uh-huh," Peyton managed, already sinking deep, deep into a black abyss, her own voice coming back to her from somewhere far away.

When she woke again, the room was dim. She parted her eyes hesitantly, but was relieved to find she could look around without her head feeling like it was being ripped apart from the inside. She put her hand on her forehead, remembering. "Ugh," she said, but only air came out. It felt like her throat was on fire, and her mouth was dry.

She sat up slowly. Her headache had faded for the most part; but dizziness had replaced it. She sat still as the room spun around her, nausea washing over her in a noxious wave. She placed her hand on her stomach, breathing, breathing until it passed. She closed her eyes. *What is wrong with me?* she wondered. She wanted Gram to come back. She wanted her Dad.

Wincing in anticipation of vertigo, she reached for her water, then brought the glass to her lips, sighing as the cool liquid wet her mouth and soothed her throat.

The door opened slowly, Gram's short grey curls poking in, followed by her curious eyes. Peyton smiled for a second, then let it fall away as another wave of nausea rolled over her. She let her head rest back against the wall. "I'm sick, Gram," she cried, tears squeezing out of her tightly shut eyes.

"Well, no kidding," Gram said, her slippers shuffling across the carpet as she crossed to the bed. She put her hand on Peyton's forehead again. "Oh, you're cooler. Good," she whispered, then sat.

Peyton opened her eyes. "So dizzy," she whispered.

Gram nodded. "What else?" "Head hurts. Throat sore. Wanna barf."

Gram was up and out the door in a flash, arriving back in the doorway in seconds, a metal garbage can in her hands. "Just in case," she said, smiling as she put the can on the floor beneath the head of the bed.

Peyton watched it all with her eyes only, sure she'd need the can if she moved at all.

"Your uncle Barry called this morning; seems both kids are sick, too."

"Thanks, Uncle Barry," Peyton croaked, closing her eyes again.

"I'm going to bring you to the doctor tomorrow; it's already set up. But today, you'll do nothing but rest."

"But I hafta pee," Peyton whined.

Gram chuckled. "Well I suppose you can do that, too. Come on," she said, already pulling the covers off of Peyton.

"Slow, slow!" Peyton said as Gram turned her legs so they dangled off the bed.

"Right, just take your time. I'll follow your lead," she said as she weaved her arm under Peyton's and around her back.

Peyton stood, Gram supporting her with more strength than Peyton had known she had. "You're strong, Gram," she said, then moaned as the room spun and dipped.

Gram froze. "I raised eight kids," Gram said breathlessly. "I've had to be."

Peyton straightened as the dizziness subsided, and they shuffled their way out of the room and down the hallway. Peyton closed her eyes whenever she felt dizzy, but she kept going, her bladder threatening to burst.

They finally stopped just outside of the bedroom at the end of the hall, and Gram untangled herself from her granddaughter, saying, "There you go, now." Peyton wavered. "Whoa, there. Should I come in with you?" Gram asked.

"Nope," Peyton said mortified at the thought, but smiling gratefully at Gram as she closed the door.

She spent the rest of the day in bed, mostly sleeping. Grandad brought her dinner up but it still sat, untouched, when Gram came up to remove the plate.

"Not hungry at all?" she asked, looking concerned.

"Sorry, Gram. I'm sure it's delicious. You can save it for me for lunch tomorrow," Peyton said quickly.

"You're not hurting my feelings, girl! I just worry you won't get well if you're not eating."

Peyton looked at the plate again.

"Just a few bites?" Gram said, then made a silly face to make Peyton smile. She crossed and took the plate, motioning for Peyton to sit up.

She complied, sighing. She looked at Gram. "Hey! I'm not dizzy!"

"Good! Then you're already healing," Gram said, placing the plate on Peyton's lap.

Mashed potatoes, some sort of meat, peas and

carrots, and gravy. Peyton scooped up some pota-toes, then ran her fork through the gravy. "Mmm." It was lukewarm, but it was good.

"Good?" Gram raised her eyebrows, and Peyton nodded.

She scooped up some peas and carrots. De-licious. "What time is the doctor tomorrow?" she asked around a mouthful of food.

"Peyton!" Gram exclaimed. "Gross!"

Peyton giggled, covering her mouth as she swallowed. "Sorry."

"Kids and their manners theses days," Gram mumbled, shaking her head disdainfully. She stood, tidying up as she talked. "Eleven," she said, answer-ing Peyton's question. "If you're well enough, we can stop at the mall afterward."

Peyton put her finger up, swallowing audibly. Gram grimaced, but with a smile. "Which mall?"

"The one in Greenwood; it's right across from the doctor's office," Gram answered as she held one of Peyton's shirts up to her nose. "Do you never sweat, child? I can't tell which are clean and which are dirty," she complained, repeating the exercise with a pair of pants she picked up off the floor.

"I'm like a flower," Peyton mumbled, her mouth not entirely empty.

Gram looked at her sideways. "I thought we'd

check out the new arts and crafts store. Have you any interest?"

Peyton nodded enthusiastically, then groaned. Her headache wasn't entirely gone, then. She put a palm to her forehead.

"OK?"

Peyton put the plate on the table again. "Yeah. Head still hurts a bit."

"Don't overdo it, Peyton. It'll take a few days for you to feel yourself again. Barry's taking the kids to the pediatrician as we speak."

"Overdo it? I nodded, Gram," Peyton replied sarcastically.

"Well, apparently that's not an option right now. And neither is that!" she pointed at Peyton as she rolled her eyes.

"Apparently not," Peyton said quietly. It really did hurt to roll her eyes. "Anyway – the arts and crafts store. I have been thinking a lot about painting."

Gram frowned. "That's an expensive hobby, dear. How about we start you off with a nice sketch pad and some good pencil crayons? And if you're still interested in a week, we'll get you paints."

Peyton shrugged. "Sounds good to me!"

"Good. We'll get you something you can fit

into that bag you're always carrying around," Gram said, motioning to Peyton's bag where it hung over the footboard.

Peyton nodded, sinking down into her covers again.

"Back to sleep?" Gram asked, her arms full of clothes for the laundry.

"Actually, I'll go brush my teeth first," Peyton replied as she slowly righted herself again. She followed Gram down the hall and accepted a hug before Gram turned to go downstairs.

She walked past the bathroom and into the bedroom with the windows overlooking the side yard. It was dark. Peyton rested her forearms on the windowsill, gazing into the trees. No bunny, no boy. Everything looked peaceful. Good. She went back to the bathroom and got ready for bed, marvelling as she brushed her teeth that she'd lost a whole day. She remembered her dream from the night before. *Maybe it's for the best,* she thought. She was less than eager to see Lex again – but she did want to talk to Jade.

She swished water around her mouth, spat into the sink. It would have to wait. The next day would be taken up by the doctor's appointment and then shopping. She looked at her reflection in the mirror. "Ick," she said aloud as she eyed her greasy hair and sunken eyes. She'd have a shower before her appointment tomorrow. Maybe getting sick had been timely. It was forcing her into a type of 'normal', after all. No ghosts to deal with, and only television and books to pass the time indoors. She smiled. *Sounds good to me,* she said again, only inwardly this time. And it did.

Her eyes widened in the mirror as she had an epiphany. She had a choice. She'd lived the first twelve years of her life thinking she was different because she *had* to be. But what if she didn't? What if she could decide to live a different life – one in which she ignored them all? All the others she could see but no one else could? Where she focused on the teacher even when someone was at the window of the classroom, staring at her? What if, because it was only happening to her and nobody else around her, she could just pretend it wasn't happening at all? And what if eventually, she didn't have to pretend anymore? What if they gave up on her and left her alone?

She frowned. Maybe that was it. And maybe even if she didn't want to ignore them, she had to, so the people in her life wouldn't give up on her and leave her alone.

CHAPTER 7 – IN SEARCH OF NORMAL

Peyton awoke the next morning feeling better than the day before, but still a bit feverish and with a very sore throat.

The headache was kept at bay with Ibuprophen – thanks, Gram – and the dizziness had subsided, only hitting her if she stood up or turned too fast. Gram had come into Peyton's room that morning to wake her, and told her that Barry had called the night before to update them on the kids. The doctor suspected strep throat.

That meant Peyton's doctor would likely swab her, too. She hated that long cotton-ended stick. A very large part of her wanted to protest - even refuse - but she fought it. She was being different, now.

True to form, the doctor took one look in Peyton's throat and pulled out that dreaded gag-stick. Peyton gagged strongly as the doctor swabbed, earning an apology and a lollipop. *Not a bad deal*, she thought with some humour.

Afterward, and as tired as her sick body was,

Peyton loved the trip to the mall. She and Gram had spent nearly an hour wandering through the aisles. Peyton lost herself in the yarn section, running her fingers along the huge selection of skeins over and over again, entranced by the textures and colors. Gram picked several things up for Grandad, thinking of his little studio in the garage. Then she'd called Peyton over to the aisle next to her. Peyton had some difficulty pulling herself away from the yarn, but found it was worth it: Gram had found a little drawing kit, complete with sketchbook, coloured pencils and even charcoal.

Peyton was thrilled, hugging Gram as they left the store with their purchases. She spent the rest of the day in her bedroom, sketching and thinking. She dutifully took her prescribed antibiotics and the Ibuprophen Gram and Grandad brought to her, and ate as well as she could force herself to, her appetite still waning.

As the natural light of the day faded into late evening, Peyton had put her sketch pad down and walked to the open window. The street was empty and quiet, only the sound of the wind in the leaves permeating the air. Peyton closed her eyes and inhaled through her nostrils. It was a beautiful night. Thinking of the bench in the fenced back yard, she grabbed her bag. She put her sketch pad and pencils inside quickly, then made her way downstairs.

"That you, Peyton?" Grandad asked from the

kitchen.

"Yep," she said, walking down the hallway and stopping as soon as she could see him. "I'm going to go sit on the bench in the back, if that's OK?" she asked.

Grandad waved the question away. "Of course, dear, if you feel well enough. Besides," he started again as she turned back toward the door. "I can see you from here," he smiled, then pointed out the kitchen window, which looked right into the fenced yard.

Peyton smiled as she turned, making a mental note not to talk to any ghost-types while she was in view of the kitchen window.

It was a cool evening. Peyton's jelly shoes crunched loudly in the gravel as the walked beside the driveway and into the back yard. She made a beeline for the bench, not even looking to the trees on the other side of the driveway, or the side yard beyond. She waved at Grandad before sitting, her back to the kitchen window.

It was gorgeous out. The light was fading fast, the sky in graduating shades of blue until she looked straight up into the navy-blackness of forever. She let her thoughts go as she took it in. For a few moments, there was nothing but her and the sky.

Something buzzed in her ear and she jumped, thinking again of Jade, but finding a mosquito. She waved it away. She pulled her sketch pad from her bag, then the black pencil crayon. She was pleased to find the light from the kitchen window gave her just enough to work with as she started drawing. She alternately looked around the yard, the trees, the sky, breathing in the evening, and then bent low over her drawing, working.

She looked back at the window once, finding both grandparents there now, drinking tea. She remembered overhearing Gram's phone conversation with her mother earlier that day. Gram had sounded encouraging, casually updating Mom on Peyton's fever and the doctor's appointment.

She'd said other things, too. Sweet things that had brought tears to Peyton's eyes. That Peyton was really blossoming here. That she'd walked to get ice cream herself. That she'd been really social with family. She'd hugged herself, such was her joy at being spoken of in such a positive way.

She took a moment to look to the right, at the driveway. Lit dimly by a lantern on the far side, it showed nothing but black pavement and trees, then the shadows of the garden beyond.

Maybe he'd given up already.

Peyton closed her sketch book, the pencil keeping her place, and stuffed it into her bag as she swatted at another mosquito with her left. The bugs were getting thick, and Peyton was tired. She rose, waving at her grandparents, and then jogged around to the door. She stopped just inside.

No Lex, she thought. And was a bit sad. She shoved it aside and kicked off her shoes, then went to say good night to her grandparents.

"There she is!" Grandad exclaimed as she went into the kitchen. They were listening to an old eight-track, the sad sounds of a clarinet filling the room. "Blue grass," Grandad said into her ear as she bent to hug him. "It's not usually this sad. There's a banjo -"

Peyton kissed his cheek, then bent to hug Gram. "I like blue grass," she said, and then, "Thank you for taking such good care of me," into Gram's hair.

Gram's arms tightened a bit. "My girl," she said.

"I'm going to bed. Still tired," Peyton said, but Gram stopped her.

"Show us what you've been drawing," she said, and Peyton startled.

"Oh! OK," she said, reaching into her bag and handing the book to Gram. "It's just stuff I've seen over the last few days.

"Oh, you've drawn the peas," Gram said, pleased. "Look, love. She's made them all delicate and curly, just like you like to describe them!" Gram held the sketch out to Grandad and he took the book, looking through his bifocals at the drawing.

"Huh. Very good," he grunted, then started flipping through the pages. Peyton bristled, remembering her drawing of Jade by her gravestone.

Grandad was scowling down at one of the pages.

"It's someone I met on my walk yesterday," she started.

Grandad turned the book around, the black pencil clattering to the floor. Gram bent to pick it up, but stopped midway, staring at the picture Peyton had been working on outside.

"Oh," she said, a bit relieved. Explaining the gravestone would have been harder.

Her grandparents looked at each other, then Gram grabbed the pencil off the floor, handing it to Grandad as she righted herself in her chair.

"Thanks," Peyton said as she watched them exchange another look. "I like to keep the pencil where I'm working. I've loved drawing today! I think I drew seven pictures – what's wrong?" she interrupted herself, the looks on her grandparent's faces confusing her.

"Who is this?" Grandad asked, pointing to the picture. Gram looked at her too, the same question in her eyes.

"Just a guy I saw," Peyton started. "Why?"

"Did you speak with him?" Gram asked.

"A – a little," Peyton stammered. "Why? Should I not?" Her mind raced. Did they know Lex? If so, what did that mean? Peyton shook her head, confused. Surely the water-spurting, alternately dry and soaking wet teenager wasn't – alive?

They looked at each other again.

"What is it?" Peyton asked, her voice escalating.

"He just looks a lot like one of the neighbor's kids," Gram said.

"They haven't seen him in a while."

"Oh," Peyton said, her eyebrows furrowed.

Grandad leaned toward her.

"If you've seen him," he started, and Peyton looked at the drawing. It was unfinished, but she liked it. She'd captured his feathered hair perfectly. "They'll want to know. And the police probably will, too," he finished.

Peyton's stomach somersaulted. "Wait, what? Why?"

"Because he's missing, love. They think he's run away. Where exactly did you see him?"

Peyton's heart was racing. "Maybe it's not

him," she started, her panic seeping into her words. "Maybe it's someone else."

Gram studied the picture again. "You're very good at this," she said. "I didn't know you could draw."

"Me neither," Peyton said quietly.

Grandad was flipping through the pages again. He held up another drawing, his eyebrows raised.

Peyton's stomach fell. It was the one of Jade. "She – that one came from my imagination. See the dress?" she spat, but she faltered. The lie was badly delivered, even to her own ears.

"Did you go to the graveyard yesterday?" Gram asked.

"Um…" She shook her head.

Gram blew out a sigh. "Just when I thought -"

"Please don't be disappointed," Peyton said quickly, tears threatening with a lump in her throat. "I really am trying hard. I only drew them -" she pointed to the picture, "- she and Lex, because I'm trying to make them – normal. Uh -" Nothing she was saying sounded right.

"Lex?" Grandad asked, turning back to the last drawing and holding it out again.

"What?" Peyton asked, then added, "I really need to pee."

Gram stood and put her hands on Peyton's shoulders. "You're not in trouble, sweetheart. We're just worried about you."

"You don't have to be -" Peyton started again, but her tears choked off her words.

Gram opened her arms, and Peyton gladly went into them. "I'm so sorry I'm weird," she cried into Gram's shoulder.

Grandad laughed behind them. "Don't ever, ever be sorry for that," he said. "Your weirdness makes you, you."

"And we love you," Gram said, her mouth moving in Peyton's hair and making her giggle as it tickled.

She took a step back. Took a breath. "I did see him," she said, finally.

"Lex?" Gram asked. Peyton nodded.

"Ok," she said, then looked at Grandad.

"We'll have to go to the police," he said.

Gram looked back at Peyton, who was still crying. "Maybe we just need to go next door first, hm?"

Peyton nodded.

"Can you tell them where you saw him?"

She nodded again, though hesitantly.

"Can you tell *us* where you saw him?"

Peyton froze.

"It's alright, darlin'" Gram said, pulling a chair out and motioning for Peyton to sit.

"The thing is -" Peyton started, her voice catching. "I don't think he's – here anymore," she finished, blowing out the rest of the air in her lungs when she got the words out.

"Here, as in – here?" Grandad asked, gesturing to their surroundings. "Or, here as in – alive?"

Gram's eyes widened, but she said nothing.

Peyton considered the choice she was faced with. In that moment – it was just a few seconds, she was sure, but it meant more than any other few seconds of her life had meant up to this point. In that moment, Peyton thought about her desire to be a normal girl. One who didn't worry everyone. One who didn't make her mother cry. She stared at the chair in front of her. She wanted to be that girl. Especially now, when she was realizing what it was she had been seeing all her life, and contemplating the meaning of it. She could hide it. She could try. She could weave her whole life with lies just to deny the truth, she wanted so badly to be that girl.

But she wasn't.

CHAPTER 8 – CHANGE

They'd stayed up talking later than Peyton had ever stayed up in her life. She felt like a zombie when Gram finally led her to her room and tucked her in, her teeth unbrushed and her day clothes still on.

She felt empty, too. She had, for the first time in her life, talked to someone about the people and things she saw, and despite her fear that it would forever shape the way her family thought of her (because surely the conversation would not be contained to the room it happened in), it had been such a relief that Peyton had been shocked at just how much it had been weighing her down.

She considered it as she lay on her pillow. She *had* talked about it before, actually. She'd been completely open to everyone about her friends when she was little. Sometimes they'd humour her, Mom even setting the table for them if Peyton begged hard enough. It never failed, though: whether her parents, teachers, or classmates humoured her or not, she'd come to realize that they never believed her. So, over time, she'd stopped talking about it.

But Gram and Grandad had taken her seriously. They'd asked questions and listened to her. Peyton hadn't told them everything – she didn't know if she'd even have the right vocabulary to tell them everything – but she had confessed much, including everything about her encounters with Lex.

And she had another epiphany as she was drifting to sleep – that although she could have chosen to keep on trying to hide who she was, the choice *not to* was valid, too. *Huh. Maybe I am changing, after all.*

In the end, Peyton and her grandparents had agreed to hold off on visiting the neighbors. Knowing what they knew at the end of the night, they thought it best to find out more first. Neither Gram nor Grandad were entirely comfortable with Peyton dealing with Lex on her own, given what she'd told them about previous encounters, but they were at a loss for how to prevent that, save one or both of them being near her always. Peyton's protests were cut off quickly; both grandparents knew they couldn't give Peyton unfair boundaries. They wanted to help her, but not by putting her in a cage.

When Peyton woke up the next morning, she took stock of how she felt. Her throat was still scratchy, but the antibiotics were doing their work; it was much better. She was sure her fever was gone, and her head didn't hurt at all.

She realized she could hear her grandparents talking outside. She went to the window, ready to say good morning to them, but stopped when she saw how serious they looked. Peyton dropped to her knees, pressing her right ear to the screen.

"What? Are you saying she's not on the spectrum at all? That instead of dealing with Autism, she's been dealing with being a – what? – psychic medium?" Grandad spoke in a low voice, but his exasperation was clear.

Gram muttered something under her breath.

Peyton turned her head a bit so she could see them better.

"No, I'm not saying anything of the sort. I'm just saying that maybe the focus has been on what's wrong with her when we should be – trying to help her? I don't know. Talking to her...learning what she already knows is different about her."

Grandad spread his huge hands beside himself in exasperation, then let them drop.

"Different, not wrong, Ed," Gram said again, then stood on her toes and tilted her face up for a kiss.

Grandad stooped to kiss her and she patted his cheek.

Peyton turned and sat, her back against the wall. *Did I make the wrong choice?* she wondered, frowning. *Or should I have been honest all along?*

She shook her head in confusion. People's reactions often seemed odd to her. Sometimes – often times – she felt clueless as to why people acted the way they did, herself included. At least her friends – *ghosts*, she reminded herself – were honest. She smiled. *Interesting that ghosts seem more real to me than the living.*

She heard Grandad's car start up in the front driveway, and a door opened downstairs. Peyton rose and slid into her new slippers, which Gram had bought for her at the mall after Peyton's doctor's appointment. She visited the bathroom, then peeked out the side window to the long driveway and the yard beyond. Nothing. She frowned. Maybe Lex really had given up on her. She felt a heavy sort of regret settle in her chest.

Feeling defeated, she went downstairs and into the kitchen.

Gram was at the stove, as usual. "Good morning, dear," she turned to smile at Peyton. "Scrambled eggs?"

Peyton nodded, then sat. Her eyes went to the outside bench she'd sat on the night before. "Nice day," she mumbled.

"It's beautiful," Gram said, putting a plate in front of Peyton. She looked down at her. "And I want you to get out in it."

Peyton looked questioningly at her grandmother. "OK?"

Gram chuckled, then sat opposite Peyton, still holding a cup towel in her hand.

Peyton scooped a giant forkful of eggs into her mouth. "Mmm, good," she mumbled in appreciation. "You put cheese in there?" she asked, raising her voice so the words could get through the eggs she was chewing. Gram pressed her lips together, and Peyton covered her mouth. "Whoops. Sorry."

"Your Grandad and I – well, we ended up talking some more after you went to bed," Gram said, sitting forward a bit. Peyton froze, her eyes on Gram. "Don't worry, love. It's nothing bad. We just – well we are worried about you, I won't lie. But even more than that, we want to help you." Peyton frowned. "You know, when I was a little girl, I saw things, too. And my mother was the same."

Now, she chewed and swallowed quickly. "Really? What about Mom?"

Gram nodded. "Her, too. But for us, right around your age, it kind of – stopped."

Peyton's eyes grew large. "You don't see anything anymore?"

"Well, I wouldn't say that, but it's certainly not like it used to be," Gram answered, her eyes on the tablecloth. "But I will say it's more of a choice now. Something I have control over."

Peyton threw her hands into the air. "Why

hasn't anyone told me before now?" Her hands came down, slapping her bare thighs beneath her jean shorts.

"I don't know!" Gram said, throwing her hands in the air, too. "When you were little and had all your imaginary friends, we joked that it was in the blood. We never thought it would intensify! We thought it would fade, just like it had for us."

Peyton sat back in her chair, looking out the window. "I wish I'd have known," she said, quietly.

"I'm telling you now, sweetheart." Gram reached across the table.

Peyton paused, then reached back. She couldn't meet Gram's eyes, though. She needed to process it all first.

"I say it faded, but it was more like -" Gram paused. "It was like I decided not to see anymore," she finished.

Peyton looked at her now, her heart speeding up. "I keep feeling like I need to make a decision, too. I tried not to see them, but it didn't work. Then I tried to just act like I couldn't see them -" she grimaced. "All I want is to be normal like everyone else," she said.

Gram looked like she might cry.

Peyton's heart kicked up another notch. She couldn't handle it if Gram cried. "Please don't be sad!" she exclaimed, squeezing Gram's fingers.

Gram shook her head. "You – you should never change for anybody, Peyton. You're a beautiful girl."

This was even worse. Peyton took her hands back and squirmed in her seat.

"I don't mean to make you uncomfortable! I just – I want you to try and gain a new perspective on things."

Peyton stared at her eggs.

"I think the things that make you different also make you who you are."

"Dad said that, too," Peyton mumbled.

"Peyton -"

Peyton forced herself to meet her grandmother's eyes.

"You said all you wanted was to be 'like everyone else,'" she continued, using air quotes. "But I think you say that because you want to please everyone around you. What about – would you be happy if you could be exactly who you are and be accepted by the people around you?"

"OF COURSE!" Peyton exclaimed. "But it doesn't seem to work that way, Gram!"

"Maybe there's a way," Gram said, and Peyton scoffed, folding her arms over her chest.

"Just give me a chance here, girl!" Gram stood up, walking to the stove. She looked at the eggs left in the pan. Picked up a morsel, then thought better of it and let it drop. She turned back to Peyton. "What if you had a few people in your life – people you were close to – that you could talk to about everything, with no fear of being ridiculed or judged?"

Peyton bit her lower lip as she considered.

"And at the same time, you could learn more about what you're seeing, feeling – whatever! - with the goal of eventually being able to work it into your daily life. School, home, work, eventually..."

Peyton shook her head now. "How, Gram?"

"Well, that's what you've got to figure out... what *we* can figure out, together."

Peyton shrugged, then picked up her fork.

"Let me help you start."

She shrugged again, scooping more eggs into her mouth. She was intrigued, but wary. It all felt jumbled and messy in her head when she thought about it.

"I'm going to give you a challenge for today," Gram said, her eyes lighting up at an idea.

Peyton raised her eyebrows and looked at her sideways.

"I want you to find Lex."

"Find him?"

"Yes. Go wherever you've seen him before, call his name, connect to him however you can."

Peyton sat up straight. She looked out the window again, toward the old oak this time.

"He was mad last time," she said quietly.

"Are you scared of him?" Peyton looked down at her eggs again.

"A little." Gram walked back to her chair and sat again, sighing.

"Oh, Peyton. I'm sorry."

"He smells bad. And he smokes. And every time he tries to say something, water shoots out of his mouth." She looked up at Gram. Her face was twisted in something like pity, or fear. Both, maybe.

"I'm sorry, love. It can't be easy."

"Sometimes it is," Peyton countered without hesitation, thinking about her friends at home. "Sometimes they're really fun and just want to play."

Gram shook her head.

"Is it OK that I tell you that? You seem upset. When you said I could talk to a few people, I thought you meant you -" Peyton talked fast to get her thoughts out, the expression on Gram's face giving her that familiar feeling of having said too much.

She shook her head to the contrary, though. "No, love. I'm not upset. And yes, I would be honored to be one of the people you feel you can share all of this with. You just have to be patient with me, OK? It's all a bit unfamiliar to me. And I forgot how emotional it could be."

Peyton nodded. "But you've seen them, too."

"Yes, but – well not like you. I never had conversations with them, much less played with them!"

"Oh," Peyton said, sinking back against her seat again. A spark of anger flaring in her unexpectedly, she yelled, "Why do I have to be so strange?"

Gram reached for her hands again, and Peyton gave them, surrendering. She started to cry. "Don't say that," Gram said, her own eyes welling up. "You're not strange; you're wonderful. I love you so much!"

Peyton let her forehead rest on the table.

"I can come with you today."

"What?" Peyton asked, her voice muffled by her hair.

"You don't have to find Lex alone. You don't have to find him at all, if you don't want to. But if you do, I'd be happy to be with you. For support."

Peyton looked up, part of her wanting to say, "Yes, yes, thank you!" But she held herself back, thinking, *if I accept her help now, I'll never get any time alone!* "No," she said simply.

"Oh. Well it was just an idea," Gram said.

"Maybe later, but not now. I don't know how to...share this the right way. Now that I know what they are, I think I need some time to figure things out on my own before I start accepting your help." She put her head back on the table. "Does that even make sense?" she asked, her voice muffled again.

Gram laughed now, and it was a welcome sound. Peyton raised her head again.

"It does, actually. It's your choice. Whatever you're comfortable with."

Peyton nodded. "Thank you."

"You'll keep me updated, though?"

She nodded again. This was going to be very... different.

Gram released Peyton's hands, then sat back in her chair. "You know – don't tell Grandad I told you this – he thinks we should be protecting you. Supervising you at all times."

Peyton gasped, her eyes widening.

Gram raised a hand before she could say anything, though. "Don't worry. That won't happen. I reminded him you've been dealing with this all your life. On your own. I'm sorry for that -"

Peyton waved the apology away. "It's OK."

"It's not anymore, though. Which is why your parents will have to be told, too."

"Uh -"

"In time," Gram added, seeing Peyton's panic. "Let's give you the time you need, first. But, sweetheart, if it really is the ghost of Lex Wheeler you're seeing...well we need to figure out what to do about that."

Peyton nodded. "I know." She stood. "I'm going to go find him."

Gram's eyes flashed with unchecked fear, but just for a second. Then, she smiled. "OK."

"If you're looking at me out the window the whole time, I'll know it," Peyton warned as she carried her plate to the sink.

"I'll be good," Gram said, watching her. "I meant to ask if you wanted some toast -"

Peyton crossed and kissed her on the cheek. "The eggs were yummy. Thank you."

Gram smiled. "You're growing up so fast."

Peyton giggled, then headed toward the side door. She turned, a thought coming to her. "Remember that little girl by the gravestone?" Gram nodded. "She offered to help me. I sort of feel like it would be better if I talk to her first."

"What?" Gram looked surprised.

"With ghost stuff," Peyton answered, then lowered her head. "I didn't realize until yesterday that I was talking to ghosts."

Gram laughed. "What did you think they were?"

Peyton shrugged. "I don't know! Aliens? Magic – people?"

"What? Why?" Gram looked thoroughly entertained.

"Ghosts are supposed to float around making '*Ooooo!*' noises!" Peyton exclaimed, raising her hands mock-menacingly. Gram laughed harder.

"Oh dear, we really should have talked about this sooner!" she got out between fits of laughter.

Peyton rolled her eyes. "They wear sheets," she finished, feeling lame.

Gram's laughter redoubled at this.

"But – I don't know if I can explain it, but something in me always did associate them with death," Peyton said then, looking thoughtful. "Just not the term, 'ghost,' as I knew it. Anyway, Jade said she could help me recognize them more quickly and stuff..."

Gram's face turned serious. "I'm sorry for laughing at you, hon. I understand why you were confused. Do you think you're feeling well enough to walk all the way to the graveyard?"

"Yeah! I feel great, actually."

"I can tell, and I'm glad, but you're still probably prone to get tired faster. Just take it easy, OK? And there's a payphone at Wilton's; call if you want Grandad to come get you."

Peyton nodded.

"Do you have a quarter?" Peyton shook her head and Gram tsk-tsked as she went to find her purse in the entryway. "What made you think of death when you were around them?" she called, her disembodied voice finding Peyton as she waited in the kitchen.

She made a face. "There's always something different about them. Lex is wet, but only sometimes. Jade – that's the girl in the graveyard – she's seven years old, but she's alone. Plus, she was sitting beside her own gravestone –"

Gram stifled a giggle as she came back to the kitchen, holding a handful of change out.

Peyton looked at her. "I know. Sometimes I just feel so dumb." She peered at the change in Gram's palm. "What's all this for?"

Gram hugged her. "Treats."

"Is it because I'm on the spectrum?"

Gram held her at arm's length, searching her eyes. "What? How you feel when you're talking to others? Maybe," she answered. "You have a hard time with people in general, don't you?"

Peyton rolled her eyes. "Always!"

Gram nodded. "Then yes, it could be because of that. But don't let it stop you, girl. You know you're nothing close to dumb. And at least we're figuring things out, now. *Then* we figure out what to do with it all."

Peyton nodded, though it all felt jumbly, still.

"To help you get along in life easier," Gram said, lifting Peyton's chin. She patted her shoulder, then turned to the stove. "Now, get! I need to eat these rubbery things," she said, peering into the frying pan again.

"No, you don't!" Peyton said, then turned, skipping out of the kitchen. "It's a choice!" She heard Gram laughing behind her.

"Smart ass," she yelled, and now Peyton was laughing. She already had her bag with all her sketching things. She started to slip on her jelly shoes, but thought better of it - she'd be walking all the way to the graveyard. She put on her runners.

"Be back by lunch! Gram called again, poking

her head into the hallway.

"I will!" Peyton said with a wave, then bounded out the door and into the sunshine of the day. "Jade first," she said out loud, and walked toward the road.

She needed all the help she could get with Lex.

CHAPTER 9 – A COMMISSION

Peyton was relieved to find Jade in the same spot as before; she'd been thinking about the absence of Lex on the way, and wondering if maybe her ability to see ghosts was fading, too, just like her mother's and her grandmother's had done at her age.

But no; Jade was there, and she waved Peyton over as soon as she noticed her. Peyton ran, but carefully, weaving around the plots with as much respect as she could.

Jade had stood up and was smiling, her dark cheeks shining in the sun. "You're back!" she said, and Peyton frowned.

"You weren't so nice yesterday," she said, and grimaced as she heard it. "I mean, you seem happy to see me. Happier than yesterday. Um…"

Jade looked at her like she was crazy. "You OK?"

Peyton sat beside the plot. "I don't know. It's been a weird couple days."

Jade sat, too, her purple dress billowing out all around her. "You look like a flower," Peyton said, gesturing at her silky skirt.

Jade smoothed the material over her lap. "I love it so much. I wish I'd had it when I was alive. Oh, check these out," she said, reaching up into her sleeves and pulling out a lacy pair of white gloves. She put them on, then held her hands out for Peyton's inspection.

"Ha, they match your socks," Peyton said.

"Funny thing is, Mom never would have let me wear this stuff before. I got dirty easily," she explained, turning her hands as she studied her gloves.

"Me too," Peyton said. Jade looked at her.

"Do they come here a lot?"

Jade shrugged. "I don't know. All I know is that I wait for them, and sometimes, they're here." She toyed with the grass as she talked. "But they can't see me. They're so sad," she trailed off.

"Don't cry," Peyton said.

Jade shook her head, but didn't raise her eyes again.

"Is it easy to – stay?"

Jade looked at her, then shook her head. "It's hard. I have to make the decision all the time. I just don't want to go, not with them so sad." She flickered and buzzed, and Peyton jumped. She'd forgotten the strange electric quality her new friend had.

"Why does that keep happening?" she asked.

Jade looked down at herself. "It scares me."

"Why?" Peyton asked, but felt the tiny hairs on her arms stand up. Her circumstances dawned on her all at once: she was in an otherwise empty graveyard, talking to a ghost, and the ghost was frightened by – herself. She fought her instinct to stand and go.

"It's the last thing I remember," Jade said, quietly. "A jolt, like I was being shaken. I was in a tree, trying to stay dry from the rain. And there was this shock. It knocked me to the ground. There was a buzzing sound in my head and nothing felt right." She looked at Peyton. "I could feel my heart beating so, so fast. And my arms and legs were shaking. I couldn't control it -"

Peyton gasped. "Lightning?"

The girl's eyes cleared. "Maybe."

"If you were in a tree and it was raining, you were probably hit by lightning," Peyton reasoned.

Jade frowned. "I never knew lightening could feel so – solid. Like, it felt like something huge hit me." She flickered again, the buzzing getting louder.

"Maybe sometimes you need an outside point

of view to help you see," Peyton muttered, trying for something comforting.

Jade smiled now. "You mean like me having to let you know you've been seeing ghosts, not aliens?"

Peyton laughed. "Like that. Yeah." She was still embarrassed, but Jade seemed so vulnerable today. Besides, it didn't feel terrible to make fun of herself a little bit. She could be vulnerable, too.

"Hmm," Jade said.

Peyton gazed around the quiet yard, then up at the sky. "Speaking of rain," she muttered, observing the dark clouds on the horizon.

Jade's head whipped in the direction Peyton was looking.

"Don't worry! I don't think you're in danger... anymore..."

Jade gave her a sarcastic, "You don't think?" sort of look.

Peyton tried laughing at herself again instead of taking offense. It felt good.

Jade shook her head. "I don't stay for the rain. Feels bad."

"Makes sense. So...you stay because your parents are too sad. And maybe because you weren't sure how it happened?" Peyton asked, trying to piece things together.

"I guess," Jade responded. She flickered again, fading for longer this time.

"Do you think I could help you?" Peyton asked. Gram and Grandad had said that from what they knew, ghosts stayed because they needed help, or to finish something important.

"It happened so fast," Jade said, looking thoughtful. "It's like they can't believe it still."

Peyton thought, furrowing her brow.

"I just wish I could say goodbye to them," Jade cried, her hands coming up to cover her face.

"Poor girl," Peyton said, feeling awkward again.

"I think it would help if I could just tell them I'm OK," Jade cried, sniffing loudly, then making an exasperated face. "It's not fair that I still have snot!" she protested, wiping her nose on the back of her hand.

Peyton grimaced, but couldn't help but giggle, too. "That really doesn't seem fair," she agreed. She looked around again. The air had gotten cooler, and the dark clouds closer.

"What's in there?" Jade asked, then hiccoughed. She was pointing to Peyton's knitted bag.

Peyton took it off. "It's my shoulder bag. I keep stuff in it when I'm going anywhere." She dug around inside and pulled out her wallet, then a bag of crushed cookies. "Ew," she muttered, and Jade giggled. Her sketchbook was next. Peyton brightened as she remembered why she'd come to the graveyard today. "Hey, remember you said you could help me?" She asked.

Jade nodded.

Peyton took a breath, mustering her courage. "There's this boy – a ghost," she stammered. "He hangs out by my grandparent's house. He seems really angry all the time."

Jade nodded again, rolling her eyes as though this was no surprise.

"Every time he tries to talk to me, water comes out of his mouth. He keeps leading me to the trees on the other side of the yard…"

"What's there?" Jade asked, wrapping her arms around her knees and squeezing them so her chin rested on them.

"I can see your underwear again."

"Oops." She crossed her legs in front of her, folding her still-gloved hands together. "Better?" She stuck her nose in the air, prim and proper.

Peyton giggled.

"So?" Jade asked again.

"Right. Oh. Trees – and the neighbor's trailer that they don't use anymore.

"What's inside?" "Nothing, I don't think." Peyton thought of the thud she'd heard, but couldn't remember whether she'd dreamt that or if it had been real.

"Maybe you should find out," Jade said. She pointed at the sketch book. "What's that?"

"Oh," Peyton said, jumping. She turned to the last picture and showed it to Jade. "That's him."

Jade wrinkled her nose. "Nice feathered hair," she remarked, then giggled. "You're really good at drawing."

"Thanks," Peyton replied, turning the pages until she came to the picture of Jade. She turned the book to face her.

Jade gasped. "Oh! You drew me!"

"Yeah."

"Wow." Jade got on her hands and knees, her face lowered to study the picture. "You probably didn't need to put the gravestone in," she smiled up at Peyton.

"Yeah, I don't think a whole lot when I draw, it turns out."

Jade giggled, then looked thoughtful. "Do you think you could draw another?" She looked at Peyton. "Without the stone?"

Peyton shrugged. "Sure." Jade smiled. "And

could I have it?"

"Uh – what for?"

"To leave here. For them."

Peyton gasped. "Your parents?"

Jade nodded, her eyes filling up again.

Peyton considered, then shrugged. "Of course."

"Make me smiling in it!"

"OK," she laughed.

"Make me look happy."

Peyton nodded. "I'll make you look just like how they need to see you."

Now Jade nodded. Thunder sounded in the distance and she jumped, squealing. Her whole body flickered and buzzed.

"It's OK!" Peyton said, but she sounded more panicked than reassuring.

Both girls stood. Jade looked at Peyton with worry in her eyes. There was that smell again. Electricity. Burning. The hairs on her arms stood on end. Jade flickered, reappeared, and flickered again, the buzzing sound intensifying. Peyton's hands flew to her ears. It was almost painful, that sound.

And then Jade was gone, flickering to nothing with a flash of white light and a crackle of static.

Peyton jumped back, a little yelp escaping her, then looked around the graveyard again. Still empty, but she didn't feel alone. The place was darkening as the clouds approached. Thunder rumbled again and Peyton looked back at Jade's plot, strangely empty now.

She stuffed her things back into her bag, then ran, that eerie feeling of being watched – or chased – fuelling her. When she reached the sidewalk, she looked back and yelped again.

Jade was still gone, but there were others, now. Some as plain as day and some hardly there at all. All of them looking at her.

She was frozen in place, not breathing, not thinking. Lightening flashed to her far right, the crack of thunder following almost instantly.

She ran.

CHAPTER 10 –
DRAWING JADE

Peyton sat up, looking over her work. She'd gotten lost in her thoughts again as she drew, and was pleasantly surprised by what she saw. She'd decided to draw Jade in different clothes than she'd been buried in; this was supposed to reassure her parents, not make them want to die, too.

Don't ever say that out loud, she said to herself.

She'd chosen mahogany for her skin, brightening her cheeks with some pink and some white, too, because they shone when she smiled. Her hair was in braids, still, but instead of being wound around her head, they fell around her face and to her shoulders. Peyton had fastened them all with baubles, but these were in different colours – blue, red, yellow and green. She'd thrown in some red barrettes, too, then scrutinized the picture, wondering if she'd taken too many liberties.

Not ready to stop drawing the pretty baubles, she turned the page and drew more in different sizes and colours. She experimented with shading and light, trying to make them appear transparent. She frowned. She hadn't mastered it yet.

She flipped back to Jade, and smiled as she saw the picture with fresh eyes. Despite the differences, it WAS Jade, her smile instantly recognizable. Peyton nodded, then kept working. She drew jean shorts, striped socks and dirty runners. She drew Jade's hands behind her back, like she was hiding something, and her smile was confident and a little impish.

"Wow," a man's voice said, and Peyton jumped, screaming, before she realized it was Grandad.

He jumped back, too. "Mother Mary," he said, his hand on his heart.

"You snuck up on me!" Peyton exclaimed. Then, "Oh, my God, you're not having a heart attack, are you?"

"No!" he looked almost offended, but took a moment to breathe, finally letting his hand drop. "I guess we scared each other. I'm sorry."

Peyton exhaled. "Thank goodness."

"I was watching you for a couple minutes, actually," he said, gesturing to her picture. "Is that the same little black girl you drew before?"

Peyton shook her head, unsure of how to react to his words. "Does it look like her?" she asked instead.

Grandad nodded. "Less fancy, but yeah. I like that you didn't draw her sitting in front of her gravestone this time," he smiled, his eyes sparkling.

Peyton rolled her eyes. "I wasn't thinking everyone was going to see it," she said a bit defensively. She picked up a deep shade of green, but hesitated, looking up at Grandad again. "She was in a tree when she died. Do you think it would be OK to put trees in the background?"

Grandad rubbed his chin. "Who are you drawing this for?" he asked.

"For Jade. Well, for her parents, really. She's helping me with Lex, so I'm helping her with her parents. They're not doing so well, I guess."

Grandad looked sad.

"I forgot to ask; do you want me to talk to you about this stuff, or would you rather not -"

Grandad waved her question away. "Of course, I do. I just – well, you can't expect me to be any sort of authority on how to handle it all."

Peyton looked back at her drawing. "I'm not either, you know," she muttered.

Grandad sat down. "You know, you're really good at this," he said, gesturing at the picture again. "I'm not just saying that because I love you; I think you have a gift."

Peyton managed a smile, but kept her eyes

lowered. Compliments were hard for her. She hadn't a clue what to do with them.

"And the more I think about it, the more I'm sure you're just about the bravest person I know," he added.

Peyton looked at him doubtfully. "Huh?" She shook her head. "You fought in a WAR!" she countered.

Grandad nodded. "I did. And I fought alongside a lot of very good people. Some of them were brave, too, but I want you to consider something."

She raised her eyebrows.

"Just because we were at war doesn't mean we were brave. Most of us were terrified, truth be told - *especially* the brave ones, if you can fathom that. We were just doing what we thought we had to do."

Peyton was confused. "I'm scared a lot, too. And I'm only just realizing I have some choices when it comes to ghosts and how I deal with them..."

Grandad put a palm on her head, and she closed her eyes at the instant warmth and smiled, giggling a little. "Your hands are too big," she said. He rubbed her forehead with his thumb. Peyton opened her eyes, and Grandad was looking intently at her. "What?" she asked, uncomfortable under his scrutiny.

"I'm proud of you," he said, and his chin trembled a bit.

"No!" Peyton said, removing his hand. "Be happy!"

He smiled. "I am happy," he said, then stood. He looked back at her. "Keep talking, girl. Don't stop." He turned to go.

"But, Grandad!"

He paused, looking at her again.

"The trees?"

"Draw the trees; she obviously loved them if she was climbing them. Maybe for the picture, though, keep her feet firmly on the ground," he winked.

"And no lightning!" Peyton added, then started on the background. Grandad walked away, muttering, "Dear God. No kid should have to..." he trailed off.

Peyton looked toward the door, considering his words. Despite his worry, he seemed glad that Peyton was sharing her secrets, and she had to admit she felt lighter for it. She hadn't even realized how much it had all ruled her until she'd unburdened herself.

She was lucky.

Her thoughts turned to Lex, who appeared to

have had less luck in life. She felt bad that she'd let her fear rule her decisions concerning him. Her eyebrows knit in her forehead. *But do I have a responsibility to him just because I can see him?* she wondered. Who could know the answer to that? She certainly didn't. Until she found someone who did, she made up her mind not to feel guilty about being scared of these spirits – especially when they were as intimidating as Lex was, with his garbled swear words and gushing water.

She nodded, reaching for the brown for the trunks, but pausing, pencil in the air as she looked toward the door again. *I may not need to feel guilty when I have a hard time helping him, but I still feel like I should do* something. She remembered Jade's advice. *Maybe I should go back to the trailer and look around some more, whether Lex is there or not.*

She rose and went to the room at the end of the hall, looking out at the yard beyond. It was raining, still, and very dark. What light there was reflected off the smooth, wet pavement of the driveway. She opened the window, then put her elbows on the sill, resting her chin in her hands. The air smelled fresh and clean, and the sounds of the rain as it hit the driveway, the roof, the leaves on the trees, was heavenly. *Not tonight*, she thought, closing the window again.

Tomorrow.

CHAPTER 11 – A HOLE IN THE FENCE

Peyton awoke to sunlight and fresh, cool air on her face. She groaned, stretching like a cat, before she opened her eyes. She'd opened the window before falling asleep the night before, wanting to hear the rain – but part of her had wanted to leave the window open for Lex, too, just in case.

"Figures he'd leave just as I realize I need to help him," she said out loud as she got out of bed and walked to the window. She hugged herself in the cool air, goosebumps prickling on her arms. Shuffling footsteps sounded from the hallway. She looked toward the door.

"Still a few grey clouds," Gram said as she came into the room, heading straight for the bedside table, where she placed a glass of water.

Peyton nodded, saying "Thank you," for the water.

"Grandad and I have some errands to run, and then we're meeting your Aunt June for lunch. Do you want to come?"

Peyton shook her head to the contrary.

"No?"

"I'll stay, if that's alright."

"Well, I suppose it is; your mom and dad told me you've been staying home alone for short periods since you turned twelve – and you're certainly alone outside much of the time -" Gram seemed to be working at convincing herself, but she looked unsure.

"I'll be OK, Gram. I'm still feeling tired, you know? And I have a lot to think about," she added.

"Oh! You've reminded me: here's your antibiotic," she said, fishing in the pocket of her jeans.

Peyton thought of lint and other, not-so-clean things that tended to live in pockets and frowned.

"There!" Gram said, holding the pill out for Peyton.

"Thanks, Gram," she said, and popped the pill into her mouth as she crossed to the glass of water. That way, she simply wouldn't have time to obsess over what types of germs she was swallowing with the pill.

"You stay in or around the house today, OK?" Gram raised her eyebrows at her.

"Of course."

"No plans to visit – what was her name?"

"Jade?"

"Right, Jade," Gram repeated, looking a bit uncomfortable.

Peyton shook her head. "I want to try to find Lex. I think I need to help him."

Gram frowned. "Do you know how you would do that?"

Peyton shrugged. "I don't know. That's what I need to find out."

Gram put a hand to her hip, thinking.

"You still believe me, right?"

Gram looked up quickly. "Of course, Peyton. Doesn't mean I have to like it, though. And I still think you should bring me or your Grandad along."

Peyton waved the comment away. "You'd be bored. And if Lex really is -"

"Dead?" Gram winced.

Peyton nodded.

"Well, we'll have to go to the neighbors and probably the police, too, as soon as you figure anything out that could help."

Peyton nodded. "He said he's not here for him, though."

"Regardless, there are people looking for him," Gram said, exasperated. She busied herself by pulling the bedsheets up, then smoothing the comforter over them with her palms.

Peyton shoved her hands in her pockets. "This is complicated, isn't it?"

Gram straightened, sighed, then smiled at Peyton. "Yep, but I think once we're used to it, it'll get easier. Right?"

Peyton considered this for a moment, then shrugged. "Maybe?"

Gram huffed. "It better," she said, then reached for the glass.

Peyton handed it over.

"There are waffles in the kitchen, and a jar of strawberry compote from last year on the counter."

Peyton did a little dance. "Woohoo!" she said, and Gram shook her head, still smiling.

"Have a good day, love. See you this afternoon," she said as she kissed Peyton's cheek.

Peyton dutifully stood still for her kiss, then continued her jig as Gram left the room, chuckling.

She changed quickly, then went to the washroom. The face that looked back at her always seemed a bit strange. Today it was strange and had a headful of brown hair that stuck together at the roots and snarled at the ends. "Ugh," Peyton uttered, resolving to shower before her grandparents returned. She ran her fingers through her hair for the time being, wincing as she pulled through the knots.

She heard the car starting in the side driveway. *Lex won't mind, considering…*she thought as she bounced down the stairs, avoiding her own reflection as she passed it.

The kitchen windows were open, the white sheers drifting listlessly in the breeze - first lifting inward, billowing lazily, then flattening against the screen. Peyton opened them further, wanting an unobstructed view into the back yard. Satisfied, she found her plate of lukewarm waffles on the counter, and grabbed the jar of compote triumphantly.

By the time she was done eating, Peyton was feeling rather accomplished and grown up. She even washed her own dishes, leaving them haphazardly in the rack to dry.

Next: Lex.

Her stomach flipped. What if he wasn't there? What if he was weird and scary? She rolled her eyes at herself. Weird and scary seemed a permanently affixed constitution for poor Lex.

She bent to stretch her jellies over her feet. *And if he's not here, I'll go back to the trailer and look around anyway,* she resolved.

But he was there.

Peyton gasped, both surprised and relieved as she went out the door to find Lex where she'd first seen him: at the edge of the trees opposite her. "Hi," she said, giving him a lame little wave.

He only stared. He wasn't wet today; his light hair perfectly feathered and held stiffly in place with – what was it called again? Aqua net? Hairspray, in any case.

She cleared her throat. "Your hair looks nice," she offered, then rolled her eyes at herself.

He followed suit, his dark eyes rolling as he gave his head a little shake.

Peyton giggled. Lex motioned for her to follow him then, and turned toward the side yard.

She jumped, scurrying to follow him, her hands flying up at her sides. The still-wet grass poked into the holes in her shoes uncomfortably, and she shuddered. She fought the urge to go back for her runners.

She found herself eager to help him. At the very least, she could try. He walked with a bit of a swagger, an air of arrogance about him, she noticed as she followed him. Then it hit her - that smell. Damp. Rot. She held her breath as they walked between the sitting area on the right and the vegetable garden on the left.

The automatic sprinklers were on. Peyton slowed, distracted by the differences she could see between the plants today and the plants when she'd picked peas for dinner. The garden had exploded with growth, the greenery tall now and starting to encroach on the spaces between the rows. She could even see some orange squash blossoms.

"The garden sure loved the rain," she muttered aloud and then startled as Lex said something from ahead of her. Though it had been garbled with that odd watery quality, Peyton was almost sure he'd said, "Come *on!*" She hop-skipped into a jog.

"Sorry," she said as she reached him.

He remained still, but pointed to the trees as he looked at her intently.

Peyton nodded, impressed he seemed to be asking, first, this time. "We can go."

He started off again, Peyton scrambling to walk beside him this time so she could breathe normally. He glanced sideways at her and they continued in silence. It probably took thirty seconds for them to reach the trees from the garden, but in that time, Peyton discovered some things about Lex. She could tell he had taken care of his looks in life. Despite the ever-present smell of rotting beneath everything else, she could smell soap. Something else – deodorant? And the hairspray, of course. She peeked at him sideways. Jeans, leather jacket, and black high-tops. Hands in pockets. His face determined and moderately annoyed, the latter Peyton recognized as being a common comportment amongst teenagers, male and female alike.

"What?" he asked, water spurting from his mouth and nose as he looked at her.

Peyton squealed, jumping further to the left. "Hey, I heard you pretty well that time!"

He stopped. "Maybe you're listening better," he gurgled.

"Bubbles," Peyton mumbled.

"What?" he asked, making the *what's wrong with you* face Peyton knew so well.

"You – you sound bubbly."

He started walking again. "Not like, chubby, giggly, happy, chatty-bubbly," she added as she rushed to catch up to him again. "More like underwater talking-bubbly."

He gave her the face again.

She inhaled sharply, preparing herself for what came next. "Are you in water?" she asked for the second time since she'd encountered him.

He stopped, and Peyton did, too, though she stumbled at the unexpectedness of it. When she looked at him, he nodded, his eyes sad. And maybe a bit angry, too. "Can I help you?" she asked, shoving a clump of hair off her face and behind her ear.

Lex's smile wasn't a happy one. He looked defeated. Hopeless. He looked toward the trees, then back at her. "Help me with this," he said, Peyton watching his thin lips shape the words as they gurgled up.

She nodded. "OK."

They reached the trees, both looking back at the greying wall of trailer, its windows thoroughly boarded up. Lex approached it, then looked back at Peyton as he pointed at one of the boarded windows. He raised his eyebrows.

Peyton joined him beside the trailer. "What?" she asked. "Is there something in there? Someone?"

He only looked at her. His hair started dripping water onto his face.

"You're wet again," she said, then looked back at the trailer to avoid the look she knew he'd give her. And when she looked back, he was gone. She heard the sound of dry leaves moving and looked down. "Oh!" she exclaimed. He wasn't gone. He was just the rabbit again. "You're much cuter that way." She giggled at her own words.

Rabbit-Lex stared at her, twitching his nose.

"Now what?" she asked, feeling silly, then realizing how odd it was that she felt stranger talking to a rabbit than a ghost.

Lex hopped to her left. Peyton was careful to keep her eyes on his soft-looking brown fur as he went. She wasn't going to lose sight of him.

He bounded along the trailer wall, now, the whiteness of his undertail flashing. He stopped where the trailer ended, then looked up at her. The trees were thicker there, and there was a green fence between the two properties. It looked new.

"Huh," she said quietly, running her fingers along the smooth diamond shapes of it. "When did this get here?"

More crunching leaves at her feet, and Peyton jumped back as she looked down again. There were two rabbits, now. She squatted, frowning at the new one. It had white fur with brown spots. "Where did you come from?"

As if in answer to her question, a third rabbit appeared from the underbrush, and he looked so much like rabbit-Lex that she looked hurriedly between them, trying to pick out distinguishing marks. A fourth rabbit appeared, then, and Peyton lowered herself further, peering through branches to where they all seemed to be coming from. A fifth rabbit suddenly hopped into her line of sight, eliciting a squeal from her, and they all startled, some freezing and some hopping away at speed.

"Sorry," she said, feeling silly again.

A brown rabbit was beside her, looking up

into her eyes. "Lex?" she asked, and he hopped into the underbrush.

Peyton lowered herself again, watching him disappear into the darkness. And then, there was a circle of light as Lex cleared the space.

There's a break in the fence, she realized. Sitting back on her heels, she frowned. *This can't be the reason Lex is here, can it? To – what? Make sure his family's rabbits don't all escape?*

The rabbits had started to follow Lex into the brush, disappearing in a neat line. Peyton looked around hurriedly, rising as she spotted something that might work as a temporary block for the fluffy little guys. It was a boulder, just heavy enough to make Peyton have to work to carry it, but stuffing it under the branches as far as her arm would go was simple, after she'd looked around to make sure no-bunny was left behind.

She giggled at her own joke, simultaneously resolving never to say that out loud, either.

She stood, looking around herself. The sun was higher in the sky; she could feel the air changing with the heat of it, the dampness within the trees thickening the air.

"Is that it?" she called out. Birdsong was her only answer.

She made her way back to the yard, glancing

behind her one last time before she went to the garden to examine its progress more closely.

A hole in the fence, she thought again, confused. It seemed an odd thing for a ghost to stick around for, but what did she know? Maybe the rabbits had been Lex's pets? *But what about Lex?* She recalled his nod after she'd asked, again, if he was in water. She shook her head. She hadn't learned much. Not much that would be of use, anyway.

She approached the garden now, and within minutes was lost in it as she wondered over new buds and blossoms, only rousing back to reality when her hair fell in front of her face again and she was reminded that she needed a shower. She skipped to the house, blissful in her solitude.

Maybe not much had been solved, but she made her mind up as she kicked off her muddy shoes to tell her grandparents everything she did know.

It was all she could do for now.

CHAPTER 12 – AN EXPLORATORY VISIT

Peyton heard Gram and Grandad downstairs when she got out of the shower. She finished up and went to greet them, and they listened intently as Peyton recalled her morning between mouthfuls of blueberry grunt, sent especially for her from Aunt June.

They looked as lost as she'd felt until she told them about the broken fence and the many rabbits that had come through it. But where it had stumped her, it inspired them.

Within minutes, she and Grandad were on the way to the Wheeler property. Peyton was pouting, her mind on what remained of her blueberry grunt in the fridge back home.

"It's the perfect excuse to snoop a little bit," Grandad said again.

Peyton shrugged. "I know," she said. Grandad took her hand. Peyton marvelled at how hers disappeared completely within his. "Are you going to say anything about Lex?" she asked, craning her neck to see his face.

"Well now, I dunno," he answered, then fell into silence, their shoes crunching along on the gravel shoulder of the road the only sound for a few minutes.

The Wheeler's mailbox was a rather spectacular metal rooster whose lower beak was also the handle for the pull-down door. Peyton pointed to it. "Yours?" she asked, and Grandad nodded. "It's beautiful," she said, a note of pride in her voice, and he squeezed her hand.

They turned down the tree-lined gravel driveway, past the large hand-painted sign for the car parts/repair business. Peyton pointed to a smaller sign erected beside it:

Rabbits 4 Sale

Grandad looked down at her, but said nothing. He waved instead, having spotted Mr. Wheeler at the end of the driveway, hosing down a very muddy jeep. He turned the hose off and came to meet them, his hands stuffed behind the bib of his overalls.

"Henry," Grandad held out a hand to greet him, and Mr. Wheeler took it, squinting at Grandad and then at Peyton.

"Ed," he said, his voice gruff. "And who do we have, here?" Grandad gestured toward Peyton.

"I guess you two have never met. This is my

granddaughter, Peyton."

"Nice to meet you, Peyton," the man said, stuffing his hand back behind his bib. "Well now, what can I do for you today, Ed?" he asked, focusing on Grandad again.

Peyton observed his thick stubble and greasy skin with a modicum of discomfort. His overalls boasted grease stains old and new, and he smelled of gasoline and stale cigarettes.

"Well, Peyton here was playing in the yard today and happened to notice the new fence you have lining the property." He pointed back toward the trailer, and Peyton's gaze followed, halting on the old mobile home. It was odd seeing it from the other side, run-down and listing slightly to the right. Further to the right of it, junked cars displaying varying degrees of disassembly rusted in the neat lines of their final resting spot.

Peyton shaded her eyes as they followed the rows as far as they could see. *They go on forever,* she marvelled inwardly. *What a sad place.*

Her attention snapped back to Mr. Wheeler suddenly, the echo of Lex's name still in her ears. "No luck finding the boy?" Grandad asked.

Mr. Wheeler shook his head, then spat in the dirt. Peyton had to fight the urge to recoil in disgust. "He ain't called, neither. The missus is out of her mind, thinking he's met his end in some big city somewhere, but I think he's shacking up with some friends nearby."

Peyton held her breath. She hadn't anticipated how it would feel to be standing on the place where Lex was supposed to be, talking to his father. Knowing he wouldn't ever be there again.

"Why would he have run?" Grandad asked.

Mr. Wheeler squinted at him. "Well now, if I knew that I probably woulda tried stopping him, isn't that right?"

Grandad nodded. "S'pose so," he said. "Well, the wife and I think of you folks often. We've known your family for years!" He paused. "We just hope it all ends well."

Mr. Wheeler looked back at the rows upon rows of cars, but said nothing.

Grandad looked sideways at Peyton. She squirmed. Part of her wanted to pipe up and say she knew him, that she'd just seen him this morning, but the new Peyton knew that wouldn't help.

It might help to tell him he's underwater, though. Peyton frowned at the thought. She wasn't sure it was valid. She needed to think.

Finally, Mr. Wheeler looked back at them. "Anyway, as I was sayin', it was Lex who took care of the rabbits. Got himself in deeper than he could handle, too. See the chicken wire around the side of the trailer, there? To the right?" Grandad squinted, but shook his head.

Peyton could make it out, but just barely. The sun reflected off of it in spots.

"That was Lex's way of trying to contain them once they started procreat'n like only rabbits can. Luckily, they like to keep to the trailer; he fed them inside of it, and spent a lot of time cleaning it, too. Sam – my eighteen-year-old - does it now, but she ain't so enthusiastic as he was, let me tell you." He rubbed at the stubble on his jaw. "I wouldn't be surprised if the critters found a way through the fence to your place; lots of green grass and a vegetable garden, if I remember right?"

Grandad nodded. "Wouldn't be a good thing to let it go on; Ada loves that garden," he said. "Let's go back and take a look at it now; Peyton says it's behind some pretty thick brush on my side."

Mr. Wheeler shook his head, planting his feet on the spot. "Not necessary. I'll get it fixed right up; Ada won't miss a single carrot from her garden," he said.

"Well, I appreciate that, Henry, but you don't even know where the breach is. Peyton could -"

Mr. Wheeler held a hand up. "It'll be easy enough to find, I imagine," he interrupted. "And I wouldn't want the little girl back there; lots of old rusty metal sticking out all over the place." He looked at Peyton. "You wouldn't want to have to get a tetanus shot on your summer vacation, would you, honey?"

Peyton shook her head no, reflexively taking a step back.

"Well, *I'm* not gonna give it to ya!" he laughed, then looked at Grandad. "Did you tell her I bite?"

Grandad smiled. "Can't blame me for warning her about that, Henry."

Mr. Wheeler's face registered surprise, quickly followed by mirth. "You got me there, Ed!" he shouted, clapping Grandad on the shoulder.

Grandad reached for Peyton's hand. "Well, we'll be on our way then, Henry. Best of luck finding your boy, eh?"

"Thanks, Ed. I'll get back to the trailer as soon as I'm done with the Jeep." He picked the hose up, giving them a wave before turning it back on, and Peyton and Grandad turned around.

Grandad looked down at her as they walked. "Well. That went -"

"Weird," Peyton finished for him, and he laughed.

"You got that right," he said, and they carried on toward home.

CHAPTER 13 – REAL, LIVE FRIENDS

Peyton finished her breakfast and then went outside with her bag slung across her, thinking she'd sketch more of the garden. It was hot, though, and before she'd even finished one sketch (a cluster of grape tomatoes, just starting to turn from green to red), she gave up, laying on her back in the cool grass, her arm over her eyes.

"You floundering, girl?" Grandad's voice penetrated her thoughts.

She raised her head. He was standing in the door to the studio, a rag in one hand and a paintbrush in the other. "Bored," she answered.

He motioned her over.

Her limbs felt heavy as she dragged herself up. "I think I was falling asleep!" she said as she approached him, grateful for the shade of the building and the trees around it.

"Why don't you take a walk?" Grandad asked.

Peyton slumped.

"What, is that too much work?" he teased.

She nodded.

"Go inside; your Gram made some lemonade. Get some of that in you, and then go."

Peyton looked in the direction of Main Street, thinking of ice cream and Jade. Grandad grumbled.

"Not that way, today. I was thinking you could go this way," he said, manoeuvring Peyton by the shoulders until she was facing the quiet back street that came off the sharp curve beside the house.

She looked up at him, eyebrows raised.

"You could walk to the school, maybe play in the park."

She scowled, unconvinced.

"Maybe meet some friends, you know? Friends who are ALIVE?"

She laughed, then looked up at him, turning serious. "It was sad yesterday, being at Lex's house."

"Sad? I thought it was just 'weird.'"

She looked down. "Well it was weird, too. But – I don't know – even after learning that he was a ghost, I never really thought of him as being really and truly – dead."

Grandad put his arm around her. "It's hard for

me to think of him that way, too. He was a bit of a punk, I won't lie." He laughed when Peyton looked at him questioningly. "I don't mean he wasn't a good kid. Though he did get into a few scrapes with the law, if I remember correctly...but he had a good heart." He looked in the direction of the trailer. "To be honest, I don't think it was very easy for him, living next door," he finished.

Peyton looked at her feet again. She thought of how she'd felt on the property and nodded. "I can see that," she said.

Grandad rubbed her head. "Go on, now. Get hydrated and then get gone. Go hang out with some real kids," he said.

Peyton slunk away. She'd comply, but she wouldn't pretend to be excited about it. Meeting new people was just not one of her favorite things to do. She didn't even like to meet familiar people.

Gram had left a tall glass of lemonade waiting for her. It was sweating onto the tablecloth, but the ice cubes were still relatively whole. Peyton could hear her humming from upstairs.

She must've told him to send me inside, she thought. Taking a long drink, she closed her eyes, letting the cold liquid spread relief down her throat. Perfectly sweet and tart at the same time. "Yum," she whispered when she finally took it from her lips. She finished it in no time, then splashed some water on her face before heading out the door again.

Refreshed, she skipped past the garage/studio and onto the street, which was shady and cool, thanks to the trees. She got lost in her thoughts, kicking a stone in front of her and humming tune-lessly.

She reached School Street in no time, then turned to the right. There was a sidewalk here – traffic was thick during the school year, of course. About halfway to the school, a little bridge spanned the creek below. Peyton leaned over the railing, watching the water flow beneath her, entranced. She knew the creek ran all the way to the river that flowed through Greenwood and into Aylesford. She made the route up in her head, imagining shady fishing spots and walking trails along the way.

By the time she got to the school, the sun was hiding behind the clouds and the air had cooled. She lifted her chin, studying the sky.

"Lose something?" a voice broke into her thoughts.

Peyton startled, jumping back.

"Sorry," the kid said. He was squatting in the dirt by the kindergarten play area, his eyes firmly on the sand in front of him. He was drawing a design in it with a stick.

Peyton went to stand behind him, curious. He'd smoothed the sand first, then had drawn an intricate circular design in furrows, its pattern mirrored in each quarter. "That's amazing," she heard herself say.

"It's a Mandala," he muttered.

"Cool," Peyton replied, though she hadn't a clue what a Mandala was.

The boy continued, the pointed stick moving evenly in the sand. Peyton watched, entranced. "So strange," she whispered.

"What?" he asked.

"If you look closely, the grains of sand are being difficult; they roll and tumble back into the lines as you go. But if you stand back and look at the bigger picture, it looks clean and neat. Perfect."

The boy paused, sitting back on his heels. "Hm," he said, then got back to it.

She watched a bit more, then started to feel awkward in the silence. "I'm going to the swings," she said, and started toward the big kids' park.

"What's your name?" he asked from behind her.

She turned. He was still focused on his drawing. She hadn't even seen his face. She bent to the side comically, trying to see him.

He looked at her, confused.

"Oh, you have green eyes!" she blurted out, then straightened up.

The boy looked back at the sand, but didn't move to draw, or do anything else, for that matter.

"You OK?" Peyton asked. This kid was strange. But then, so was she.

"Mmhm," he answered, and lifted his stick, seemingly considering where to start again.

"I'm Peyton," she said. She had the feeling she'd lost him. He'd only looked at her for a second, and now he was immersed in his drawing again. She turned away, half expecting him to call after her again, but he didn't.

Two girls came into view when she rounded the corner, their red and blonde heads lowered as they drew on the pavement.

Peyton stopped suddenly, the urge to turn back around intense.

"Hi," the blonde one waved.

Too late. They'd seen her. Peyton reconsidered backtracking – this wasn't her school; she'd probably never see these kids again. She inwardly kicked herself and moved toward them, mustering a smile. "Hey," she said, trying for casual and achieving robotic.

They both smiled. "Wanna play?" the red-haired one asked, gesturing toward the foursquare chalk outline they were working on.

"Sure!" Peyton answered, excited at her luck. She loved the game; it was something she was good at. "Do you have a ball?"

"Josh has it," the redhead said, looking in the direction from which Peyton had come.

"The black-haired kid?" Peyton asked, realizing it would be more convenient to call them by their names rather than the colour of their hair.

Redhead nodded. "That's my big brother." She looked up at Peyton again. "How old are you?"

"Twelve," she answered, feeling lucky again. Being the bigger kid, and having the respect that came along with it, would surely afford her some wiggle room when it came to how clumsy she was likely to be in her interactions with these kids. Then she thought of Jade and the feeling went away.

"He's thirteen," redhead said. "He's autistic, though," she added, as though it was a tempering thing.

Peyton's stomach somersaulted. She searched frantically for something to say but came up empty.

The blonde one looked up at her. "He's nice, don't worry," she said. "Just weird with people. Really smart, though." She went back to her chalk.

Peyton felt even worse at that. Is this how she'd be judged? "Should I get him?" she asked, her voice cracking.

Redhead stood up. She wore a flowery sundress. "Sure. I'm Sonia, by the way."

"Peyton," she answered, smiling.

"That's my best friend, Stella," Sonia added, pointing to the blonde, who looked up, giving a little wave hello.

"I love the name Peyton," she said absently as she finished off a corner of the square.

"Thanks," Peyton replied.

"He might not come to play," Sonia said, now. "It's hard for him to stop doing something when he's into it, so just get the ball if he doesn't want to come."

Peyton nodded, her heart racing. She thought about how she felt when she had to stop doing something – anything – abruptly. "You sound like a really good sister," she said, surprised at the words as they escaped her. She looked toward the swings, wishing she was there.

"Wow, thanks," Sonia said, smiling, then went back to the chalked square. "Hey, you finished it. Looks great!" she said to Stella.

Peyton thought they might be ten or eleven. She watched them for a moment, then caught herself getting distracted by her thoughts. She turned quickly, jogging back to the corner of the building and rounding it, smashing solidly into Josh, who had been carrying the ball in front of him, effectively bouncing Peyton backward when she hit it.

She landed hard on her bum, her tailbone sending a shot of pain down her thighs to her knees. "Ooooh!" she cried, her eyes clenched tightly shut. She opened them a sliver. "How did you not fall?" she exclaimed when she saw Josh, the ball still held in front of him.

"I... bounced backward and banged into the school," he replied, his face blank.

"Oh my gosh," she muttered as she got herself back up to standing. Josh was looking somewhere off to her left.

Peyton glanced in that direction and saw the girls looking at them.

"Are you OK?" Sonia yelled.

Peyton rubbed her tailbone.

"She hurt her butt," Josh called.

Peyton sent him a withering look, but his eyes were still to the left of her. "Thanks to you," Peyton said, embarrassed and upset.

Josh's eyes lowered but his expression remained impassive.

Peyton shook her head.

"Come on, guys!" Stella called, beckoning them forward.

Josh started toward them, but Peyton remained on the spot. Everything inside her was telling her to turn and leave. But she had made a promise. She was trying to be different. She grimaced. *This is hard.*

"Peyton! Come on!"

She didn't let herself hesitate anymore. She started toward them, trying a hop into a jog and slowing quickly. That hurt. She reached the kids and stepped into square two.

"You OK?" Sonia asked. She was holding the ball in the fourth square to Peyton's right.

Peyton nodded. "Let's play!"

With that, the game was on. Sonia served the ball to Josh in Square one, who instantly whipped it into Stella's square with a spin. Stella yelled in frustration, but a smile stretched across her face. She hadn't had a chance.

"Wow!" Peyton exclaimed.

"Josh's really good," Sonia said, as Stella went after the ball and Josh moved into square three.

Stella returned and bounced the ball to Sonia, then went to the brick siding of the school. "Don't serve to Josh first! She warned, clapping.

Peyton turned her attention to Sonia. Predictably, she served to Peyton and Peyton bounced it back with ease. Sonia hit it into Josh's square and he spun it again, his front leg bending low as he arced his pass. It hit the corner of Sonia's square, but she was ready. Low to the ground, she swatted at it and it came toward Peyton.

"Whoa, it's squirrelly!" Stella yelled and Peyton screwed her face up in determination. Stella was right; the ball was wild, wobbling from being knocked out of its spin. She dipped low, her palm contacting the ball solidly and sending it in an easy arch to Josh's square. He pounced on it, pushing his elbow back and then shooting his arm forward to smash it into his sister's square. Sonia squealed and grabbed for it clumsily, the back of her hand knocking it out of bounds.

"Aaaah!" she cried, stomping off to join Stella at the wall. "You can beat him, Peyton!" She cheered.

Peyton moved to square three as Josh took four. He was smiling. Peyton was taken aback at the difference it made, compared with the blank look that had seemed stuck there earlier. He regarded her, his smile faltering. She got into a ready position, her breathing shallow as she prepared for his serve.

"Serve!" one of the girls yelled, and he glanced toward them, looking nervous.

"Come on!" another shout from the wall came.

Peyton bounced a bit on the spot, her tailbone aching. Josh looked back at her, his eyes changing. He bounced an easy serve to her. Peyton frowned, hitting the serve viciously, the ball swerving hard to the right. He'd have to dive to get it. Peyton leaned forward to get ready for the rebound; from what she'd seen, he was more than capable. But he didn't even try. The ball bounced sadly into square one, then dribbled to a roll.

Peyton threw her hands up, exasperated. "You didn't even try!" she accused, and the girls echoed her sentiment from behind them.

Josh looked down at his feet, then hopped out of square four. "You win," he said, gesturing for Peyton to take the square. His eyes never met hers. Peyton scoffed. "Doesn't feel like a win when someone totally gives it to you," she said, squinting at him as the sun reappeared.

Josh blushed.

Peyton rubbed her tailbone again. It was aching, and her head was hurting now, too. She looked back at the girls. "My butt hurts more than I realized," she said, and they broke into fits of giggles. Peyton smiled. "I think I'll head for home," she finished.

"Aw!" Stella said, then stuck her lower lip out. "It's so much better when four people play."

"Sorry, guys," Peyton said, and smiled again. She felt like running as fast as she could, her headache worsening by the minute. "I think the fall gave me a headache, too. Delayed reaction," she said.

"OK, well thanks for playing with us. Are you coming back tomorrow?" Sonia asked.

Peyton felt a warmth in her chest. She was asking her back. "Maybe," she said, then, "Probably!" She started toward the side playground, waving behind her as she went.

"Why'd you do that?" she heard Sonia behind her. She must've been talking to her brother.

She rounded the school, then broke into a jog, each step sending little shocks of pain into her butt cheeks. *Of all the body parts I could have hurt,* she thought, shaking her head as she slowed to a walk. She reached the road and turned toward the bridge, swinging her arms as she walked. She looked forward to telling Gram and Grandad how well she'd done with real, live kids.

Heavy footfalls approached behind her, and she moved to the right, making room for the runner to pass. It took her a moment to realize they'd slowed and walked beside her. She looked sideways, frowning. It was Josh. "Uh, hi," she said.

Josh, hands in his pockets, focused on the sidewalk, head down. His black hair hung limply over his face. He ran his fingers through it nervously, and Peyton saw freckles on his cheeks and thick, dark eyelashes framing his downcast gaze.

"So, what are you doing?" she asked, more gently.

He stopped in his tracks and Peyton did, too, turning to face him. "I just wanted to apologize for knocking you down. I didn't mean to. I feel really bad that you got hurt," he said, his eyes on the ground between them.

Peyton inhaled, her mind racing. His effort to catch up to her and then to apologize was touching, especially if he felt anywhere near as nervous as she did when approaching someone. "It's OK," she replied after a few seconds. She felt a little teary, the nice gesture just a little too much after getting hurt and having tried so hard not to act too weird in front of Josh and the girls. She felt ashamed of her feelings and kicked the pebbles at her feet as she got hold of herself. When she felt steady enough, she asked, "Is that why you let me win?" with a smile.

Josh looked across the street to his right, a small smile fighting to take over his face, as well.

Peyton laughed as he fought it. "It was kind of obvious," she said, and he let a laugh escape, his hand coming up to cover his mouth.

"You're really good though, he said, shoving both hands back into his pockets.

"Thanks."

He glanced back toward the school. "I told Sonia I'd walk you home and get back to the park. Where do you live?" He raised his eyes to hers briefly, squinting, then closing, holding his hand over them, though the sun was on his back.

Peyton made an effort to smile, but had to look away. Knowing how hard it was for him to look at her made it even harder for her to meet his eyes. She had always fought the discomfort of making eye contact, having noticed others doing it as though it were completely natural. It was work, though. Something she had to be mindful of. "You don't have to do that," she said. "I'm staying with my grandparents on Hazel Street," she gestured behind her.

"I know that road. We walk down there to get to Main Street sometimes," he said, his hand still shading his eyes, but his gaze on the sidewalk again.

Peyton had the sudden, overwhelming urge to hug him. Everything he displayed, she worked to hide every day. She wanted to tell him she understood. She wanted to thank him for proving she wasn't alone. Instead, she remained glued to the spot, trembling slightly.

"Are you OK?" he asked.

She could only nod.

"Can I walk you?" he asked.

She shook her head no, now.

He looked disappointed, and Peyton took a step toward him. "Not because I'm mad or I don't like you or anything like that," she said quickly. "It's because I'm not feeling…good…right now. I have a headache and -" she looked toward some movement in the trees to her right, and spotted a cardinal. "Look!" she said, pointing.

It trilled its signature song and she heard Josh gasp. "I like how it sings," he said.

"It's a male cardinal," Peyton said, and he laughed.

"I know."

She looked back at him, softening. "You can walk me."

"OK."

They walked to Hazel in silence, both of them kicking the occasional rock in their path. As they approached the corner, Peyton pointed. "That's my grandparent's house."

He raised his head. "Oh, I know that place. Are you staying for long?"

Peyton nodded. "My parents are on vacation until the end of August, almost. We live in Kentville."

"Why didn't they just take the whole summer?" he asked.

They'd stopped at the foot of the side driveway. Peyton looked at him, getting a glimpse of his green eyes again. She noticed dark flecks in them. "I have to meet with the doctors again," she answered absently. She'd noticed that Sonia's eyes were green, too. *Josh's must stand out more because of his dark hair,* she thought.

"Are you sick?" he asked.

She shook her head. "What? Oh, no. I mean, not – physically." She looked toward the house, feeling awkward.

He studied her, seemingly waiting for an explanation and she perceptively wilted under his scrutiny.

"I should go in," she said.

He turned and started walking away. She looked after him, baffled, then followed suit, walking toward the house, the thought of lemonade popping into her mind.

"I'll come back tomorrow," she heard Josh call behind her.

She turned. "What?" He was still walking in

the other direction.

"I'll come back tomorrow," he said, turning his head to yell back.

"I'm on the spectrum, too," she yelled, then cursed inwardly. *What the heck?*

She heard him laugh, even saw him bend a bit at the middle. "Sorry I'm an idiot!" she called again, then clapped a hand to her mouth to prevent herself from calling out further atrocities.

He turned this time, walking backwards and laughing. He waved, then turned around again, his hands back in his pockets.

She watched him until he turned right at the end of the street. She seemed frozen on the spot. *What the -?* She questioned herself again, but had to smile this time, for she had no answer and it was either that or cry. She turned, then skipped to the house, her pain momentarily forgotten.

CHAPTER 14 – WAKING NIGHTMARE

Peyton shot upright in bed. It took her a few seconds to realize the whimpering sound she could hear was coming from her. She stopped, then focused on catching her breath. It took a minute.

When her heart no longer pounded in her ears, she ran her fingers through her hair. She became aware of how stiff her lower back and tailbone was and remembered how hard she'd fallen at the school. Gram and Grandad had let her eat dinner on the couch, Gram bringing her hot chocolate afterward. They were so thrilled Peyton had met some kids to play with, they and hadn't spoken about Lex at all.

She swung her legs over the side of the bed, glancing at the digital clock. 3:03AM. She frowned. Wasn't that what time she'd woken up after she'd dreamt of Lex the last time? She rubbed her temples, trying to recall what she'd been dreaming about to have woken so scared. Lex had been in it. That she knew, and nothing else.

She got up and padded toward the bathroom,

yawning. When she was done, she stopped at the doorway to the room on her right, looking at the window. The motion sensor light that was mounted on the outside of the garage was on, the trees opposite in its glow. Grandad had been talking about taking it down; a strong breeze could activate it, he'd said.

Peyton crossed through the room to the window, opening it to breathe in the air without pausing. She could see nothing that would have set the sensor off, but that didn't mean anything. It was a gorgeous night, the breeze rustling through the trees gently. An idea coming to her, she hurried back to her room. She grabbed her bag with her sketching stuff inside and slung it across herself, then went back down the hallway to the stairs.

In her excitement, she didn't think about how Gram and Grandad would feel about her nighttime excursion; her mind was on the stars. She slipped on her jellies and went out the unlocked door (nobody locked their doors in sleepy Kingston), already fumbling in her bag and wondering what colors one should use to draw the sky.

She looked up as she stepped onto the driveway, but the motion sensor light went on again, making it difficult to see the sky. She walked past the garage and into the side yard, squirming as the cool, damp grass poked at her feet through the openings in her shoes. Why she'd ever wanted a pair of these things escaped her now. She reached the garden just as the light flicked off, and looked up.

"Wow," she whispered, overcome by the sparkling expanse above her. She couldn't remember ever seeing the sky so spectacularly adorned with stars. Then again, she couldn't remember ever being outside at 3 am, either.

She sat on the grass, her nightgown stretching over her knees. The ambient light was enough for her to roughly sketch by but not much else; she used the first pencil she touched to mark out constellations on the page, unable to discern the color, after all. She'd do more with them by the light of day.

By the time she remembered she should get some more sleep, she'd filled two pages, circling each constellation so she could pick them out when she came back to them. She lay back, breathing deeply the crisp night air and sending gratitude to the sky.

Lex bent over her, his face both obstructing her view and nearly making her pee her pants in shock. She covered her mouth as a scream escaped, sat up, then scrambled to turn around as she stood. "Lex!" she said, breathlessly. "Do NOT do that!"

He grinned, and it wasn't altogether regretful. Amused, more like.

"Mean!" Peyton whispered loudly.

He held his palms out and mouthed, *sorry*. A bit of water dribbled onto his chin and he wiped it away.

Peyton caught her breath, staring into the trees to her right. "Man, oh man," she whispered. "You can't just pop up like that. Holy." She looked back as he gurgle-talked.

"Why aren't you sleeping?" he asked, leaning his head to the side and closing his eyes as he said it.

Peyton noted the care he was taking to communicate with her with interest. "I had a nightmare," she answered.

He raised his eyebrows, but didn't look entirely surprised.

"I think you were in it."

He looked toward the trees as he took his lighter out of his jacket pocket and lit it. Lit it again. And again.

"Can you tell me what happened to you?" she asked, stepping toward him.

He stopped with the lighter, turning his gaze back to her, then shaking his head no slowly.

"I – I saw your dad. He needs to know – your whole family does," she continued, a note of desperation in her voice.

He motioned for her to come with him, then

turned toward the trees at the end of the yard.

She knew this routine. She followed, sighing. "I already saw the bunnies, and the broken fence. Your father was supposed to fix it already -" she trailed off as they went into the trees. "You know, my Gram and Grandad are letting me be pretty independent. I don't think they'd like it if they found me following a - you - into the trees in the middle of the night."

Lex stopped at the trailer and looked back at her. He pointed to the same boarded-up window as before.

Peyton looked at him questioningly. "What do you want me to do? Your dad didn't even let us go back to show him the fence," she said.

He gestured at the window again. "What's in there?" she asked, then gasped. "Are you in there? Oh, My God. Are you dead in there? Are the rabbits trying to tell me something?" She was starting to panic, remembering what Mr. Wheeler had said about how his daughter didn't take good care of the rabbits. Gasping, she exclaimed, "ARE YOU BEING EATEN BY YOUR OWN RABBITS?"

Lex rolled his eyes dramatically.

"What?" Peyton asked. "Talk to me!"

"Not me," he blubbed, water gushing this time.

Peyton didn't react; this was routine now, too. "OK – is someone else in there?"

His eyes lit up, and Peyton's stomach flipped sickeningly.

"Wait. Is someone dead in there?" she whispered, suddenly horrified.

He shook his head no, but his eyes were sad. "Not yet," he said. Peyton took a step back.

"I have to go." Peyton's heart pounded almost painfully in her chest.

He stepped toward her, his eyes wide.

She held up her hand. "Don't worry, Lex. I got it, OK?"

He shook his head, going back to the trailer. He reached up, tucking the fingers of his left hand under one of the boards. Peyton was still, her mind racing along with her heart.

He pulled, but nothing budged. He braced a foot against the trailer wall, stuffing the fingers of his other hand under the board, too. He pulled, his jacket rising stiffly, and groaned as he did, water bubbling up and out of his body in a torrent.

Peyton covered her mouth again.

The board made a cracking noise, then came off entirely, falling to the ground with Lex. He pushed himself back up to sitting, resting on his hands and gasping for air.

How hard must a ghost have to work to do something like that, she wondered, the question taking some of her fear away. She walked toward the dark, filthy glass that had been revealed between the remaining boards on the window. If it was important enough for Lex to work so hard, the least she could do was look.

The window was higher than her, so she stayed back a bit, her gaze never leaving the glass.

And then she was there.

Peyton shrieked and tumbled backward, landing painfully on her already-sore tailbone. Her eyes were locked on the pale vision at the window, her mind skipping over the pain in its shock.

A woman, her white hair wild around her head, her skin loose on the bones of her face, looked back at her blankly. In the darkness, she appeared entirely grey and white, the dust and grime of the window exaggerating her unearthly appearance.

Peyton's body began to move before she consciously bade it to do so, her hands and feet pushing her backward. Away from the window, from the woman, the trees. She remembered Lex, and searched the trees around her.

He was gone.

When she looked back at the window, there

was a white hand on it, as gnarled as ancient tree bark. That was all she needed. She turned, stood, and ran all the way back to the house, and then up the stairs to her room. Rethinking, she hurried back to the door.

And locked it.

CHAPTER 15 – JUST TWO NORMAL KIDS WHO HAPPEN TO BE AUTISTIC

Peyton and Josh sat in the side yard the next afternoon, each with a velvet bag full of marbles. Josh had brought them both, offering one to Peyton to apologize again for their collision.

Gram had fussed over them as they had a snack at the kitchen table. Poor Josh had looked like he wanted to flee the whole time, practically inhaling his oatmeal raisin cookies in an effort to get out of there quickly. Peyton had stifled her giggles, but barely.

It felt incredible to be able to relate to someone like her.

They'd escaped to the yard at last, Gram calling after them to stay close to the house. After a thorough tour of the garden (Josh was as enchanted by it as Peyton), they'd sat in the grass, pulling their marbles out one by one to examine them. They were silent, both intent on their task, but somehow together, still.

When Josh pointed toward the trailer beyond the trees, asking, "What's back there?" Peyton was caught off guard.

Remembering the night before, she grimaced. Not only had she woken with a surreal sense of what had gone on – to the point of questioning whether it, too, had been a dream – but she'd decided to keep it to herself for the time being. She'd gone about her morning, diving into her tasks with gusto just to distract herself. Gram had been thrilled to have help with the dusting and the dishes, but started asking questions when Peyton had joined her to fold laundry.

"Alright, what's up?" she'd asked and Peyton had looked at her innocently.

"What?" she'd asked.

"This is just getting weird now," Gram had replied, and Peyton laughed.

When Josh had showed up at the door, Gram brought him right in, ushering him to the kitchen table for milk and cookies. And now he looked at her expectantly, his question still hanging between them.

"It's the old mobile home the Wheelers next door lived in," she said. She studied one of her marbles. The brown and black horsehair twist within it was beautiful.

Josh continued to look toward the trees.

"Where'd you get so many of these?" Peyton asked in an attempt to distract him from the trailer.

"That would be a great clubhouse," he said, then looked at his marbles. "I play marbles at school with anyone who has some. It's fun."

"I guess you win a lot."

He shrugged.

"Thank you for mine."

Another shrug. "What's inside it?"

Peyton sighed. "Rabbits, actually."

Josh whipped his head up. "Really?" he asked.

Peyton had to laugh. "I swear," she answered, crossing her heart.

Josh was up and jogging toward the trees before she could stop him.

"Wait!"

He didn't wait.

Peyton groaned in defeat and hoisted herself up. He was at the trailer in no time, but Peyton froze at the edge of the trees, her eyes on the gap of darkness between the boards of the window where the woman's face had been during the night. *So, it was real.*

Josh was going along the base of the wall.

"Are you looking for holes?"

He didn't answer; just continued along the bottom of the wall.

"There aren't any. There used to be a hole in the fence -"

"What fence?" he cut in, his eyes still on the ground where the trailer met it.

Peyton groaned, reluctant to go any further.

He looked at her. When she still didn't answer, he peered toward the end of the trailer, then started toward it, to Peyton's dismay.

She watched him press the underbrush to the side, then reach out to touch the green diamonds of the fence.

He looked back at her again. "I can see where it's been fixed."

Peyton nodded, relief flooding through her. Maybe he'd give up. "Let's go back," she said, turning her body sideways in the hope he'd be compelled to follow her.

"What's wrong?" he asked.

She hesitated to answer, but turned back to face him fully.

"What?" he prodded.

She looked at the gap between the boards again. "Have you ever seen a ghost?" she asked.

Josh was standing in no time flat. He followed Peyton's gaze, the words, "No, WHY?" shooting from his mouth, his voice cracking almost comically.

"You haven't?" she asked, incredulous.

He shook his head. "Of course not, are you crazy?"

"A little."

He looked back at her. It was strange to get the "You're weird" look from someone who also had a spectrum diagnosis.

Peyton's stomach dropped as a thud sounded from the trailer, and Josh rebounded from it like he'd been burned. He lost his balance and fell, his arms turning in the air like a cartoon character before he crashed down. "*Aaah!*" he screamed, pushing himself off the ground and running toward Peyton.

She stepped to the side, the tiniest of smiles playing at her lips as he passed her.

"Run!" he demanded, and she did, following him. Only because he demanded it, though. Her tailbone protested forcefully, and she slowed within the first few steps.

"Josh, wait!" she yelled.

He stopped at the far end of the garden. "Did you hear that?" he shouted.

Peyton nodded, then stopped beside the marbles, sitting. More protests from her tailbone had her rolling to her stomach right away. She folded her forearms and rested her head on them.

Josh soon made his way back to her, his shuffling footfalls sounding through the grass. He sat. "You should have warned me," he said, breathless.

She switched sides, resting the opposite cheek on her arms so she could look at him. "I told you there were rabbits inside!"

Josh picked up a marble, blushing. Peyton giggled. "OK, but then you asked me about *ghosts!*" he exclaimed, his green eyes meeting hers for a moment.

She sighed. "I thought – because we're both – the same kind of weird, that you'd be able to see them, too.

"Asperger's doesn't automatically mean you can see ghosts," he chuckled. "Imagine," he continued; "Signs and symptoms: difficulty in social situations and complaints of ghost sightings."

Peyton sighed, pressing her forehead against her forearms now. The grass tickled her nose, though, and she pressed herself up to sitting.

Josh froze, his eyes back toward the trailer. "So, you see ghosts?"

Peyton scrubbed her face with her hands, palms rubbing against her cheeks rather forcefully.

"Stop that."

She stopped.

"I won't tell anyone."

She looked at him. "But will you believe me?"

He looked to the trailer, then down at the grass, then at her again. He nodded.

Peyton registered that, looking down.

"You've seen one back there?" he asked, pointing toward the trees.

She nodded.

"Wow. In that case, my cowardly escape wasn't so dumb, after all."

Peyton laughed.

His eyes were on the grass, but he did, too.

She slung her bag over her shoulder. "I need to get back to that trailer, but on the Wheeler's side, she said, almost absently. I know something is wrong in there, but I can't really do anything until I know what."

"You said you have a sketchbook in there?" he

asked, pointing at her bag.

She shook her head, the sudden turn in conversation throwing her for a loop. "Yeah, I just started. I really like it," she said, pulling it out of the bag, then holding it, closed, on her lap.

"Do you draw the ghosts you see?"

She didn't answer.

He reached for the book, and she let it go.

"You may not believe this," he said, flipping through the pages, but then he was distracted. "Wow, this is cool," he said when he got to the end, the jumbled pages of constellations affirming once more that last night had happened.

"I need to do more with them."

"Constellations?" he asked.

"Yeah. I did them in the dark," she added, gesturing toward the purple-colored stars.

"You could just *not* draw the stars," he mumbled. Observing Peyton's confused look, he went on, "You could do a pencil mark for where you want to place each star, then colour the rest of the page black, leaving the page white where the marks are, you know? It would be a lot of work -"

Peyton brightened. "Not with paint!"

He met her eyes again. "Yeah!"

She smiled and his eyes darted back to the book.

"What were you saying about me not believing something?" "Oh. I was going to tell you that my mother said I could have a pet," he paused, going back to the latest picture of Jade. "This is beautiful, you know."

"No way," Peyton said. "Not a rabbit."

He smiled. "It was actually my second choice, behind monitor lizard."

Peyton made a face. "What? They're as different as you can get!" she said, amused again.

"I know, but I like all animals, really. Anyway, the point is that Mom agreed to the rabbit when I revealed choice number one."

Peyton only continued to stare at him, disbelieving.

"Can I write in the back?" he asked, pointing to the book.

She handed him a pencil.

He wrote his name, and then his phone number. Handing it back to her, he said, "Just in case."

"OK," Peyton said awkwardly.

He stood. "I have to go. I'll bring her back tomorrow."

"What? Who? Your mom?" Peyton asked, looking up at him.

"Yep. You can go over with us."

"Uh, wait a sec," Peyton said, but she was unable to think up a reason not to. In fact, part of her was glad. This could be the perfect opportunity to get a closer look at the trailer. She shuddered, the old woman's face popping into her mind. "It's actually a good idea. Thank you."

He nodded. "You can tell me about your ghosts whenever you want," he said, his gaze on the road.

"OK," she nodded, looking at the picture of Jade again. She was happy with it.

"Bye," Josh said, abruptly turning.

Peyton wondered if she'd done that, too – suddenly cutting things short when people didn't expect it, leaving them hanging.

She imagined she did.

CHAPTER 16 – BUYING A BUNNY

"Stop pacing, child!" Gram exclaimed.

Peyton stopped. "Sorry," she said, standing still in the middle of the second floor TV room for a couple seconds and then starting up again.

"Peyton!"

She stopped again.

Gram laughed. "Did he say when they'd be here?"

Peyton shook her head. Josh's quick retreat the day before had been on her mind ever since. What if he left so fast because of the ghost talk? What if he wasn't coming today? What if he thought she was much crazier than him and she'd never see him again?

"Come sit," Gram said, patting the couch beside her.

Peyton sighed, then crossed to the couch. The phone rang before she could sit, though, making them both jump.

"Lord have mercy," Gram muttered, grabbing it off the end table. "Hello?"

Peyton turned, then walked to the room at the end of the hall. She went to the window and looked out. Nothing. Not even Grandad's car. She briefly wondered where he was.

Gram's voice reached Peyton, snatches of this end of the conversation piquing her interest. She realized it was her mother on the other end and went back to Gram, sitting beside her anxiously.

"We'll talk about it more when you two come get her," Gram was saying. She caught Peyton's eyes and smiled, giving her a thumbs-up. "Hmm? Oh, sure; she's right beside me." Gram handed the phone over, Peyton covering the mouthpiece.

"What did you tell her?" she asked.

"I told her you've really been coming out of yourself and that you've opened up to us about some things that have been going on with you. That's it!"

Peyton nodded, then brought the phone to her ear. "Mom?"

"Hi, baby! We miss you!"

"Are you having fun?"

"It's wonderful, Pey. Really relaxing."

"Good. How's the baby?"

"Active!"

They caught up quickly, Peyton's dislike for talking on the phone on both of their minds.

"Your Gram says you're doing really well," Mom said to wind down the conversation.

"I'm having a good summer, Mom. I've started drawing."

"Oh? That's wonderful!"

"I really want some paints and brushes," she said, hoping to steer clear of anything that would make her lie about the ghosts. She'd have to; if she told her mother the truth about what she'd been seeing – what she'd always seen – she'd surely panic.

"I'm sure we can manage that when we get back."

"Thanks, Mom." The doorbell sounded and Gram reached for the phone. "I have to give you back to Gram, Mom. My friend is here," she spat, then handed the phone over, perhaps a bit too forcefully, for Gram nearly dropped it.

"Peyton!"

Peyton turned.

"Was that necessary?"

"I'm sorry, Gram!" she said, but danced on the spot in her eagerness to reach the door.

"What? Oh, nothing, dear, I just fumbled the handoff a bit." Gram said into the phone. She moved the mouthpiece down, her eyes on Peyton. She whispered, "You're to come right back here after you're done next door."

Peyton nodded and Gram blew her a kiss, then shooed her away. She was down the stairs in a flash. She peered out the side door, but saw nobody. Picking up her runners, she bolted through the kitchen, impressed at her foresight. *Jelly shoes probably wouldn't mix well with rabbit poop,* she thought.

Her stomach dipped as she thought of possibly of catching sight of the old woman in the trailer. At least she wouldn't be alone if she did see her again. *And I'll know for sure whether she was a ghost or not,* she said to herself.

She reached the entryway and a woman with straight, black hair smiled at her through the screen. "You must be Peyton?" she asked.

Peyton dropped her shoes, then stuffed her feet into them. "Hi, Mrs. – Josh's mom?" she replied as she used a finger to unfold the backs of her shoes from under her heels. She opened the door and saw Josh near the road, hands in pockets. "Hi, Josh," she called, and he raised his hand briefly before stuffing it back into his pocket. Peyton looked at the tall woman beside her. "You're so pretty," she said, then bit the insides of her cheeks to prevent herself from saying anything else.

But the woman brightened, her smile spreading even further across her cheeks. "Aw, thank you. And you can call me Fran," she said.

Peyton nodded as she squatted to tie her shoes.

"So, you're certain they're selling the rabbits next door?" Fran asked, gripping the shoulder strap of her purse with both hands.

Peyton stood, then swatted a mosquito on her arm, already fat with her blood. "Ew," she said as it exploded, her own blood spurting onto her arm. She looked at Fran apologetically. "Sorry; I didn't know it was already – full."

Fran was fishing in her purse. "Don't apologize, honey. I've seen worse," she said, then handed Peyton a Kleenex.

"Thanks." They started down the front driveway toward Josh.

"Um, the rabbits?" Fran asked again, and Peyton gasped, cutting her off.

"Oh! Sorry! Yes, they're for sale. Lex used to take care of them, but they weren't all pets. To be honest," she continued, looking at Fran, "I think there's more than they can handle."

"No surprise there, considering." They reached Josh. "OK to park here in front of the house? Fran asked.

Peyton looked at the car, considering. "Actually, you might be better off parking in the driveway. That corner is a tough one." Fran nodded.

"I avoid it at all costs, but I wasn't sure if I'd be blocking your grandparents."

"Nope; there's a side driveway, too," Peyton said. She and Josh stood to the side as his mother pulled into the driveway.

"Nice day," Josh muttered.

Peyton looked around. "Sure."

"I sort of realized I didn't give you much of a choice about this. Are you OK with coming?"

"Yeah. I'm not sure he'll let us back to the trailer, though."

"He'll have to if he wants to sell a rabbit, he said.

Peyton smiled. "I was hoping you'd say that."

Fran joined them and they started toward the Wheeler property, Fran asking questions about Peyton and Peyton trying hard to answer them politely. She felt she was doing well until she asked about Lex.

"You said Lex - their son? - used to take care of the rabbits," she started.

Peyton held her breath. She hadn't even realized she'd mentioned him.

"Why doesn't he anymore?"

Peyton paused, considering her options. She chose the simplest version of the truth. "He's missing."

"Oh, that's right!" Fran answered. "Oh, no; I'd forgotten about that. I heard from a friend of mine – she has a police scanner – that they suspect he ran off. His car was missing too, I think?"

Peyton shrugged. "I don't know much about it. Mr. Wheeler thinks he's staying at a friends' house."

Fran shook her head. "Only seventeen. I hope nothing bad's happened."

They fell silent, each to their own thoughts.

"Here it is," Peyton said, gesturing toward the long driveway.

"Great mailbox," Josh said.

"Didn't your Grandad make that, Peyton?" Fran asked.

She was proud her Grandad's work was well known. "Yep!" she said, puffing up a bit.

Nobody was in the yard today; they had to knock at the house.

"Oh!" Fran said when a tall, thin girl answered. Half her head was shaved and the other was pink at the ends. "Hi, you must be Sam?" Fran asked.

The girl nodded, chewing loudly on her gum. Peyton couldn't stop looking at the girl's eyes. They looked weird. It wasn't the heavy makeup so much as the glassy quality they had. She wondered if she'd been crying, or sneezing.

"Well! Are either of your parents home?" Fran carried on, her voice light.

This time she shook her head no.

"Oh." Fran seemed momentarily flummoxed. She glanced at Josh, then Peyton.

"We were wondering about the rabbits," Peyton said, desperate to end the awkward moment.

"Yes!" Fran agreed, looking back at Sam.

"Just a sec," the girl mumbled, closing the door.

"Well," Fran sighed, backing away from the door. "Not sure what that means."

"Lex's dad said she takes care of them now, but I don't think she likes it much."

Fran nodded. She seemed uncomfortable. "Maybe we should go. We should probably deal with Mr. or Mrs. Wheeler."

Josh seemed to wake up beside Peyton. "Aw, no way!"

"Well, Josh, I don't know if we'll even be able to take one with us until the parents know about it, anyway!" Fran said in a low voice.

Josh opened his mouth to protest, but the door opened. Sam had put a pair of unlaced high-tops on. "You want a boy or a girl?" she asked, looking at Fran.

Fran looked at Josh. "Doesn't matter," he said, shuffling his feet. Sam started off, then turned back. "Brown OK?"

Josh looked up. "I get to pick one myself, right?"

Peyton watched Sam anxiously. She blew a bubble then sucked, popping it loudly. She looked back at the trailer and then at Josh. "I'm not supposed to let anyone back there," she said. "It's dangerous, with all the cars and junk." She waved her arm across the back as though she was presenting it on a game show.

Josh hung his head. Just as Peyton was going to cut in, he spoke. "I don't think I'll get one if I can't pick it out."

Sam rolled her eyes. "OK, come on," she said, but paused, holding up a finger. "Just stay back when I tell you to."

They all nodded, and Peyton's heart sped up. She hadn't let herself believe they'd get back there. They all started toward the trailer, Sam muttering, "Dad's gonna kill me."

"He won't find out," Josh said quietly, and Sam shrugged as she walked.

"Better not." She stopped them about six feet away from the chicken wire fence.

Josh lost himself in his excitement, exclaiming over the rabbits. Babies and adults alike slept or hopped about, twitching their noses at the ground.

"Might as well feed them while I'm here," Sam said. She went to a plastic barrel beside the trailer and pulled a large plastic scoop off a hook on the wall. She filled it, then walked slowly to a gate. The scoop wobbled as she tried the latch, forcing her hand back on it to hold it steady. Peyton saw her chance. She rushed to the gate, opening the latch before Sam could react.

"Thanks," Sam muttered, looking sideways at her. "Close it behind me?"

She nodded eagerly. As soon as Sam's back was turned, Peyton scanned the whole area. She noted that the door to the trailer was open, bunnies going in and out of the broken-down building freely. The windows along this side of the building weren't boarded over. Peyton saw that they were all open to the screens.

Sam was spreading the food around quickly, casting the scoop forward, then to the sides, the rabbits scampering around her feet excitedly. Josh and Fran had approached the fence, Peyton saw.

Josh was squatting, his fingers wiggling between the wire.

Sam started back to the gate, motioning Peyton to open it for her. She slid out quickly, the scoop held behind her back, then stopped, her eyes on Josh and his mother. She looked confused, and really tired.

"Will they stay in the trailer over the Winter?" Peyton asked, hoping to distract her. Sam looked at the trailer, then down at Peyton. "I don't know," she said quietly. She went around the side of the building and replaced the scoop and the lid to the barrel.

Peyton's head was on a swivel, taking in everything she could. Really, she needed to see inside the trailer. She joined Josh and Fran. "Find your bunny yet?" she asked, her eyes on the open trailer door. She moved to the other side of them, squinting. She could see cupboards on the far wall, but just barely; it was that dark inside. She wondered if it had electricity.

"I really like this guy," Josh said.

Peyton kept her eyes on the door and rounded the fence. She could see a table. Strange thing to keep in a rabbit shelter.

"Don't you want a little one?" Fran said.

"Hey," Sam's voice cut into Peyton's concentration as well as Josh and Fran's discussion. "You guys can't be here."

Josh stood up and Fran backed away. Peyton watched the door.

"You!" Sam called, and Peyton walked back to the group, knowing that was directed at her. "Back up. What are you looking at?" she asked, and Peyton backed up.

Sam seemed surprised they'd approached, though they'd been there for minutes. Peyton saw something else, too – Sam seemed scared.

"Sorry," Peyton said. "I was just trying to see the ones inside."

"Well, you can't see inside, got it?"

Peyton nodded, her eyes on the ground.

"We'll take the big grey one, there," Fran pointed.

Peyton got her first look at Josh's choice and had to giggle. He was the biggest one of the lot. Even his cheeks were big. His other distinguishing feature were his ears; they flopped long and heavy on either side of his head.

"Bub? The grey?" Sam asked, pointing.

Josh nodded.

Sam laughed. "You can't take him, he's our best male."

"Oh," Fran said.

A lightbulb went off in Peyton's head. "Ah, so it's him making all these babies!" she exclaimed.

Josh looked at her, his eyes confused, then something like impressed. Sam, on the other hand, looked like she'd won the lottery.

"I guess you wouldn't want your best breeder sold," Fran said. "Can you pick one of the babies, Josh? There are so many to choose from!"

Peyton smiled at Fran. She was liking her more and more.

"Wait!" Sam said. Everyone froze as she considered her choices. She looked around the fenced yard, then at the trailer for a long time. Finally, she muttered, "Screw it" and opened the gate. Bub was already hopping toward her when she squatted and said his name.

A throaty laugh came from within the trailer, and Peyton's eyes were back on the door at once. Sam's were, too.

"Is there someone in the trailer?" Fran asked, stepping toward the chicken wire again.

"Back off!" Sam said, her eyes wide. Then she yelled, "Open the door for me!"

Fran, who had started to back away, jumped, then hurried forward to unlatch the gate.

Sam came out, Bub seeming to overflow over her arms.

"Your father's gonna be mad!" came a voice through the open door, and suddenly she was there: the woman from the window.

Peyton looked at Josh, desperate. "Can you see her?" she asked.

He nodded, his eyes fixed on the spot where the frail-looking woman stood.

Sam latched the door, then walked double-fast to Peyton and Josh. "Here," she said, dumping the oversized fluffball into Josh's waiting arms. He was instantly entranced, seemingly forgetting the old woman completely.

Peyton, who was still absorbing the fact that the woman was real, watched Sam rush back to the fence and whisper, "Get back inside!" to the woman in the trailer door. She waved a bony hand at Sam.

Peyton remembered her hand on the window. The woman was real. The woman needed help.

"Is that your grandmother?" Fran asked.

"OK, that's it. Let's go," Sam said, her voice high and wavering as she walked toward them, her arms outstretched and motioning them back.

Fran shot a questioning look at Peyton.

"Let's go," Peyton said quietly.

Fran nodded, her eyebrows still furrowed in her forehead. She cleared her throat. "What do we owe you?" she asked, looking back at Sam.

"Just wait around front!" Sam spat, jogging ahead and disappearing through the side door where they'd first met her.

Fran glanced behind them again, and Peyton followed suit. The woman was still there, her dirty skirt ruffling in the breeze like a wisp of milkweed, her bony knees visible beneath the thin fabric. She grasped the door frame as though it was the only thing holding her up.

They went to the front yard to wait for Sam. Josh was lost to them, deep in conversation with Bub, who, interestingly, seemed quite taken with Josh, too.

"He's so fat," Peyton heard herself say.

Sam burst out of the front door, a plastic bag in one hand. The screen door rebounded at the hinges and slammed loudly in its frame as Sam descended the stairs. She approached them. "Twenty bucks because he's our best male," she said, her eyes challenging Fran.

"That's fine," Fran said casually, her wallet already open in her hand.

Peyton watched her. She knew all the questions Fran wanted to ask, but silently willed her to keep them to herself. Fran handed a twenty to Sam, no questions asked.

Sam stuffed it into her pocket, muttering something unintelligible, then thrust the plastic bag at the older woman. "This is some food. Mix it half and half with whatever you get him," she said, then paused. "My Granny takes care of the rabbits. She likes to sit in the trailer while she's watching them."

Peyton thought her eyes looked scared again.

Fran opened her mouth to reply, but Sam ran past them and then around the corner of the house.

Peyton imagined she was going to corral the old woman and shook her head. Fran looked at her, the same look of confusion and worry in her eyes as Peyton imagined was in her own.

"That woman in the trailer - she didn't look good, did she?"

Peyton shook her head no. "I'm going to tell my Gram and Grandad. I don't think she's back there to take care of the rabbits."

Fran nodded. "Will you tell them today?"

"As soon as I get back." "Good. Because I'll call the police if they don't."

"Josh wrote his phone number in my sketch book yesterday. I'll get my Gram to call you after."

Fran nodded, satisfied.

"Let's go, then," Josh piped up, and Peyton startled. He hadn't said a word to them since he'd taken his rabbit from Sam. She looked at him. Eyes still lovingly on Bub, he appeared distant. "Come on," he said, and started down the driveway.

"I thought he wasn't listening," Peyton said to Fran.

"It may look like that, but he hears everything, trust me," she replied, her eyes on Josh's back.

"I have Asperger's too," Peyton confessed, again to her own surprise.

Fran stopped. Peyton did too, though she wasn't sure why.

"You know that doesn't mean anything, right?" Fran asked, her eyes intently on Peyton's.

Peyton looked at Josh. He'd turned around and was waiting for them.

"You know that's just a label that makes them more comfortable," Fran continued. "A way to explain why you seem different. But it doesn't shape who you are in any way."

Peyton looked at her feet. "It's pretty new to me. I don't really understand it yet."

"You'll learn more, I'm sure. But don't let it define you, you know?"

Peyton nodded, tucking Fran's words safely into her memory so she could come back to them later.

They started walking again.

"Thank you," Peyton said. And something – she'd never be able to articulate what – made her reach for Fran's hand. Fran took it, and Peyton was simultaneously appalled at herself and filled with happiness. She brought Fran's hand to her mouth, kissed it, and then let it go, taking off at a run to catch up to Josh and his monstrous rabbit. She heard Fran let out a laugh behind her, and it was a joyful one. She wasn't laughing at Peyton. *She was laughing*, Peyton thought, *because I surprised her*.

And as odd as it seemed to Peyton in this moment, she knew somehow that it was a good thing, too.

CHAPTER 17 –
REPORTING A CRIME

Reporting what they'd seen at the Wheelers' to her grandparents had been easy, as had the subsequent calls to the police – Grandad picked the phone up before Peyton had even finished talking about the old woman – and Fran.

Gram had taken care of the latter, filling Josh's mom in on Grandad's conversation with the police. From what Peyton could tell, it had been short. An officer had taken the information, then had promised that someone would go out to the Wheeler property to investigate.

The hard part had come after that, when Gram and Grandad sat down with Peyton and asked her to tell them everything. After dancing around the details, she eventually broken down and told all – from the first time she'd heard a thud from the trailer to Josh's visit and the subsequent trip to get him a rabbit with Fran.

The part where Peyton had first seen the woman proved to be a sticking point. Peyton told them everything, unable to see another option that would prevent them from finding out the truth, anyway. She'd been thinking about that night non-stop since she'd waved goodbye to Josh and Fran as they backed out of the driveway. It was, in fact, the first time she thought about how the truth of it would reflect on her.

She recalled the meeting she and her parents had earlier in the summer with the team of doctors. How Mom had stiffened in particular when they talked about impulsive behaviour. When she said that she and Peyton's father had been struggling to help Peyton with her impulse control, Peyton had been genuinely confused. Until that point, it hadn't even crossed her mind that the decisions she made could be dangerous, much less have an impact on her parents, or anyone else. She hadn't, in fact, even realized her parents had been 'struggling' with it. It was one of the things they'd be tackling at the end of the summer, Peyton knew.

Since then, she truly had been observing her decisions and actions more carefully. It had been one of the catalysts in her decision to try and be "normal". But now, when she was faced with confessing that she'd first seen the old woman in the dead middle of the night, when she'd ventured out into the dark – and then into the trees – alone and without consideration of the consequences, Peyton came face to face with the fact that she was ill-equipped to handle this on her own.

Once they'd squeezed every detail out of her (which, Peyton had been grateful for at the time, but would come back and haunt her later, involved Lex), they'd both sat back on the couch, silently considering everything Peyton had told them. Grandad had eventually asked Peyton to leave the room, but Peyton had refused, crying that she was being open with them, so they had to do the same for her. Gram had agreed, and at length, Grandad gave in, no other choice presenting itself. They then discussed what this could mean for Peyton, should it be reflected back to her parents as Peyton had told it.

And Peyton made another discovery: adults sometimes lied. It might've seemed a ridiculously late epiphany to other kids her age, but it was truly a revelation for her. And hence, the three of them crafted the version of the truth which would be told to Peyton's parents.

In the end, all they'd done was add in some realization in Peyton that it wasn't the best decision at the time, and emphasize the fact that it hadn't been Lex that had coaxed her out in the first place. The fact that he was the one leading her back to the woods all the time couldn't, they decided, be altered if they wanted Peyton's parents to know about her ghosts.

It was late in the evening when the three had finally decided that they'd talked it through enough for one day, and they'd stood, stretching and declaring they were starving, all. As they sat down for a simple thrown-together meal of peanut butter and jelly sandwiches, slices of cheese, some crackers and a communal bowl of grapes which sat in the middle of the table, Peyton felt completely wrung out and beyond her tolerance for human interaction for at least the rest of the night.

"Can I please take this to my room?"

Gram and Grandad looked at her, their faces displaying identical combinations of concern and surrender. "Of course," Gram finally said. "You OK after such a crazy day, love?"

Peyton shrugged, which, despite appearing very casual, was the only thing she could do without breaking down into a puddle of exhaustion on the floor.

"You know we're very proud of you, don't you?" Grandad asked, his voice soft.

Peyton was so stricken by the sentiment that she froze, wide eyes on her grandfather. It crossed her mind, fleetingly, that he appeared tired, too. She looked at Gram and found similar traces of exhaustion on her face.

"I'm not sure if you realize how brave you are," Grandad continued. "And I hope you understand now that we have to worry a little – it's our job as members of a family who loves you so, so much – about whether you understand the danger of some of the situations you find yourself in."

Peyton nodded.

Gram took her hand. "You can learn this, dear. And you won't be learning it alone. We – Grandad, myself, and both your parents – will be with you every step of the way."

Peyton nodded again, desperate to find some solitude so she could decompress. She felt so full of emotion, and hadn't a clue how to sort it all out, or even handle it without breaking down.

"OK, go," Gram said, and Peyton went, her plate feeling heavy in her hands, and the events of the day heavy on her heart.

When she reached her room, she felt lost. Deciding whether to go to the window or sit on the bed seemed impossible, so she sat where she stood, just inside the door. She put the plate on the floor, then ate mouthful upon mouthful until it was gone, not tasting it, not gauging whether she was hungry or full; just doing it to do it. After that, she burped loudly, then lay down where she was, the deep pile carpet providing a modicum of comfort.

Then she cried. She let everything that was built up inside her flow out on a steady stream of tears, feeling pleasantly empty when she was done. At that moment, the distant but distinct sound of the doorbell came to her, and she forced herself to her hands and knees and crawled to the top of the stairs.

A man's voice spoke in an authoritative tone. "Tomorrow would be fine, yes. Just give me a call – here's my card – before you come down to the station with your granddaughter.

Peyton broke into a sweat, her gut clenching as the man referred to her.

"I just want to make sure of one thing, Officer, before we see you again tomorrow," Grandad's voice cut in, now.

Peyton had put a hand over her mouth, covering a gasp at Grandad's words, "officer," in particular.

"What's that?"

"That we – or at least one of us – can be present the entire time she'll be talking to you folks."

"Well, given that her parents are away, it makes sense, of course. No problem."

"And I want you to understand that we'll step in or cut it short if we feel she's too stressed." Grandad added.

Peyton's eyes filled with grateful tears.

"Sir, I completely understand your concern, but we're not grilling her - or anything close to it!" the officer laughed. "We just need to add every bit of information we can gather to the file."

"That's fine, but Peyton's had some rough news this summer, and in general, she gets over-stimulated easily." Grandad said, and Peyton felt a little strange listening to him describe her in such a way.

"Ah, I see. If you don't mind my asking, is there something we should be sensitive to when we're interacting with her?"

Peyton held her breath.

"She's got Asperger's, so she's sensitive. If you could just be aware that pushing her in any way won't get you anywhere -"

Gram interrupted, "And don't rush her; she's incredibly bright and a perfectly capable girl, but sometimes, when it looks like she hasn't heard you, she's just going over her response in her own mind. Be patient, and I promise, she'll give you higher quality responses than you can expect from just about anyone you interview."

Peyton exhaled. She fought an urge to run down to the landing and throw her arms around her grandparents.

"I understand, ma'am. My nephew is autistic, so I've got first-hand experience -"

"Oh! Then you understand. Peyton's quite high-functioning. In fact, she's gifted -" Gram interrupted again, and Peyton's love for her filled her entirely.

"No worries, Ma'am. I think the world of my nephew. I'll make sure to interview her myself. Sound good?"

Peyton heard no reply.

"Good. We'll see you tomorrow, then?"

"Wait," Grandad said, an edge to his voice. "I want to know what's happened next door."

"Of course. We'll fill you in more tomorrow once we've solidified next steps, and some of this is, of course, confidential. But what I can tell you, given what your granddaughter saw, is that she's most likely saved Mrs. Wheeler's life."

Peyton felt the blood drain from her face. A wave of dizziness rolled over her.

"Mrs. Wheeler – Sandy?"

"No, this is Mr. Wheeler's mother, Joan."

Peyton could hear her grandmother gasp. "But Joan's at the home; the one in Middleton!"

"She was, but I'm sad to say that Mr. Wheeler removed her several months ago. Seems payment was a problem, especially while they ran into some issues during the building of their new house. Ultimately, rather than rack up an astronomical bill in addition to the costs they were incurring for their building project, they took her home."

"Oh, my," Gram said.

"Problem is, instead of giving her the guest room in their nice, new house, they put her in the old trailer, there; the one bordering your property."

"Oh, my God," Grandad muttered.

"Seems they'd rather forget about her than take care of her. I won't go into detail about the inside of the trailer, but I will say that those rabbits she's been living with are much better cared for than she's been.

An odd, high-pitched sound echoed up the stairs. Crying.

"I'm very sorry to upset you, ma'am, but I think it's important you know that without the intervention of your granddaughter and her friends today, Mrs. Wheeler surely wouldn't have lived out the summer. So, you can rest assured that when I'm gathering information from her tomorrow, she'll be treated like the hero she is."

Peyton turned, crawling back to her room, her head spinning. She stood when she reached the door, inwardly wondering why she'd chosen to crawl, and then sat on her bed.

She thought of Josh and Fran with gratitude, and then of Lex, whom she hadn't seen since that night in the woods.

"I hope I did what you wanted, Lex," she whispered, then lay down, relishing the softness of her pillow. And she let the warmth of the gentle fall into unconsciousness seep in, letting go, finally, of the day.

CHAPTER 18 – JADE LETS GO

Peyton was so absorbed in her ice cream – black raspberry cheesecake again – that when she finally looked up, she'd reached the intersection of Main and Deveau, the graveyard behind her. She rolled her eyes at herself and turned back.

The cedar hedges bordering the graveyard were at the height of the season, full, green and tall. Peyton finished her cone with her eyes on them and started jogging, no hint of lingering pain from her tailbone.

She thought of the day she'd met Josh and the girls with gratitude. If she and Josh hadn't collided around the corner of the school, they most likely wouldn't be such good friends now. They'd seen each other almost every day since the police station, where they'd been allowed to talk to the officer - Officer Johnson – that had spoken to Gram and Grandad the night before, together. It had been more like a group meeting; Peyton, Josh, Fran and Peyton's grandparents sitting around a table with Officer Johnson and a detective to "round out the file," as they put it.

Happily for Peyton, the story had started with Josh's first visit to her and his discovery that rabbits were for sale next door. No mention of Peyton's first encounter with the woman. But they did talk about Lex: Officer Johnson told them that Sam was full of remorse over not going to the police sooner, and that in fact, Lex had left over a fight with his father about his grandmother. Apparently, he'd been threatening to go to the police as he left.

And nobody had seen him again.

Peyton hadn't, either. But the police had let them all know that they were going to investigate his disappearance much more seriously. They hadn't before, because his father had been so adamant that he'd be with his friends and would return soon. And his mother apparently wasn't involved at all. She'd left shortly before Lex's disappearance, too, but the police weren't able to tell them why.

She approached the archway wishing, for the umpteenth time since that day, that there was some way that she could help him, too. While he'd insisted that he wasn't there for himself, and Peyton felt good about helping his grandmother, she couldn't shake the feeling that she needed to do more for him.

But today was for Jade. Peyton had fallen into a routine over the last few weeks, playing outside with her friends, enduring frequent visits from family, drawing and just enjoying her vacation. It had been so "normal" that Peyton had easily held off returning to see Jade.

The graveyard was deserted, to Peyton's relief. She recalled the last time she was here: the day of the thunderstorm. Each time she thought about it, the memory of how Jade had fizzled out returned to her, followed relentlessly by the many other ghosts that had appeared as she was leaving.

But she saw no one today, not even Jade. She made her way to her stone, then knelt on the plot, as intent on talking to her friend, even if she wasn't here, as she'd been before.

"Hey," she started, feeling a little silly.

"Hey," Jade answered, suddenly kneeling beside her.

Peyton screamed, falling to her side and rolling, her scream ending in a fit of giggles. "WHY did you DO that?" she yelled.

Jade put her hands over her mouth, but was unable to control her own giggles. She ended up on her side, too.

"I'm happy to see you," Jade said, finally. Both girls were still laying in the cool grass, facing each other. Jade on her plot and Peyton beside her, in between Jade's plot and the next.

"I'm sorry it's been so long. A lot has happened," Peyton said, her voice sincere.

Jade shrugged the shoulder that wasn't in the grass. "You're here now."

Peyton sat up. "I brought something for you," she said, her stomach doing a somersault. She hoped Jade liked her picture; she'd gone back to it time and again to make it better.

"Oooh!" Jade sat up, too, clapping her hands. She crossed her legs and leaned toward Peyton eagerly.

Peyton looked at her, a realization crystallizing. "I knew something was different. You're not buzzing or flickering!"

Jade looked down at herself, then at Peyton. "Huh!"

"It was scary seeing you flicker out last time," Peyton admitted.

"I'm sorry." Jade looked thoughtful. "But you know, I felt so much better after I told you how – it happened. And after you left that day, after I'd gotten so scared about the storm, I kind of stuck around. I didn't -" she scrunched up her face as she searched for the words, "– go, completely."

"I'm not sure what that means, but OK!" Peyton said, smiling.

Jade smiled, too. "And you know what?"

"What?"

"It wasn't scary like before," Jade finished, looking content.

"Wow, that's really cool," Peyton said, the satisfaction of having helped Jade tempering her regret over Lex just a little. "Thank you for telling me that."

"Well thank YOU, actually," Jade said. She looked so cute, her smile revealing slightly crooked adult teeth.

She was so young. The reality of it in that moment was painful for Peyton, whose heart ached in her chest. "I wish -" she paused, wanting to say it right. "I wish you could come home and play with me," she said, and it sounded exactly how she felt.

Jade looked down, fiddling with the grass. "Does it make you feel any better that from what I've seen, it's really nice where I am?"

Peyton considered her words for a moment before nodding, saying, "Yeah, it does. Does that mean you'll be, um, moving on?"

"Not yet," Jade said. And then she was looking over Peyton's shoulder and exclaiming, "Oh!"

Peyton followed her gaze. A couple was coming toward them, holding hands. The man was tall and well-dressed, with ebony skin, and the woman was – well she looked to Peyton like an adult version of the little girl beside her. She was carrying a beautiful bouquet of flowers.

Peyton looked back at Jade. "Your parents?"

Jade did flicker a little bit, then, nodding. Her smile was huge, but it was offset by the tears in her eyes.

"I'm going to go," Peyton said, not wanting to intrude. Also not wanting to have to explain to Jade's parents why she was here.

Jade said nothing for a moment, her eyes glued to her parents, but when Peyton started to walk away, she yelled, "WAIT!"

She stopped, looking back.

"What did you have for me?" she asked.

Peyton looked at Jade's parents, who had arrived at the plot, blindly standing ever so close to the daughter they'd lost. They looked back at her, their eyes curious.

Peyton wished the ground would swallow her up, then remembered where she was and took it back, wishing instead to be transported to her grandparents' house.

"Hi," the woman said.

Peyton froze, as though being still could render her invisible to them, too.

When she didn't reply, the woman stepped

toward her. "Were you – visiting Jade?"

Peyton looked at Jade, who was jumping up and down. "Say yes!" she said.

She cleared her throat. "Uh. Yes."

"That's so nice," the woman said. She looked at her husband, then back at Peyton. "Did you know her from school?"

Peyton looked at Jade again. Jade only shrugged this time.

"What are you looking at?" her father asked. Peyton panicked.

"Nothing. I, uh...I have Asperger's," she blurted.

Jade rolled her eyes dramatically.

Her parents looked at each other, suddenly awkward.

"It's on the autism spectrum..." Peyton said, lamely, then, feeling the need to apologize, said, "I'm sorry."

The woman smiled. "There's no need to be sorry, dear. We're here to visit Jade, too. She's our daughter."

"I'm very sorry she left you at such a young age," Peyton said.

Jade put a hand to her hip, her head cocked to

the side as she stared at Peyton. "You made it sound like I chose to die!"

"Sorry," Peyton said, then inhaled sharply, as though she could suck the word back in.

Peyton's father followed her gaze again. He looked suspicious.

"I-I h-have to go," Peyton stammered.

"Wait," the man said, holding his hand out. "You didn't tell us how you knew her," he said, and Peyton noticed a slight accent.

"I like your accent," she said. Then she looked at Jade's mother. "I met her, um...she told me about the tree, and the lightening." She remembered the drawing. "Oh! I have this. She wanted me to do it for you, so you could see that she's OK. She's happy." She pulled out the framed drawing.

"Oh, you framed it!" Jade exclaimed, craning her neck to see it.

Peyton turned it around so she could easily admire it, then realized she must look like a loon to Jade's parents. Completely flummoxed, she said, "She hasn't seen this one yet." She heard herself as she said it, and tears welled up in her eyes. She was messing this up, big time. "I'm so sorry. You must think I'm a nut," she said, a tear escaping. She held the frame out.

Jade's mother, who seemed fascinated by Peyton's face, reached out and took it in slow motion. She looked at it and smiled, then showed Jade's father. Then she started to cry.

"I'm sorry," Peyton said again, then looked at Jade.

"Thank you," Jade said. Then, "Can I say that I love you?"

Peyton, already well beyond her coping abilities, let a sob escape. "I love you, too," she said, past caring how it looked.

Jade's parents looked back again, following Peyton's gaze. Seeing nothing, they looked back at Peyton.

"She's OK? She's happy?" Jade's mother asked.

Peyton nodded, just barely holding back a major cry.

"Thank you," the father said. "We will cherish this picture, and your words, forever."

The woman nodded. "Can I hug you?" she asked.

Peyton, who in any other circumstance would have declined, went to the woman, her arms open. She was enveloped instantly, surrounded in warmth and a subtle flowery smell. When she was released, Peyton looked one last time at Jade, who had moved closer during the hug, a look of longing twisting her features.

"I can go now," she said.

Peyton nodded, then turned to go, herself.

"What's your name?" the woman called.

She turned. "Peyton. I'm staying with my grandparents on Hazel street, on the corner. I'm telling you just in case you ever want to talk to me about Jade, you know? I'm there almost every weekend."

Their faces brightened. "Really?" the woman asked.

Peyton nodded. "It's the house on the big corner?"

They both nodded.

Jade waved.

Peyton waved back, then blew her a kiss.

"Will you still talk to me?" Jade asked.

Peyton wasn't sure how that would work. "How?"

"How, what?" the woman asked.

"I won't be far," Jade replied. "Just talk to me."

"OK," Peyton said.

"Tell them I love them. Oh, and that I love my stupid brothers, too!"

"I'm not saying that!"

"OK, then tell them I love my...challenging brothers, too. That's what Dad was always suggesting I call them instead of stupid!" She giggled.

Peyton smiled, then looked at Jade's parents again. "She wants me to tell you that she loves you, and she loves her 'challenging' brothers, too," Peyton used air quotes around 'challenging'.

Jade's father fell to his knees, crying.

Peyton thought of grass stains.

"Thank you. Oh, thank you so much," her mother said. She walked to Peyton, then held out the flowers. "We brought these for Jade, but if I know my baby girl, she'll want you to take them as much as we do."

Jade was jumping up and down again. She stopped when Peyton looked at her, then smiled, nodding.

Peyton accepted the flowers. "Thank you," she said.

Jade's mother went to her husband, kneeling to comfort him.

Peyton gave Jade one last look, then turned and ran. She didn't look back or stop running until she was too out of breath to both cry and run. She walked the rest of the way home, cradling her bouquet with care. She was overwhelmed, but satisfied at the same time.

This may be weird, and it may be hard, but it's me, she thought. *It's my life, and it's my gift, and if seeing ghosts means interacting with people so I can help them, even when I don't know exactly how to do that like someone without Asperger's would, then I'm just going to do my best. Because that's all I can do. I can only be who I am – it's all I have the energy for.*

Besides, I'm happy with who I am, she decided, right then and there.

CHAPTER 19 – SAYING GOODBYE

The night before Peyton's parents would come to take her home, Gram and Grandad had a party of sorts in the side yard.

Uncle Barry and Aunt Lois were there with Peyton's cousins, and so were several of her other Aunts and Uncles. Her Gram had called Fran to invite she, Josh and Sonia herself, telling Fran that Sonia should bring Stella, too.

Grandad was the master chef, manning the barbeque with gusto.

Gram had set up a long, rented table with Peyton's help, and each guest had brought something to share. There were bowls of pasta salad and spinach salad with mandarin oranges and sliced almonds, plates of sandwiches, pans of potato and pasta casserole, and desserts - oh, the desserts!

Peyton and the other kids had studied them all in anticipation of loading their dessert plates after dinner. There were rocky road bars, lemon squares, cookies galore, and a chocolate sheet cake with bright blue frosting. Peyton had insisted that the party not be all about her leaving; it would make her the center of attention, which was the opposite of what she wanted. Gram had understood completely, making it into an "end of summer" party. The cake, therefore, had the words, *Thank You for A Magical Summer!* written on it in all the colours of the rainbow. Peyton thought it was perfect.

It was a happy affair. The adults drank beer and wine and the kids had popsicles and were allowed cans of pop. Stella, Sonia and Peyton made a hopscotch board on the driveway with the chalk Sonia had brought, and then they'd played four-square, all the cousins getting in on the action, too. Josh was reigning champion in the end, of course.

By the time they'd cut the cake and a fire was going in the fire pit, Peyton was exhausted. She sat beside Josh on a log bench and they alternately shared a companionable silence or talked until Fran said it was time for them to go home.

Before they left, Fran hugged Peyton tight. "I hope to see a lot more of you, sweetheart," she said, and Peyton felt pure, unfettered happiness.

Josh stood awkwardly to the side, hands in his pockets, until Fran released Peyton, and then he opened his arms for a hug, too, raising his eyebrows in a question as he looked at her.

Peyton giggled, then hugged him. It was awkward, but sweet, too. They were both smiling when they separated.

"I won't miss you," he said, his eyes on the ground. He was smiling a little.

"Uh -" Peyton looked at Fran.

"Because I'm going to see you soon," Josh finished, pointing at her.

"Right," she said.

Fran was smiling.

"You will, I promise. I'll call you every time I'm here."

She watched them walk around the house, where Fran had parked their car, Stella and Sonia waving back at her.

"See ya, Peyton!" Sonia yelled.

Peyton hugged herself.

"What a nice group of kids," Gram said as she came to stand beside Peyton. Peyton hugged her, now. "What's this for?" Gram asked, sounding pleased.

"It's because I love you. And because you helped me so much all summer," Peyton said.

"Well I love you too, my darling girl," Gram replied, her voice a bit wobbly with emotion.

"I'm going to go in, I think," Peyton said as she stepped back. "Oh, unless you need help cleaning up?"

"Aunt Sheri's already at it," Gram motioned toward the long table. "I don't think the night's ended for the family just yet, anyway," she added. "You go on, have some quiet time just for you."

It was exactly what she needed.

When she thought of seeing her parents the following day, her heart sped up with both excitement and apprehension. Gram and Grandad had committed to giving them a rundown of the summer, first. They'd be the ones to tell Mom and Dad about the Wheelers, Jade, and Lex. But they'd also tell them how Peyton had made some good friends, and how she'd ended her vacation with more confidence and self-esteem than she'd ever had.

After that, Peyton would be on her own with her parents. She purposefully hadn't planned anything to say to them. She didn't want to be rehearsed. She wanted to be herself. It was going to be - she thought of Jade's description of her brothers - challenging.

She wound down in the bathtub before going to bed, the warm water easing her tension. She felt utterly exhausted when she hit the pillow, and her grandparents told her the next day that by the time they came to tuck her in for the last time that summer, she was fast asleep.

CHAPTER 20 –
RESOLUTION

Peyton surveyed her room. It was clean of her belongings; she'd packed her suitcases before going downstairs for breakfast that morning. She'd made the bed, too, though she couldn't get it to look neat and crisp like Gram could. Still, she'd tried.

She stood her suitcase up, then checked the drawers once more. Empty. She was ready to go home.

She thrilled at the thought of returning home. Her bedroom, her things, her comfy, happy place. She thought, too, about her long-time ghost friends and roommates. How would things change now that she realized what they were? *Man, do I have some questions for them!* she thought.

She perked her ears up. She couldn't hear the voices of her parents and grandparents anymore; maybe it'd be alright if she went downstairs. As she reached the landing, she realized her bad timing; their voices were just lower, now. She couldn't make out what they were saying, but her mother sounded like she was crying. Unsure of where to go or what to do, Peyton stood awkwardly on the landing.

She looked back at the staircase, then down at the shoe rack. Both her jellies and her runners were still there. Slipping into her jelly shoes, she grabbed her runners and went out the door, intent on putting them in the car so she wouldn't forget them. She wandered a bit after that, inwardly saying goodbye to her surroundings, though she'd surely be back soon. It would be different, though. It wouldn't all be hers anymore.

She walked along the garden, but her eyes were on the trees. Thinking of Lex, she walked toward them, then into them, marvelling at the change in temperature. It was cool in here, and utterly quiet. Not a sound from the trailer at the back of the trees, and no rabbits to speak of, ghost or otherwise.

"I'm sorry, Lex," she muttered, still wishing she'd done more than help his grandmother. She turned and left. The space felt entirely different, now.

Her father was waiting for her in the doorway. "There's my girl," he said as she approached.

"Hi, Daddy."

"You sad to be going?"

Peyton looked around again. "Only a little."

"We missed you."

Peyton smiled.

He held her at arm's length. "You know, I'm looking at you and I can see that you've grown. Not just taller, but inside, too. As a person."

Peyton looked at him, squinting in the sunlight.

"I'm very, very proud of you, Pey."

"Everyone grows," Peyton shrugged.

"Not everyone accomplishes what you have this summer. I think your mom and I have to start looking at you as a young woman in addition to being our little girl."

"I haven't changed completely, Dad," Peyton felt the need to protest, these new words from her father feeling alien.

"Thank goodness," he smiled.

"You're really tan," she said, and he looked down at himself.

"I'm really happy, too. We had a great vacation."

"And Mom's belly is so big!" Peyton exclaimed, remembering the shock of seeing her after so many weeks away.

Her father laughed. "I know. Not long now," he said, shaking his head. "Life's about to change again, Peypey."

Peyton studied her shoes. "I can handle it," she said, finally.

Her father looked like he had no doubts that she could.

Peyton pretended to sleep on the drive home. Her parents were talking in hushed voices, mostly about Peyton's ghosts.

"Do you think it's all true?" her mother asked.

"I think we have to, considering what's happened!" her father replied.

"I don't mean – of course I don't think she's lying, Charlie. But maybe she perceives things differently, or interprets things differently. I don't know."

Peyton cracked an eyelid. Her mother was pinching the bridge of her nose.

"Babe, I know it would be easier to believe that. Hell, I've never known what to think about all this – stuff. But personally, I can't deny everything we've heard. The Wheeler grandmother? The girl in the graveyard? And it's got to be hard on her – I think at the very least, we owe it to her to keep an open mind."

"You're right," her mother sighed. "I just wish – ugh, she's got enough to deal with! Now she has to deal with ghosts, too?"

"Now? Honey, think about it. This isn't new."

There was a pause. "My God. You're right."

They fell silent.

Peyton cracked her eyes again, this time looking out the window. They were on the treacherously winding road between Greenwood and Aylesford. She wondered why her parents had gone the long way, then opened her eyes fully, sitting up.

There was a boy. A boy in a leather jacket, walking on the side of the road. He was soaking wet.

"OK, hon?" Mom asked, turning to look back at her.

They sped past him, and Peyton saw his face. His eyes fixed on hers.

"Stop!"

"What?" Dad glanced in the rear-view mirror.

"Stop! Please!" Peyton knew she was yelling, but couldn't help herself. She twisted in her seat, searching for Lex out the rear window, but they'd turned one of the many curves of the road.

"I can't stop, love! The shoulder is too narrow and there's a sharp drop to the trees."

"It's dangerous, hon," Mom agreed, still looking back at her.

Peyton panicked, then had an idea. "Daddy you have to stop RIGHT NOW or I'm going to throw up all over the car!"

He pulled over.

Peyton had the door open before he'd even stopped, and she could hear her mother screaming after her as she burst out of the car and broke into a run. She could no longer see Lex, but she knew she had to go back.

"Peyton!" her father yelled, and her heart squeezed at the panic in his voice.

Still, she ran, willing her legs to carry her faster. She was just rounding the corner when she heard running footsteps behind her. Leaning forward, she drove her energy into her legs, refusing to stop until she found Lex again.

The corner finally behind her, she slowed. She turned on the spot, gasping for air. There was nobody.

"*Lex!*" she screamed, her voice desperate.

Her father caught up to her and stopped, bending over to catch his breath.

"LEX! Where are you?" she screamed again.

"Jesus Christ, Peyton! What's gotten into you?" her father gasped, his eyes wide.

"I saw him, Dad!"

"Saw WHO?"

"Lex!"

"Lex Wheeler? The missing boy?"

"Yes. He was here!"

"Honey -" her father started to reach for her.

"NO! I have to find him, Dad. Please!" Peyton was screaming still, and she felt tears on her cheeks, though she didn't remember starting to cry. "Please, Daddy," she said again, her voice high-pitched and wavering.

"Christ," he whispered, glancing uncomfortably into the woods and then at the road. He put his hands on his hips. "OK let's do this, but fast. Your mother is probably crapping her pants right now."

Peyton laughed, despite her tears.

"Where do we look?" her father asked her.

Peyton focused. Her father was taking her lead. This was new. She walked past him, listening, Birdsong. A breeze in the trees. And the sound of the creek, just ahead.

Are you in water?

Her question to Lex echoed back to her.

"This way," she said, running.

"Wait!" her father called, but she was already there. The sounds of the water were louder, now. She looked into the trees, squinting into the dark. Her father had been right; the land dropped at a steep incline beside the road.

"Why isn't there a fence here?" she wondered aloud.

Her father skidded to a stop. "Do you see something?"

"Not yet," she answered, taking small steps forward. Her eyes were on the trees, and on the spaces between them. The sound of the water increased as she walked, but then she heard a car, too.

Her father reached out for her, pulling her into his grasp as the car sped around the corner and swiftly past them, the horn blaring. The wind from it whipped Peyton's hair and set her anxiety level to "high".

"This is too dangerous, Peyton," her father said into her hair.

"I know," she said back. She turned her head, peering downward into the trees from beneath her father's armpit. She could see something. A spark of light. "A reflection," she said out loud.

Her father released her and followed her gaze. "What is that?"

Peyton took a few more steps along the road, her eyes riveted to that one little spot of light. And then, she saw it. A car. "Daddy!" she exclaimed, pointing. Still, she kept her eyes glued to the spot, for fear of losing it.

He approached her, then looked, his hand

shielding his eyes from the sun. "My God," he said.

"It's flipped, Daddy."

He looked at her. "You saw him?"

She nodded. "He must have gone off the road that day he left to go to the police," her father said.

Her tears renewed, she let them loose. She finally let herself cry for Lex.

"We have to find a phone," her father said as he draped an arm around her. "And we have to go back to your mother, or there'll be another accident. He looked down at her. "OK?"

"He's down there, Daddy. Oh, my God. He died down there!" Peyton covered her face, the pain almost unbearable.

Her father's arms went around her again, strong and sure. "If he's down there, love, he'll be found, now. Because of you."

She took a deep breath. Let that sink in. "Oh, Lex," she said, but she was quiet, now.

Her father stepped back, looked at her. "OK?"

She nodded, once. He put his arm around her again, and they started back to the car.

Peyton's mother was beside herself. As soon as they rounded the corner, they saw her. She was standing beside the car looking in their direction and wringing her hands. When she saw them, her arms went up and she called to them, relief flooding her voice.

Peyton ran again, straight into her arms. "We found him, Mommy."

Her mother held her at arm's length so she could meet her eyes. "Found who, baby?"

"Lex. We found his car, and he's down there, too. I know he is."

Her mother's eyes registered shock, but she nodded, then gathered Peyton into her arms again. Her father joined in when he reached them.

Another car whizzed past them and they separated, Peyton's mom smiling and wiping her tears away. "Shall we?" she asked, and received no protests.

They got into the car.

Peyton buckled her seatbelt. "Can we just go to the police station right now, Dad?"

He nodded, looking at her in the rear-view mirror again.

Peyton turned and looked out the back window once more, and this time she found Lex instantly.

He was standing on the shoulder about twenty feet away, and he looked to be dry as a bone. He smiled at her. It made his face beautiful. Then he lifted a hand and waved. "Thank you," he mouthed, and Peyton heard it like he was next to her, as clear as a bell. And this time, no water gushed from his mouth.

She had helped him, after all.

The End

STAY IN TOUCH

Stay up-to-date on Theresa Dale's books; email paperdollpublishing@outlook.com with the word SUBSCRIBE in the subject line.

Be part of the community! Follow Rose's Ghost on Facebook and theresadaleauthor on Instagram.

Thanks for reading!